Keith Ridgway was born in author of the novella *Horses*, *The Long Falling* (winner of the Prix Femina Etranger in France) published in 1998; the short story collection *Standard Time* (winner of the Rooney Prize for Irish Literature) published in 2001; and the novel *The Parts*, published in 2003. He lives in London.

www.keithridgway.com

Visit www.AuthorTracker.co.uk for exclusive information on your favourite HarperCollins authors.

From the reviews of *Animals*:

'Like Nicholson Baker Ridgway has the descriptive power to locate the sublime, hidden inside mundane minutiae. And like Paul Auster, he knows how the accretion of ordinariness can be made to seem overwhelming and sinister to a bewildered narrator. The result is that *Animals* is both a very funny and surprising inspection of the detail of modern life, and an affecting portrait of a man trying to make sense of it'
Independent on Sunday

'Ridgway's most tonally intimate prose to date ... a first-person story in a style so impressively compressed and rhythmic' *Irish Times*

'This strange, beautiful and deeply troubling novel makes the grade as genuine art ... [Ridgway is] writing fiction as radically new and provocative as any of the current gener-ation of writers around the world, literary darlings with such exotic names as Eugenides, Hemon, Houellebecq, Kunzru, Murakami, and of course Mr McSweeney's himself, Dave Eggars' *Sunday Independent*

'*Animals* is a story about the shapes of all our human stuff once you take the skin off ... Ridgway's compassionate, intelligent, forensic approach eschews pat answers. It haunts the reader, insisting he think a little more, be a little more cautious, look a little deeper' *Daily Telegraph*

'He turns people inside out, detailing their quirks and vulnerabilities with engaging perceptiveness ... a concatenation of anecdotes and dream revelations ... unnerving in their odd accuracy' *The Times*

'Showing the disintegration of a subject is not an easy task but Ridgway pulls it off. This is not an easy or comforting read but, surrounded by ease and comfort as we are, it is all the more crucial for that' *Scotsman*

'The almost stream of consciousness deluge of paranoia and urban myth made real that constitute his recollection of these events is darkly, grimly hilarious ... deeply unsettling but utterly absorbing' *Metro*

'At once comic and tragic, bright and solemn, this is a tremendous work' *Dubliner*

By the same author

Horses
The Long Falling
Standard Time
The Parts

KEITH RIDGWAY

Animals

HARPER PERENNIAL
London, New York, Toronto and Sydney

Harper Perennial
An imprint of HarperCollins*Publishers*
77–85 Fulham Palace Road,
Hammersmith, London W6 8JB

www.harperperennial.co.uk

This edition published by Harper Perennial 2007

First published in Great Britain by Fourth Estate in 2006

Copyright © Keith Ridgway 2006

Keith Ridgway asserts the moral right to
be identified as the author of this work

A catalogue record for this book
is available from the British Library

ISBN-13 978-0-00-721332 0

Typeset in Sabon by
Palimpsest Book Production Limited, Grangemouth, Stirlingshire

Several people helped in the writing of this book, sometimes knowingly, often not. I'd like to thank the following
for their support, friendship, patience, advice and hospi-
tality:

Kenneth Armstrong, David Miller, Clare Reihill, Michèle
Ridgway, Geneviève Lynam, Andre and Ailbhe Troubetzkoi,
Hilary and David Marshall, Diane Hamer, Liz Naylor, Ed
Firth, Stephen Lyons, David Ong, Evelyn Conlon and Sean
O'Reilly.

I'd like to thank Peter Sirr at the Liffey Project, whose re-
quest for a short piece for their website (www.liffeyproject.net)
provoked an early version of what became the first chapter
of *Animals*.

I would also like to acknowledge the generous support
of the Authors' Foundation.

Keith Ridgway, July 2005

The Mouse

All of this happened about a week ago. There had been rain, on and off, and I was worried about dreams. Not my dreams in particular, but all of our dreams. I'm not talking about aspirations or anything. I mean our actual dreams – dreams we have when we fall asleep. I think there's something wrong with them.

Before that, though, I have to tell you about what I saw on the morning of the first day, the Friday. I saw a dead mouse. I saw other things as well, and I'll come to them, but chiefly, at the beginning, I saw the mouse. If anything is at the beginning then that is. I'm actually tempted to start somewhere else – with Catherine Anderson, for example (yes, *the* Catherine Anderson), or with BOX and all that Australia nonsense, or even with my friend David and his tiny writing. But none of that makes much sense really unless I tell you about what happened with K; and what happened with K doesn't make any sense *at all* until I tell you about the mouse (and may not make much sense even then), and lunch with Michael, and a little bit about Rachel, and the thing about the strange rain. And the

1

swimming pool, obviously. So I have to start with the mouse. Which is not ideal, because it's not exactly what you'd call very exciting, in itself, even though, the more I think about it, the more it sums up everything else; and in a way, if I was brave, and if my bravery was confident of your bravery, I should just tell you about the mouse and leave it at that. Because, you know, the rest of it is just *human*. But none of us are brave any more.

I left my umbrella at home. I left it standing upright in the thick glass vase on the floor of our hall, leaning against K's umbrella – two tall question marks asking me if I was sure. There had been constant showers for days – some of them quite heavy. Fat black clouds scuttled over the grey sky as fast as birds, bringing cold bursts of rain that drenched people, took them by surprise – because before they happened they were hard to imagine, and because we never learn. But I thought that this day looked a little brighter. I usually watch the weather forecast on the television in the mornings. But on the Friday I slept late – in fact, I was barely out of bed – and I had just had a chance to bathe and get dressed before it was time to leave the flat. So I decided that an umbrella wasn't needed. I opened the front door and saw a strip of blue sky torn through the grey, and I decided I didn't need an umbrella and I stepped out into the world as it is.

Our neighbourhood is generally sedate but can get a little agitated sometimes, and then you can feel a minor disturbance in the air, as if you've walked into a room where people have just stopped talking about you. I felt it that morning. There were some kids walking up the road towards me – about three or four of them, white and black and sullen, school age but not interested, obviously, in that, and they just looked like they were up to something – some kind of kiddie evil. I watched them carefully. Sometimes they can play that ancient joke of pushing one of their friends into a passing stranger, and I hate that – I never know which kid to be angry with, or how angry I should be. But these ones hushed their talk and parted for me as I passed through them. I glanced back and saw one of them spit, and two of the others glanced back at me, twisting themselves round in their hoodies and their low jeans with their boxers showing. They're harmless really, though they'd hate to hear it said. They have their swagger ready-made for them in some East Asian sweat shop, and they wear it with the label showing. They are fully owned.

As I turned away though, and looked where I was going, there was a sudden flurry of activity behind me, where the boys were, which sounded like they had scattered, voicelessly, all limbs and splitting up, like they were a flock of pigeons disturbed. I spun round and sure enough, they had disappeared. I was startled and stopped in my tracks, and my eyes ran over the street looking for some sign of them because it seemed uncanny that they could have vanished so completely, so quickly. I thought I saw the shape of a shoulder, a hooded head, slip behind a wall on my left. There's a small lane there which leads to a road which runs parallel to ours. But I saw nothing else. I thought it strange. I stayed where I was for a minute or so, looking around, patting my bag and my pocket where my wallet was. I couldn't figure it out. Perhaps I had hesitated for longer than I'd realised before turning. Perhaps I'd been nervous about what the noise had meant, fearing that they were running towards me and not away from me. But surely that would have caused me to turn even sooner – so that I could be certain. So that I'd know as soon as possible what I was up against. Or, if I'd thought that I

3

was going to be attacked in some way, surely I'd have started running myself, without turning round at all. We have instincts after all – flight or fight. I think I tend towards flight, although, to be honest, I've never been particularly tested in that way. But I hadn't even considered running when I heard the noise. Maybe a third instinct had kicked in – that of pretending that nothing is happening for as long as is humanly possible, thinking that ignorance might be a shield. I shrugged and went on.

I nodded hello at a woman from across the road who was making her way home with the shopping, and I had a long look at two separate elderly men who waited at the bus stop, ignoring everything but the corner from where the bus would come, when it came. I stood with them for a while, and looked at my watch, and decided to risk going into Eric's.

There is actually no one in Eric's called Eric, as far as I can make out, although the very pleasant Turkish man who runs it seems happy to answer to the name. Sometimes there is also a woman who I assume is his wife, and sometimes a son, who I have also heard being called Eric, though he doesn't seem to like it very much. They stock groceries and newspapers and sweets, and some general small-scale DIY stuff like nails and screws and hammers and other tools, and watering cans and ropes and drain unblockers and sink plungers and bulbs and batteries and smoke alarms and mouse traps. Eric's is the first port of call for the entire neighbourhood when some small domestic crisis hits. It can be annoying sometimes when you go in just to get a newspaper or some milk and you have to wait while Eric whose name is not Eric rummages around for an ancient fuse for a customer whose dinner depends on it. When I went in this time, I thought I'd been unlucky. Eric whose

4

name is not Eric was standing at the back of the shop with a large woman I didn't recognise. They were looking at mousetraps – an old-fashioned one with a spring-loaded neck-breaking bar, and a more modern one, involving an adhesive-floored box.

—They get stuck, you see, not-Eric was saying. Stuck there, they cannot move.

—And it's alive?

—They're trapped. They die of a heart attack or something. Who can know? They just die.

—And how do you get it out?

—You don't get it out, you just throw the box away. No problem.

—Oh, I don't know. Seems a bit cruel, doesn't it?

She was laughing a little uneasily and looked at me. I smiled. Luckily, Mrs Eric who is not Mrs Eric appeared out of the back room and took for my newspaper and bottle of mineral water.

—The other snaps their neck, it's not cruel?

—Well, it's quick at least. Which one is cheaper?

—The more cruel is the cheaper. It's always the way.

On the bus, I read, and drank my water and forgot entirely about mice and the vanishing boys. I read lazily, yawning, and glanced at the rooftops and the arches and at the signs that line the routes here, and at the teeth of scaffold and at the wires. It was all a blur. I made sense of nothing, but I was content I think. I have a smallish life. It doesn't need much. There were seven different stories on the front page. Nothing specific seemed to be occurring anywhere.

The bus went quickly and I got off in the centre, a couple of stops early, thinking that it was nice, I could walk, I could get some fresh air and look in the windows and think about things. I wanted to draw a quick sketch. I rummaged in my bag and found my sketchbook and my pen, and standing where I was, on some street somewhere near the centre, about ten minutes' walk from where I was going, I drew a rough cartoon of a daffodil running through a field of children, knocking off their heads. I frowned at it for a moment, wondering if maybe it wasn't an idea at all, but a memory of something I'd seen before. Oh well. One thing follows another. It was when I put away the sketchbook and the pen, and turned to cross the road, my head down watching my hands fiddle with the bag, that I saw it.

I saw a dead mouse. Guttered, up dead against the kerb. A silky little thing, like a purse. Shut down, remarkably unruffled, thoroughly dead. There wasn't even the slightest hesitation. I did not think, *There is a mouse, oh, it's dead*. I thought, *There is a dead mouse*. He lay on his side, with his belly exposed towards me, and his limbs, with their little feet, stretched out from either end. He was a grey brown. With the underside lighter. You'd think, against the ground, the belly would be black with dirt. They are probably clean little things, in their world. Proud little cleansers. His eyes were closed. His mouth slightly open, with the smallest hint of a tooth. His claws at prayer, almost clasped together, above his head. The way he lay, I fancied he had fallen off the footpath. I could see no injury. I could see no blemish on his body at all. From what I know. I say he. I could see no genitalia. I was not aware of any genitalia in what I was seeing. But he was furry around the end regions. I found it hard to see, to tell. I peered at the thing. A stretched tiny creature, in-explicably ended, at the side of the road.

I thought of course, though not with any great focus,

of the woman in Eric's looking for a mousetrap. It was a minor little coincidence. I noted it and paid it the deference I thought it was due (not very much) and put it out of my head.

I wanted to prod it with my umbrella. An instinct in my arm, a twitch, so that I actually looked down at my side, as if for an umbrella, as if there was a chance that one of them, either K's or mine, might have come with me, might have attached itself somehow, out of wisdom and the never-ending question. I had no umbrella. I had not brought one. I stood and stared down. I crouched a little. The thing was crying out to be prodded.

I rummaged in my bag for something to touch it with. This small thing. Small dead creature. Just a touch. A little poke. Just to see. Just to feel. But in my bag there was nothing of any use. A novel, an address book, a half-empty bottle of water, half an apple in a tissue, a hat against cold, a glasses case, with sunglasses inside, my telephone, my camera, my sketchbook, my pen. I could see immediately of course how I might proceed: the pen. But I had only the one pen with me – and using a pen is what I do, it's my role, I'm an illustrator and cartoonist, it's what I do for a living, and I like to be able to sketch at any time and in any place – and I wasn't that keen on using my pen on the mouse. Not really. So. I sought other options. I could take out the sunglasses, extend an arm, touch it like that. But I was afraid, frankly. Afraid of spillage. Of guts and ooze. I was afraid of what the touch would leave me with. And even if there was no obvious detritus left clinging to my glasses, I was not sure that I would want to wrap that arm around my ear, once I knew that it had prodded a dead mouse. The water bottle then. I could throw it away. But it was one of those wide-mouthed things, built to latch on to our own mouths, and it was too wide and bulky and awkward. I was sure it wouldn't communicate to me anything of what I was after. What I was after was the body sense, the heft of it. The weight and the resistance. Things, I think, like that. So I would use the pen. I mean, I could buy another, if I really, suddenly, desperately needed to sketch something. Take the pen and poke the mouse and throw the pen away. Simply leave it there on the ground – a bewilderment for whoever came after. It would look, what, like the mouse had been hit from above by a falling pen. Maybe. Or that it had carried its pen as far it could before its miniature heart gave out. That the writing had killed it in the end. Some such thoughts might go through some kind of mind when I was gone. That's what I thought.

I could touch the mouse with the pen and then leave the pen by the mouse's side. I put the pen in my hand. It was a nice pen, new or newish. It would be a shame. But I needed to know. I needed to touch the corpse. I needed to know the level of quiver and give, the degree of rigidity; the liquidity, possibly, of the innards. I took the pen in my hand. Which end? It was a rollerblade. No, excuse me, a rollerball. With a decent rubberised grip mid-shaft which would plainly be useless. I would be on one end of this pen, and the mouse on the distant other. One poke. One prod. That's all. I decided on the butt end. I would hold to the rear. Clutch the base of it, the arse of it. Cap on or cap off? There was a danger I thought that if I used, as it were, the sharp end – the nib, or the ball in this case – that I would puncture something. That I would puncture the mouse. That there would be a barely discernible hiss of gaseous escape; an emission of mousey . . . life, followed in all likelihood by ooze – watery pink animal blood from grey string veins. About a mouthful in all, of bile and suppurations. I didn't want that. And there was the remoter danger too (I looked around, the street was fairly quiet) of an explosion. Of a simple hideous pop. It didn't look swollen, but how many dead mice have I seen? I would leave the cap on.

I gripped the pen with my thumb and first two fingers. Right hand. Was there enough sensation there? Should I use the left for the sake of novelty? For the superior sensation from the lesser used limb? No. There was risk that the inexperienced left hand would over-poke or over-prod, and a resultant increased possibility of puncture or pop. Oh, I was just being stupid now. I thought of calling K. I put it off.

I crouched, my coat skirting the ground, tenting my legs. My ribs rested on my thighs. My left hand held my bag beyond harm. My right hand went out. I was closer to it now, of course. Its claws were stretched up above its head. Yawning. Its forearms. Forelimbs. Why are we so unclear on the body parts of other creatures? Of how to name them. As if we're a little embarrassed to let them have the same things we have. Arms. Hands. Feet. Belly. It looked like it . . . I can't call him *it*. It's *him*. I thought of him as a him, I still do. I could see nothing to confirm it, even this close, but I thought of him as *him*. I don't know why. His arms stretched up over his head. His hands close to clasping. He looked like he'd surrendered, or been swimming. Perhaps he had been caught in a flood in the gutter. A sudden deluge, taking him and bringing him here, as helpless as a paper boat, choked in his little lungs and unable to hold. Or perhaps he *had* simply surrendered. Given up. Abandoned the fight. His belly was pathetic. It was open to anything. He lay there like a puppy waiting to be tickled, or a lamb waiting to be slaughtered, and either way he didn't know and he didn't care and he was better off in not knowing and not caring and in generally not being. Something stilled around me. I don't know what I mean. I think I mean the city came to a halt. Which it didn't. But I lost it for a moment. Lost the city and the city's noise, and the world, and the world's sorry items. Something got in the way. Just for a second. Something got in the way of my curiosity for details, facts, experiences. Something minutely sad. Something small and terribly strange. That pause in living. Sadness, I think it is. Sadness. All right.

I thought of calling K. I put it off.

I extended my pen. I sent it on its way, across that patch of air, that polluted patch. And all my sudden sadness went with it, expanded with it, pushed out from me like sound, and I wondered if I could carry on.

It did quiver to the touch. And seemed to shrink. Its small extended limbs seemed to come in, to try to close, to try to cover its vulnerable front. It was as if a shadow briefly crossed its dream. Its uncontaminated dream. A slight disturbance in its sleep. A breeze rippled something that was closed, and lifted, for a second, an opening of sorts. A memory of something. A dim recall in the dirty street. It was nothing, was it? I prodded a dead mouse with my pen. There in the street. I crouched and touched its corpse. I felt a small resistance. Give and no give and give – a weak bundle of death on the end of my pen. I could have flicked it in the air with barely an effort. It was nothing. Nothing. It should have been nothing. It should have been utterly nothing.

But since that, all of this.

I tried once more. What was I trying for? I poked it again. Perhaps a little harder. Or perhaps a little softer, overcom-

pensating against the risks run by attempting to go a little
harder. There was the same small contraction, protective-
looking, awful really, and the return then, the relax, like a
last breath breathed again. It looked like it had looked when
I'd found it. Let it be. Leave it in peace. I imagined I saw
a tiny indentation left in its belly by the tip of my capped
pen. I paused again. The world paused again. I felt something shift inside me, a worrisome realignment.

I thought of calling K. I put it off.

There was certainly an indentation. There certainly was.
A pockmark in the shape of a pen cap. It seemed to shimmer
like a morning puddle on the pale flesh. It was a sort of
greyish shadow. I looked at the pen, and saw, much to my
weird guilt, that there had indeed been some kind of small
secretion. A minutely cluttered sheen of moisture clung
to the smoothness of the plastic like a grimy sweat. It
caught the light, and I could even see a tiny bead of it roll
around the shaft, in and out of the almost microscopic
debris of what must have been the first symptoms of rot.
And I thought I could detect a mild smell to go with it. A
sort of warm sweet sickness, very light, but present, like
a childish bad breath. I remembered measles and chicken-
pox. My mouth dried.

I laid the pen on the ground.

There must have been more than that. That's what I
think now. I think that I don't have enough detail, and the
detail I have is the wrong kind of detail – that it misses the
point. Because although there was seepage and although
there was a smell, these things did not, at the time, get in
the way of the feeling I had that this was a very interesting
and, in some obscure way, meaningful encounter. So the
corpse was a bit yucky. So what? It was a corpse after all.
It was not nearly so repugnant as it was striking. But it's

difficult now, if I'm honest, to say whether I genuinely thought that it was striking, or whether I just wanted it to be striking. Perhaps the significance comes later. Perhaps it wasn't there then. But I think it was. I really do think it was.

So I think about the face. The face of the mouse. Its eyes and nostril nose and its mouth and its teeth and its whiskers. What were all of them doing while I prodded its belly? I don't know. I can't remember. Did I even look? I mean, I only poked him twice, and my eyes have only so many things they can look at. But you'd imagine, would you not, that the face would be the obvious thing to monitor? We have that instinct. We look at faces. Do mice have faces? Something about that word 'mice' worries me. It is unlike what it describes. It has been corrupted and diminished by cartoons, and by its pronunciation as 'meece' in some of those cartoons. And the idea of mice faces, as well, is ruined somewhat by cartoons. Even now, trying to remember the face, I am interfered with by features entirely unmouselike but forever associated with mice because of the consistent use to which mice have been put in the last one hundred or so years. Mouse as Everyman. Cute resourceful little fellow with a twitchy whiskered nose and a spunky sense of humour. Why? I have never drawn mice. Never. They're a devalued currency really, in terms of illustration. I draw all sorts of other creatures, but not mice. I've never liked them anyway. Crouching in the street poking this dead one was the closest I have ever willingly been to a mouse. That I know of. Something about their speed, their size, their ability to infiltrate, their capacity for turning up anywhere, at any time, has always half terrified me. I do mean *half* terrified. Because I feel the start of full terror but close it off quickly, with the thought that it's only a mouse, it's only a little mouse, mice are harmless, they're not like *rats*. If rats did not exist would we feel the same about mice? I don't think so. They are blurred things. Uneasy little shapes that flash by, on our periphery, on the sidelines, like a scratch on the surface of the eye, like fat black clouds across the grey sky. They cling to skirting boards and kerbs and edges. They come looking for the food we drop without noticing – the crumbs that fall from us daily, the rain of our chewing and our fumbling and our bad-mannered lives. They know something about us that we don't fully comprehend. Mice is the wrong word for them.

When I try to remember his face now I get a composite of memory and Disney and fear, and the backwards assignation of things that hadn't happened yet. There's a childish scrunch to it, a sort of *eek-a-mouse* fright. I see the mouth, and a glint of inner whites and pinks, God, and the nose, which is really no more than two wet nostril holes in the grey fur, at the point of the whiskered snout. The eyes must have been closed. Either that or I have blanked them out. Either that or something else. It all goes forward, leans out, presses out ahead of the body. They are pointed little creatures – missiles, arrowheads. No wonder they move at such speed. He looked like a child that had bitten something bitter. Something horrid and yuck. Perhaps he was poisoned? Perhaps they lay some toxin down here on the streets. Or perhaps just one of our idle by-products did for it. Some accidental spillage or fume.

—It's me.
—Yes.
—I saw a dead mouse.
—Did you eat the apple?

—I ate half of it.

—All right. That's a start. I suppose.

—I saw, I see, I'm looking at a dead mouse.

—Oh shit.

—No, no, I'm not at home. I'm out on the street. In town I mean.

—Oh, OK.

—It's just lying here, in the gutter.

—Right. Are you sure it's dead?

—Yes.

—You don't want to attempt some CPR? Call an ambulance?

—I can't figure out how it died.

—Old age maybe.

—Do mice die of old age?

—I'm sure some of them must do.

—On the street?

—What, you think they should have a sacred place where they go to die?

—I find the whole thing quite moving.

—Aw. That's sweet. I think.

—I mean, it looks somehow significant. Or, not significant, that's not what I mean. It looks somehow terrible, as if, you know, here, in the midst of all this, all this life, there's this dead thing. This death.

—This mouse.

—Yes.

—Are you still meeting Michael? For lunch?

—Yes. I suppose.

—Life hasn't suddenly ceased to have any meaning or anything?

—No.

—Where are you going?

14

—To the place, the café place that he likes, I don't know what it's called. You know.

—Well, you're going to be late.

What I wanted to tell K, what I wanted to say to K then was, *I don't want to leave the mouse*. The sentence assembled on my tongue and started forward. I said, *I* . . . But it was of course a ridiculous thing to say. To even consider saying. It was mad. And of the alternatives which presented themselves, as *don't* began to pass through my lips, *I don't want to leave the house* seemed if anything even more suggestive of some kind of half-arsed melodrama. And anyway, I had already left the house. *Want* came out. *I don't want to leave you now* simply made no sense at all. In fact, it suggested meanings and thoughts and even agendas which were simply not in my head. Out tumbled *to*. I bit down on *leave*, truncated it by a syllable. *I don't want to lee* . . . and then corrected myself with an impatient little sigh. *I don't want to be, I don't want to be late*. Even that was suspicious. It was a thing I just wouldn't say. K picked up on it.

—Is it squished?

—What?

—The mouse. Is it squished and horrible?

—No. No, not at all. Well . . .

I couldn't bring myself to talk about the poking.

—Not much. Not at all really. It's very passive, peaceful. It looks unhurt. Its face looks a little, you know, *oh, I'm dying now*. But there's no injury. No wounds. That I can see.

—No blunt-force trauma?

—No . . .

—Have you drawn it?

Funny that it never occurred to me to draw it. That I

used the pen to poke rather than draw. That what you would have thought of as my natural instinct had been somehow redirected towards touch.

—Eh, no. No. I don't have a sketchbook. Or a . . . I have a sketchbook. I don't have a pen.

—Well, have you got your camera?

—Yes.

—Then take a photo.

—Why?

—What do you mean, why? You're transfixed by it. Record it. You might use it for something.

—I'm not transfixed by it.

—Yes you are. You've called me up to tell me you're standing in the street staring at a dead mouse and you've gone all metaphysical. Of course you're transfixed. Now take a photograph of it and go and have lunch with Michael. You'll be late.

The truth was that I didn't want to take its photograph. It didn't seem right. But I couldn't say that to K, who would have laughed.

—All right.

—All right. Call me again later. Minus dead things ideally. OK?

—Yeah. OK. Sorry.

—I love you.

—I love you too.

I didn't want to take a photograph. His photograph. Something about the scene was irreducible. To take out my camera and point and click would be an act of censorship. I would be editing out the noise of the traffic, the voices, the shuffle of feet on the pavement, the high rumble of the airplanes, the sound of the world as it is. I would be editing out the spring confusion of a clear fresh day and exhaust fumes; the low lumpen scent of the burger bar at my back; the ineffable musk of the city, never mind of the mouse itself. I would also be editing out my own reaction to this scene, which was, now that I had talked to K, beginning to strike me as immensely strange. I would be editing out the sadness. I would be reduced, I knew it even then, to showing a photograph of a dead mouse to the people I love, in an attempted explanation. For all of this blurred impossible. This life.

To say it even now sounds ridiculous.

But K had told me what to do. Not to do it would mean having to explain not doing it. I couldn't quite grasp the explanation for taking a picture or the explanation for not taking one. Perhaps they were the same explanation, differently sized. Proportionate. But proportionate to what? To what they explained, or to our capacity for explanations like that? Maybe it's better to reduce. To short-circuit the direct experience, to minimise memory's chances of messing things up. If I had a photograph, maybe I would only have a photograph. A picture of a dead mouse. What could be simpler, smaller, more stupid, less significant? Really, it was nothing.

I took out my camera. There was an amount of fumbling. Doing this always makes me feel like a tourist, like a visitor here. It is one of those cheap but clever digital cameras – it looks like a toy. The size of it is supposed to make it compact, discreet, easy, but it seems to me always awkward, unwieldy, and I feel I'm forever on the verge of dropping it. It has a bag that is not really a bag at all, more a jacket, an overcoat, which has to be taken off, the Velcro ripped and then the thing itself slipped out, balancing it in one hand, and the so-called bag in the other, and then the lens cap, which is just badly designed, and is attached to the body of the camera by a silver string, and all of this is important because it was distracting me, it was shifting my mind two thoughts away from where it was properly supposed to be. I put the camera around my neck. Hung it there. I think I still held the cover in my hands. I think my shoulder bag was hanging from my shoulder. Not what you'd call the relaxed demeanour of a regular photographer. I sorted it out somehow. Maybe I clenched the cover between my knees, or under my elbow. Maybe I put my bag at my feet. Somehow. All of my accessories, arranged and disassembled. I switched on the camera, heard its reassuring mechanical whirring and its patter of soft beeps. I raised it to my eye. I looked through the viewfinder. There was the mouse. I zoomed a little, let it focus, snapped. Did the mouse flinch? I looked at it naturally again, the camera lowered. I didn't think so. But I seemed to be involved in something oddly resuscitative. I felt like a television doctor. I mouthed *clear* as I focused again, and felt the electricity, the shock of the exposure, travel the air between the mouse and me.

The pen made it look like I had staged it, that I had put the pen down there to give the whole thing some scale. I took four photographs of the dead mouse beside the pen before I reached down, gingerly picked up the smeared pen, moved it, put it somewhere else, and took another seven photographs. That is all I can say that I remember. That I put the pen somewhere else. There I am, crouching in the street with a camera, documenting the death of a mouse, with my bag and the camera cover and my coat all getting in the way, and the badly designed lens cap swinging this and that way, and I picked up the pen because it made the scene look staged, and I put it somewhere else. I put the pen somewhere else. Even now, especially now, after all that has happened since, I find it hard to believe that my mind was so deflected, so absent, that I put the pen, the pen that had poked the mouse, the pen that had touched death – the death-stained pen – into my bag. But that, it seems, is exactly what I did.

Seven or eight more photographs. I think. About that. I took them as simply as I could, framing the dead mouse against the grey of the road, against the scattered blotches of faded yellow paint that went to form a double line. They look so clear, so solid, from a distance – those yellow lines. Up close though, they're ruined. I filled the frame with the dead mouse. Then I zoomed out to lend more context. In one of the shots you can see the tip of my left shoe. Then I zoomed in as close as I could on the face, the claws, the limbs, the tail, the head, the snout, the eyes, the feet, the mouth, the whiskers. I documented fully the mouse in death. Perhaps it was by way of a compromise between my fear of strong memory and its associations – and my knowledge that the photograph subverts and undermines such memories. I wanted, I think, the least bad thing. The possibility of appropriate placement, of getting everything in perspective, eventually. That's probably how we live.

Look at me. I met a dead mouse in the street. I stared at it. I prodded it with my pen. I called K. I photographed the mouse. I stared at it a little more. I glanced at my watch, and my shoulders rose and fell, and I went and had lunch with Michael.

Afterwards, after lunch, I passed that way again. I looked carefully, and in several places in case I was mistaken, but the mouse was gone.

That was it. That was how it started.

Rachel and Michael

Rachel had called the night before to tell us that she was going to go to Poland. Apparently she'd had some strange sort of communication from *an old school friend of her brother's*, and she wanted to investigate. She was pretty vague about it all, but sounded cheerful enough; excited that it's happening yet again. I find it difficult to tell with Rachel though. K is better at identifying her humours. I think she fakes it with me sometimes – probably because she picks up on my frustration and unease about her, and particularly about her Max project. She's an artist, I suppose. Well, actually, I don't suppose it – she is an artist, of course she is. She works mostly with photography, but also with film and audio, and with longer-term projects in which she usually perpetrates some kind of deception and then documents what happens. In the past these have been fairly playful and quite fun. She spent a month last year telephoning random people from the phone book, greeting them by name and telling them that she'd just called up for a chat. She recorded the conversations. Most of them ended pretty abruptly with a *Who the hell are you?* kind of response. But a surprising number evolved into long dialogues, or monologues, some of them quite revealing. Rachel was never sure sometimes whether people believed they knew her, or didn't care and talked anyway.

Hi there [xxxx], it's Rachel. Just thought I'd call for a chat. How are you?

Her best-known project is the one that no one knows she's responsible for. Until now, I suppose. It's the Double-Decker Slasher rumour. She started that. It took off to such an extent that I think it freaked her out a bit. I suppose paranoia is a fairly easy thing to generate, or feed off, these days, and half the city seemed to believe at various times last year that people were having their throats cut on the upstairs of double-decker buses. It was an elaborate set-up and she did it really well. But it got out of hand and she has more or less disowned it now. Originally there had been plans for a show, but I haven't heard anything about that lately. She has lots of eerie photographs taken on the upper decks of city buses, and she was going to show them, along with the fake evening newspaper front pages that she printed and left lying about all over the place, and she was going to record people's accounts of the rumour, as they'd heard it, as they'd embellished it, and have the audio playing on a loop. But I think she's shelved all that.

Upstairs only, on buses that are about half full – less than half full, a quarter full; the point is that they don't have to be empty, and you sit upstairs, towards the back; you're aware that there are people sitting behind you but you haven't really paid them any attention, you haven't picked them out at all – maybe one or two, probably one man, two women, something like that, two on the left, two on the right, and you sit down and you read your book or

*your newspaper or listen to your iPod or you look out the
window, or you do all of these things because you can and
the day is good and buses are nice, you can see the city go
by, and then you feel something, at your shoulder maybe,
what can that be, as if someone has brushed up against
you, and then a sudden cold sensation across your throat,
one that ends all the sounds that you've been hearing, one
that seems to stop the world still, a thin abrupt clarity, as
if you have plunged into cold water up to your neck, and
you look down, you can't seem to help looking down, and
you are wearing, how strange, a flowing apron of dark
blood, and you know in a slowing-down instant, in the last
of your sight, out of nowhere, on such a nice day, that
you're dead.*

I was one of the team on the Double-Decker Slasher
project. I don't know how many of us there were, but I'm
not sure it was that many really. I was told to drop it into
conversations, casually, precisely. I wasn't allowed to give
any details. I was to ask a question rather than impart
information. *Did you hear something about someone on
a number 38 getting their throat cut? The other day? No?
Well, I don't know, I heard something, oh, maybe I heard
it wrong, never mind.* No more than that. And when I
was with her, when we were in a pub or having lunch, or
on a bus, we would have the conversation, and she was
very good at lowering her voice in such a way that it would
attract attention from people within eavesdropping range.

—*I heard there was another slashing last weekend.*

—*You're joking.*

—*No. The number 7. Some middle-aged woman. A
passenger climbed the stairs and found her bleeding to
death, throat cut from ear to ear, two people sitting three
seats in front of her hadn't heard a thing.*

—*Jesus.*

—*And the camera not working of course. And the conductor sitting downstairs reading the paper. Of course. It's the third.*

—*My God.*

—*They don't want to start a panic. It may be al-Qaeda. But it's going to get out. City like this. People talk.*

She shut it down when the bus companies issued a joint statement saying that the rumours were no more than rumours, and that they suspected a malicious intent and a single source, and had asked the police to investigate. There was real panic then for a few days as Rachel made all of us swear a vow of silence – convinced that one of us had overplayed it, or that the fake newspaper pages she'd printed would somehow be traced back to her. But she'd used a printer friend, Serbian Stan, and I think practically his entire life is illegal and virtually invisible anyway, and she had no real reason to worry. For a while there were ripples in the (real) newspapers and on the radio about rumour-mongering and the climate of fear, before there was another wave of terrorist arrests and talk of a dirty bomb, and everyone forgot about old-fashioned throat-cutting and was terrified again for real.

But the major thing that Rachel's been doing, for about eighteen months now, is to pretend she has a missing brother. She's given him the name Max. She has concocted photographs, using a picture of her uncle as a young man, altered digitally in a couple of respects – removing the moustache for example, changing the colour of the eyes, restyling the hair and updating the clothes. Her uncle is dead and she doesn't actually have any brothers, so there is absolutely no one real to find. She's given Max something of a biography, but she's left most of the details

23

blank. He was born in 1970, left school in 1987, spent some time travelling all over Europe and possibly North America and possibly the Far East, and possibly anywhere else that might come in handy, and returned here in 1992, possibly, where he lived at various addresses, mostly unknown, doing various jobs, mostly unknown, until disappearing completely in 1994, at the age of twenty-four. So she has a website about him, and she has these little posters that she sticks up, and she'll sometimes go around asking all the people in a particular street or block of flats or bar or something, saying that she's found out recently that he might have lived in the area or been a regular in the bar. And what she's looking for really is exactly what she gets – people screwed up in various ways sufficient to make them believe that they knew this non-existent Max, and to offer Rachel hints and clues and insights, not into her fictional brother, but into themselves, which she duly records in some way, and stores, cross-indexed, neat, until she's ready to stick it all in an exhibition.

Anyway. Rachel called to say she was going to Poland, in connection with the Max project. This is not the first trip abroad that she's undertaken in the course of this. She's already been to Spain and Morocco, and to Israel twice. She makes quite a good living out of magazine photography. And I think her father was a pretty successful businessman. He's either dead or has retired to Israel, I actually can't remember. I think he's retired to Israel.

During lunch, Michael told me the story of the BOX building ghost. But before that, he wanted to talk about Rachel. He admires Rachel a great deal. He thinks she's a great artist. Michael has strong views on these things.

—She's off to Warsaw, you know.

—Yes, I know. She called last night.

—Oh.

He was a bit put out that she'd told us. That his news wasn't news. He made a sulky face. He makes a lot of faces, Michael. And he does voices. I think sitting at a desk all day doesn't suit him.

—Well, he whined. —Did she tell you what it was?

—An old school friend?

—Isn't that marvellous? You know, this is about the seventh or eighth one who's claimed to be a schoolmate. This chap though also claims to have seen a photograph of him, of Max, behind a bar somewhere outside Warsaw. Some hideous little Polish dump full of vodka alcoholics and toothless Catholics, can you just imagine? He lives out there now, some EU chappie. Swears that it's Max. On his life. Poor sod. And the really pathetic thing is that this fellow has told Rachel that he saw the photograph months and months ago, and recognised it then, and even pointed it out to his wife, or girlfriend or what have you, as in, *Look, how strange, there's a photograph of an old school chum, good old Max, wonder what he was doing here,* and that it wasn't until last week that he finally got around to searching for Max on the Internet and found Rachel's website and discovered he was missing.

—Jesus. That's quite elaborate.

—Isn't it? People are elaborate, though. People are Byzantine.

I'm sure that one of these days the Max project is going to go seriously off the rails. Someone is going to find out that they're being taken for a ride and they're going to get really angry. Of course Rachel insists that such a thing could never happen because such a person would, were Rachel genuine, actually be taking Rachel for a ride, and a much crueller and more disturbing one, and anger, should it all break down, would be entirely Rachel's prerogative. She insists that the room for mistaken identity is slim. The photographs, while slightly altered, are photographs of an actual distinctive person, with distinguishing features (a small scar over the left eyebrow, what looks like a mole on the lower right cheek, a handsome gap between the two front teeth), and could not be easily mistaken for somebody else. Similarly, the name she has given her missing brother, Max Poe, is sufficiently unusual to rule out that kind of confusion. And the dates she has come up with – of birth and departure and return and disappearance – are unalterable. Put all of this together, says Rachel, and it simply doesn't fit any actual missing person. She's checked. And when someone does approach her with some story about Max, Rachel goes through (so she tells us) a complicated checking procedure to ensure that it doesn't amount to valuable information about somebody who is genuinely missing. By which I think she means that she checks any checkable details against files for those who went missing at the same time and the same age as Max did not.

But of course no one is deceiving her on purpose. What would be the point? Any deception involved is total, in the sense that the people who claim to have seen Max, or who claim to have known him either before or after he didn't disappear, are deceiving themselves. Completely and utterly – almost religiously. And they're doing it for a reason – it's in their interest to deceive themselves. Because they are divided against themselves, like nations. They're disturbed. And Rachel is flying out to Poland to have a chat with them. It makes me nervous.

Of course she's aware of all of this, she's talked about it. It seems to be the point of it, in many ways. I once tried to tell her that I was worried on her behalf, but I think it came across quite badly, as if I had accused her of something, which I suppose I had. Well, I don't suppose. I did accuse her. I actually accused her of abuse – of the abuse of vulnerable, lonely people. She was astonished, and angry, and in turn she suggested that I was jealous of her – artistically jealous – and that if I wasn't fulfilled by *cartooning* I shouldn't take it out on her. Which of course may be true to some extent – I'm not really sure – but it distracted me and confused me and I lost sight of the point that I was trying to make, which was that someone at some time was going to discover that the Max they claimed to know didn't actually exist, and they would feel fooled, and they might become angry, even dangerously so. After the argument with Rachel I went over all the same ground with K, who immediately saw what I had been trying to say, but insisted that the disturbing nature of the Max project was exactly the point of it, that Rachel was that kind of artist, and that her work was for that reason hugely interesting, and that her friends should really only offer support, that anything else would be useless, that she was a grown woman who was completely aware of what she was doing, and that it would be patronising to tell her to be careful. Which, as I'm sure you can imagine, didn't exactly comfort me. I was still nervous, and added to it now was a new nervousness, about myself and my own motivations and my own worth in terms of what I do and what I manage to understand. It left me feeling rather stupid, to tell you the truth.

Michael never seems nervous at all. Or stupid. I imagine that appearing stupid would be the worst imaginable thing for Michael. Ever. I think he would rather die than appear stupid. I envy him really. He seems to exist without any difficulty, as if everything is easy. He is a very calm man, a sort of still point, who's always at the centre of some derangement or other. His mother is Catherine Anderson, who I mentioned – *the* Catherine Anderson, the actress. His father, estranged from both of them, is currently serving a jail term for a ridiculous fraud perpetrated against a children's charity somewhere in France, or Switzerland maybe. I think Michael is quite embarrassed about his parents. It's difficult to get him to talk about them, though I'm always trying, just because I'm so curious. I think they're fascinating. He *will* talk about his father sometimes, in a disparaging tone, full of distance and tired amusement, as if he's talking about the latest misadventures of a character from a soap opera. Even then he'll only talk about him while we're alone or with other close friends. About his mother he was never very voluble. I used to think that was a kind of modesty, as if he was afraid that people would think he was making himself interesting by invoking her name. But I don't think that now. I just don't think he likes her very much. We used to get the occasional reference to whatever it was that she was up to, and annoyance that she had turned up to see him unannounced, or that she'd wanted him to accompany her to some function or party or other and how he felt obliged but resentful, as if it was her who was using him. But lately, he doesn't mention her at all – not since she gave a long interview to a Sunday newspaper in which she detailed her elaborate sexual history. I don't think they're talking.

So, over lunch, Michael told me the story of the building ghost. Or should that be the ghost building? Michael is an architect. He works for Edwards Patten Associates – the people who designed the Lacon Tower, among other things, and the new Technology Museum which won a big

award last year. I like the museum. At least, I like the
photographs I've seen of it. It seems rather elegant. The
Lacon Tower, on the other hand, always looks to me like
it's about to fall down. It makes my stomach lurch a little
every time I see it. I don't like heights. Michael tells me
that it contains movement in its line. He has a voice he
adopts when he talks about his work, and I'm never sure
if it's just another one of his voices or whether it's actually the real one. It's quieter, more intense. He tells me
that the design of the Lacon Tower is intended to convey
forward momentum, like the bold cursive script of a self-
confident person. I asked Michael about this, about
whether it is really possible to speak about a building in
other terms – to say that building design, architecture, is
like something else, like people or water or air or handwriting. He admitted to me that he never thought of architecture in that way – as being like other things. He thought
of it simply as itself – as function and line and, to some
degree, *intellectual occupation of a space*. He thought about
architecture – in other words, in the language of architecture – without the need to translate. He tells me that the
similes of architecture are simply an interface with the lay
community. A way of talking to the likes of me. Do you
think that is true? I don't know whether it's true or whether
he's just teasing me. I don't know any other architects.

Comparisons make life easier, I suppose. We have two
eyes. We see things in double before we can see them at
all. In double and upside down, as far as I can remember.
They are projected on to the backs of our inner skulls,
and some process of the brain makes sense of them. We
can't see one thing unless it's next to another.

Michael told me about a building project that the practice has been involved with at quite a superficial, technical

level. A small team, which doesn't include Michael, have designed a necessarily complicated access route, vehicle and pedestrian, from street to underground car park, in a new office building in some previously anonymous inner suburb which is now attracting a number of fairly prestigious media consultancy companies for a reason which Michael, he said, knows but has forgotten. I'm not entirely sure what a 'media consultancy company' is, but I didn't ask. If I asked Michael to explain all the terms he uses we'd never finish a conversation. The project is a new build on the site of a nondescript, three-storey office and retail unit which had been destroyed by fire. The principal architects designed an attractive (though dated, said Michael) strip-windowed affair, with the name of the commissioning company, BOX, in art-deco pushpin steel lettering on one side, vertically, at the front. Actually, I know about BOX. I thought they were an advertising company. I know about them because I know someone who works for them. Not very well. But I do know her. And we had talked once about the possibility of my doing some work for them. Or *with* them, as she put it. She had asked me to send her a portfolio, which I never did. I interrupted Michael to tell him this, and he frowned at me.

—Why didn't you?

—Why didn't I what?

—Send them your stuff? Could have been something there, you know.

—They're advertisers.

—Oh, no one is an *advertiser* any more. They're brand presentation, media strategy, perception creation – all that.

—Well, I don't do that.

—No, I know you don't *do* that, of course you don't *do* that, but the fact is you *can* do that, you can do it in your sleep. Visuals, I mean – the striking image, the simple stroke that conjures up a world of complexity. Don't laugh at me. That's their language. Could have been good money in it, you know. They're worth a fortune. Why else would they be getting us in to make their bloody underground car park tunnel all lovely and light and poncing *inspirational*. The word was in the brief. Still might be money in it, for you I mean. If this whole thing doesn't knock them off line. You should send them something.

The building, Michael went on, is one storey higher than its predecessor, and was completed on time and within budget. But it's empty, unused. Because, Michael said, hunched down over his plate, eyes wide, putting on a voice, it's *haunted*. Haunted by the building it's replaced.

I had to wait until Michael went and got himself another pot of tea before I heard any more. It might be possible to guess that he's the son of an actress and a con man if you didn't already know. K gets quite bored with it all sometimes, but I enjoy spending time with Michael. I'm not sure what it is in life that he takes seriously. His work, perhaps. He likes films and music and always knows what's new without ever describing it as anything other than old hat. And he wears, as it happens, old hats. Especially in this kind of weather. I can't ever imagine him with an umbrella. He has a terrible fear of seeming very enthusiastic, and you can see him sometimes, taking a breath, calming himself down, dampening everything. And at the same time, he has a fear of not having anything to say. He looks stereotypically alternative, with his close-cropped hair, his experiments with beards, moustaches and sideburns, his black-framed glasses, his shoulder bag and his clever T-shirts and his canny shoes. A lot of our friends look like this. Vaguely arty, mildly unconventional, conscious of the irony but incorporating it. They incorporate everything really. And, of course, they are wholly incorporated.

The first manifestation of the haunting, Michael told me, was the inability of the lifts to reach the top floor. The first time this had happened the lift engineers quickly solved, or seemed to solve, the problem. But within hours, the malfunction recurred. Each time the lift attempted to rise above the third floor it stalled and would not budge. Endless diagnoses were made. Electronic problems, gear mechanisms that were faulty or misaligned, magnetic interference, inadvertent vacuums – all were blamed in turn and then discounted. Every time they changed something it seemed they had fixed it – the lift would climb to the fourth floor – and then it would stall again, within a day, or within hours, or within minutes. A fortune was spent on delicate sensors and measuring machines, and countless man hours were invested in analysing the data. The architects went through their plans again and again, the lift engineers removed the entire cabling system. The builders rebuilt part of the lift shaft. The cabling system was reinstalled. It worked for three days. And then, to the despair of everyone involved, and much to Michael's amusement, the lift would once more climb no higher than the third floor. As if there wasn't a fourth.

I told Michael that it sounded like an interesting engineering problem, rather than a poltergeist. No, he told me. There was more. While they tried to work out what to do with the lifts, and everyone started reaching for their lawyers, various other strange things began to occur.

- The telephone lines on the fourth floor misbehaved. They would go dead. Or, while working, would pick up crossed lines in unison, so that from each extension could be heard a sample section of the city's babble.

- Two electricians, called in on a Saturday to sort out the non-functioning sockets in one of the fourth-floor offices, contacted the project manager to report the fourth floor inaccessible due to some joker having bricked up the stairwell on the third-floor landing. The project manager arrived and met the electricians downstairs. Together they took the lift to the third floor because, well, that was as far as it would take them, and went into the adjacent stairwell. The brick wall had vanished. Both electricians fled, upset, ashen (*distraught*, said Michael), and had refused to work in the building since.

- Four workmen from the roofing contractors were asked to explain their presence on the fourth floor one morning – they could be clearly seen from the ground, moving around behind the windows, and at one point firing up a welding gun, by at least half a dozen people. They insisted that they had been where they were supposed to be – on the roof – the entire time. And indeed, as revealed by subsequent checks, they had no access to the fourth floor. The lift didn't go there, and the door from the stairwell had been locked the night before by a security guard who reported that he had felt 'uneasy' patrolling there, and had sealed it off.

- Carpets on the fourth floor had been replaced three times due to unexplained staining before they just gave up and left them as they were, including one with a strange Australia-shaped discoloration.

- When the CEO of BOX came on his first visit he got out of his car, stared up at the building and asked why there were only three storeys. Those accompanying him, including the chief architect, the project manager and the main contractor, looked from him to the building and back again. But there are four storeys, they told him. He looked at the building and he looked at them, and he looked at the building again. No there are not, he insisted. Then they had that argument, Michael laughed – *that* argument – about whether a four-storey building was a ground floor and three above it, or whether a four-storey building was a ground floor and four above it, and what was the difference anyway between a storey and a floor. It was only when the CEO used his finger to point and count that they all finally agreed that there was a fourth floor. Inside the building, the CEO remained silent throughout the tour, until, on the fourth floor, he was taken ill and had to leave. The nature of the illness, Michael had not been able to determine. It was simply reported that he had been taken ill, a phrase which, as Michael pointed out, covers everything from the shits to a stroke.

The CEO had not been back since. In fact, Michael believed, there had been efforts made to get BOX out of the deal entirely, and this having apparently failed, the company appeared now to be trying to sell the place without ever having taken up residency, and while still operating out of a cramped two-storey lease in the impossible city centre. But word was out, said Michael, and a sale would be difficult. He was surprised, Michael was, that it hadn't made the papers yet.

Actually, I am myself unclear about the difference between a storey and a floor – if there is one – and I get very confused by all talk of an x-storeyed building. Where do you start counting? Surely you include the ground floor as a storey? But if so, why is the first floor not the second floor? Because surely the ground floor has to be the first floor – as in Storey 1 – rather than the zero floor, the nought floor – Storey 0. Because if the ground floor is just that – the ground floor – and the first floor is the first storey, then a four-storey building, such as the BOX offices which Michael had described, was a building with five levels. A ground floor, and four storeys above it. Or was it a four-*level* building – with a ground floor and three storeys above it?

I opened my mouth to voice this puzzlement to Michael, but shut it again because I was suddenly sure that we had already had this conversation at some previous time, and I was sure also that he had explained it to me and that I had forgotten. Then I opened my mouth again to suggest that the building wasn't haunted at all, it was just jinxed by the fact that no one ever knew what other people meant when they said 'a four-storey building'. But I shut it immediately. That was just stupid.

I have a very amateur interest in architecture. By which, Michael tells me, I mean that I like buildings. He has explained to me that what I like is actually not really architecture at all, it is the placement of people against things. He insists that I am far too interested in people to really have any proper appreciation of architecture. Most of the time of course he is joking with me, teasing, but I think that he does actually, in truth, have quite a condescending attitude towards my interest in his profession. Which, I suppose, is fair enough. Architecture is probably one of those things that we all feel entitled to discuss without ever really understanding the principles. What I'm not so sure about is just how serious he is when he insists that architecture cannot concern itself too much with people. With actual real people and their physical needs and their practical necessities. These are technical matters, and should be given only minor, cursory attention. Sometimes I think he is not serious at all, that he can't be. Other times I'm convinced that this is what he really thinks, and that he dresses it up in deniable humour because he is ashamed of it. Maybe it is a cross between the two. Part of one thing and part of the other.

I was impressed, though, by Michael's story of an old building refusing to allow a new one to take its place. I liked the idea that the space had been defined at a certain height, and the new construction would not be allowed to go any higher – that it did not have metaphysical planning permission. I thought it reminded me of a film I had seen once, though I couldn't remember the details. I mentioned this to Michael.

—Oh, I know what you mean.

He was fiddling with his phone, reading a text I think.

—It's a Bob Hope thing, isn't it? he said.

—No, it's European, subtitles, German maybe.

—Fassbinder? Not like him I don't think. Who was in it?

—Oh, I can barely remember. Something about a house and the house is actually the one doing –

—*The Haunting*.

—Yeah . . .

—Well, that's American.

—It wasn't American. It was in German or something.

—Well, *The Haunting* is an American film.

—No, it wasn't called that.

—You just said it was.

—I didn't. I said that in this film the house was the one doing the haunting, and that the film was German.

Michael was replying to his text.

36

—You're thinking of *The Haunting*.

—I'm not! Is *The Haunting* German?

—No, it's American.

—Then why were there subtitles?

—Are you thinking of Tarkovsky? There's a bit in *Stalker* –

—I don't know who that is.

—There was a creepy Yugoslavian thing called *The House*. From what I remember. All bony hands on banisters.

—Oh, I don't know. It doesn't matter.

—Menzel?

—What?

—*Closely Observed Trains*?

—What?

—Not that one obviously. He had another one. Powerful. Powerful film-maker. Must get it on DVD actually – *Trains*. Lovely film. The boy in the bath, all that. There.

Just as he finished whatever it was that he was doing on his phone, and I was about to give out to him for doing it, there was a sudden cloudburst outside. I'm not sure if there was thunder. But a wave of darkness raced through the café, bringing hush and hesitation, and then the rain hit the ground like debris. The two of us watched as people ran for cover, some of them screeching between laughter and alarm, a couple of them coming into the café for shelter, others making it across the road to a second-hand record shop. The rain was torrential. It came down so hard that after a couple of minutes we could no longer see the other side of the street. We stared out at what I can't really call rain at all. We stared out at falling water, as if we had been transported to some jungle and were crouched in a cave behind a waterfall, mute in fear and ignorance, cold little apes in the crevice. The café was becalmed. There was no noise of voices. The radio had

37

disappeared. There was no clatter of dishes or cutlery or cooking, no ring of the register, no tunes from phones, no movement. Only the hysterical drumming of the rain, and the gathering rattle of running water. We stared and waited, as if there was a chance that this time, this time, it might not stop. Or this time, this time, it might presage something worse. The darkness covered us, and I was afraid. It was hard in the noisy gloom to pick out Michael sitting beside me. His telephone too went dark, its little lights vanishing in his hand. On my face I could feel a kind of paralysis, as if I had neglected to blink, or breathe. I thought that it would not stop. I thought that it would never stop, not now. But it did. After just a couple of minutes. The light returned. The water became rain again. And then the rain slowly ceased.

Michael broke the human silence with his laugh. He stopped, made a wide-eyed face of mock fear and laughed again. In the rest of the café, people relaxed. Others laughed too, some shook their heads, rolled their eyes, muttered. Conversations resumed, the hubbub rose unaltered.

Then a dog appeared, walking down the centre of the road; a large, dark dog that moved with a great swagger, slowly – almost, it seemed to me, in slow motion – right down the middle of the sodden roadway, as if it was in charge here. I'm not sure anyone else noticed. Michael was fiddling again with his phone. The dog's big head bounced gently, its powerful shoulders rolled and rippled and its tongue seemed to glisten and ooze over its pointed teeth like a bag of blood. It glanced this way and that with huge cloudy eyes, and paused, and went on, and looked, as it passed, directly into the café – directly, it seemed, at me – registering my stare, taking note of me, its hard, intelligent mind considering and then dismissing me. It went from view. A huge, loathsome dog, a deep shadow in the damp sunlight, uncollared, unkept. Dry as a bone.

I took a sip of my very cold tea.

I can't remember anything else about lunch with Michael. We talked about Rachel. We talked about a building haunted by another building. We watched the rain. I saw a dog. I think Michael enjoyed meeting me. Perhaps I was a little quieter than usual. I had the mouse on my mind, still. And I was a little depressed by the news of Rachel's trip to Poland. And at the end, after the rain and the dog, I was uneasy, a little nervous. I don't really like dogs. But I think Michael had a good enough time talking with me.

It is often impossible, however, to know very much about Michael. He is rather opaque.

The Swimming Pool

The mouse's corpse was washed away by the rain, I suppose. All the gutters were raging when I left the café. But a few streets away they were calmer, and when I got to the place where I'd seen the mouse, the ground was almost dry. I don't know if that meant that the rain had been very localised or that the sun was very hot. It didn't feel very hot.

I was feeling, by this time, if I'm honest, a little perplexed. I know that when I list the things that happened that day, they don't seem to amount to very much. And they don't. But nevertheless, I was, even by the time I left Michael after lunch, feeling somewhat rattled – on edge. Stress had crept into me. Even stepping out of the café I moved very slowly, nervously, afraid that the dog might still be around. So much so that I think Michael had to nudge me in the back to get me into the street. I think it was mostly the dog. The rain and the dog. They had, both of them, unsettled me slightly, but I wasn't sure why, and maybe I was simply, unconsciously, the victim of various automatic associations that had no relevance to me personally. Michael was going to the left, and it made sense for me to go to the left as well, as there was a bus stop in that direction from where I could catch a bus home. But it was also the way the dog had gone. I can't remember what I told Michael now – that I wanted to look in some shops or something – but I made an excuse, said my goodbyes and walked instead to the right.

I wonder now why I didn't tell Michael about the mouse. Perhaps because I knew that he'd have wanted to look at the photographs stored on my camera, and that he would have had some wry way of making the whole thing seem a lot less strange, a lot more unremarkable. He would have been quick to puncture what would have seemed to him a typically inflated sense of significance and drama which I had attached, not for the first time, to something banal. I regret it now. Because that is probably exactly what I needed just then, and it may have proved useful later on. *Delete the photographs if they bother you. Forget all about it. Put it out of your mind.* But of course, as you know, I kept it to myself. Which is typical and predictable. But I shouldn't make the mistake now of believing that my failure to talk to Michael – and the consequent failure to be convinced of the insignificance of the mouse – was in itself significant. There's no point is replacing the ridiculous *Oh my God a dead mouse* with the equally ridiculous *Oh my God I didn't tell Michael about the dead mouse.*

In any case, I have no way of knowing that telling Michael would have made any difference anyway. He might have had the same reaction as me. He might have been moved by the same odd mechanism and been knocked off balance – reinforcing my sense of peculiarity and low-level but elaborate menace. I was stuck with my weird mouse reaction. Nothing had defused it. And if you add to it my reawakened worries for Rachel and the slightly disconcerting talk of building ghosts (though, to be honest, Michael's story hadn't really made its full impact on me at that point), plus the rather biblical rain and the demon dog, then I think it's fair to say that I had a head full of negative thoughts. I felt a little queasy.

I decided to go for a swim.

I took a bus home, dropped off my bag (I left it on a chair in the kitchen), changed out of my shoes into some trainers, picked up my swimming things, and walked to the quiet end of our street and through the park to the sports centre. It's a brand new centre, and the local council has spent a lot of money on it, but it has been very badly designed, or perhaps very badly built (Michael suggests a little of both) and already it looks somewhat dilapidated. Most days when I go, some part of the changing rooms, or the reception, or the gym, is inevitably cordoned off – due to leaks or problems with ceiling tiles falling down or the floor buckling or otherwise giving way. One day I was in the communal shower area when a large tile fell from the wall, coming away as neatly as if it had been pushed out from the other side, and it shattered on the floor in a cloud of dust and fragments. Luckily, no one had been standing close to it at the time. Despite all these problems, and the huge controversy which they have engendered, I still love going to the pool. You don't have to be a member or anything, you just have to pay a small per-use fee. You have to be careful with timing of course. Sometimes it's not open access, it's booked up by clubs or schools. Or some days, especially on warm days, it can be very busy, and after-school hours can be filled with noisy kids. This time of day, though, is usually perfect, and when I got there I was cheered up greatly by the fact that there were only a handful of people in the changing room, and all of them seemed to be getting dressed, having finished their swims.

I love to swim. I always have. It calms me, soothes me. I don't really know what it is about it that has such a positive effect on me, but it's not unusual I suppose. It's sensual of course – being almost naked, surrounded by warm water; and it's exercise, the only exercise I get really; and it's also the only physical activity that I do relatively well. Perhaps it was for all these fairly mundane but sensible reasons that I decided to go for a swim. But I remember wondering, as I undressed, whether it wasn't something as well to do with the rain I'd seen from the café during lunch with Michael. I wondered whether what I was actually doing was attempting to reassert myself over the element. As if I needed to reassure myself that I had the measure of it, that I had it tamed, that I could be a master of water – that it was, after all, only water, and that it was there for me to use and enjoy and not to fear. The thought made me laugh as I stepped beneath the lukewarm shower and slipped my goggles over my head. Then I made my way carefully through to the poolside, thinking that mine is a daft psychology, and that I would make K laugh later that evening with an account of my redemptive exorcism down at the sports centre.

There was a middle-aged woman swimming slow, sedate lengths, and a young girl and her father, clinging to the side, chatting. They were all in the slow lane, and there was no one else. I had never known the pool to be so empty. I think I probably grinned as I walked to the middle lane at the deep end. I nodded to the bored-looking lifeguard slumped in his high chair and asked him if it was all right if I dived in. He nodded, unconcerned. Normally

I ease myself into the pool, most of the time I use one of the ladders at the sides, and then swim to the middle lane. But I felt today that the more exuberantly I took the opportunity to enjoy myself, the better I would be able to clear my head of all my concerns and my worries.

I dived. I'm not a great diver, but still, I dived this dive well, and my body went into the water as it should do – hands, arms, shoulders, head, chest, and then the rest of me, slicing into the water neatly, quickly, cleanly. It was a good dive. Something has to go through your mind at a moment like that. It is like a moment of violence almost – like a knife into skin, or the moment of an accident. It is heightened. I mean, things go through our minds all the time, endlessly, but there are certain moments when the thought gets caught, amplified, recorded. It's like someone takes a photograph. And always, after that, you remember what it was you were thinking when whatever happened happened. When your car hit the kerb; when you lost your footing; when you heard the news; when you heard the bang; the moment you jumped; the moment you dived. I'm not saying that anything other than the dive happened. I just mean that a dive into a swimming pool, as you force your body to trust your brain – if you're not used to doing it – is just such a moment. As with a trauma moment, the shock, or the adrenalin, or whatever it is, captures your thought and shows it to you in rare clarity, and stores it with those other heightened moments and their associated thoughts. And when I dived into the swimming pool that day, the thought I caught myself thinking was this one: *the stain was shaped like Australia.*

It was what Michael had said, when he told me about the building ghost. That there was a stain on the carpet of the fourth floor and it wouldn't go away and it was shaped like Australia. I couldn't remember really what emphasis he'd given it, if any, and didn't even know whether it was accurate or something he'd added himself as an evocative phrase, not knowing in truth what the stain looked like at all, thinking that it would assist me in visualising something. And perhaps he'd chosen Australia just because it has a distinctive shape, and also because it suggests something of considerable scale. You don't really think of something shaped like Australia as being small. At least, I don't. If it was something that someone had actually said to him, that had been reported to *him* as an accurate description, and which he had in turn reported accurately to *me*, did that mean that it was accurate in fact? That the stain really did look like Australia? Perhaps someone earlier in the reporting chain had added it as an embellishment, Chinese-whisper-style, and it had stuck. It might have been the person who told the story to Michael, or it might have been the person before that; it could in fact have been anyone at all in the chain, at any point, close to the original source or not. Even if it had been applied by one of the people who had actually been in the building, who had been to the fourth floor and had seen the stain on the carpet there – even then, how accurate was it? Shapes are fairly objective things, once you get past circles and squares and triangles. One person can look at a cloud and see the outline of a face. A second person can look at the same cloud and see the shape of a sailboat. A third person can look at the same cloud and see nothing but a cloud – shapeless, meaningless and fleeting. Even if you were to assume that several people had seen the stain and that they had all agreed that its shape resembled that of Australia, could it not be said that all stains, almost inevitably, look like Australia? It's something about the large irregular blob-ness of it, with the single separate smaller blob underneath, Tasmania. Knock your cup of coffee and have a look at the resulting mess. From some angle, somehow, it will look a little like Australia.

I don't know why all of this suddenly seemed so important, but it did. I realised it with a sort of annoyance, a kind of underwater sigh of impatience, and a slight tilting of the head and a brief rolling of the eyes, as I dived down into the deep brightness of the pool, which felt to me less warm than I thought it should have, but which was, nevertheless, wonderfully refreshing. I knew that I'd have to call Michael and find out whether it was true, whether it was definitely the case that the stain on the fourth-floor carpet of the BOX building was shaped like Australia. I felt it was vital that I find this out, and I couldn't believe that I hadn't asked him at the time. My body was fully immersed by then. I was pointing downwards, head first, towards the bottom of the pool, still moving, and all the water seemed to panic around me, as if I was a catastrophe here. It seemed terribly significant – the matter of Australia, I mean. Significant in terms of what, I had no idea, and why it should occur to me that it was significant I had no idea either. But there was something in the notion of Australia. It wasn't about the stain per se, or the idea that it remained, despite constant attempts to remove it. What was significant, if it was true, was its shape. I've never been to Australia. I know some Australians of course – it's inevitable – but it's not a country I know very much about or have very much interest in. And I did not know at that time, I think, what I could or would do with the knowledge – if it was forthcoming from Michael – that the stain was indeed, definitely and clearly and objectively, shaped like Australia. But I knew I had to find out.

My momentum slowed. I kicked my legs briefly and did a quick breaststroke to keep myself going down. Why did I want to keep going down? I suppose I was exhilarated by the water, by being out of the world for a moment, by being so completely and alertly *elsewhere*. But really – the bottom of a swimming pool is a terrible place. There are tricks and corners there. There are hidden catches. There is the noise. The pool in the sports centre is white-tiled. It has black lane markers – elongated *I*s that attempt a kind of orientation, and fail, or fail me at least, providing only a mild sense of vertigo and a vague disappointment at the impossibility of falling. There is a slope in the middle somewhere, as the deep end becomes the shallow end. There are randomly spaced plastic covers over drains or filters or some such. There are the shadows of the lane ropes and their measured-out floaters, bobbing. There is the water: bubbles and distortions, glints of light, minute clouds of particles, debris, human dust, debris. We are disintegrating. Sometimes the sparkle of an earring or an unmissed bracelet or an unreachable delicate chain with cross or locket or twist. I don't think I had been to the bottom of the sports centre pool before. And I think it was only when I reached it, my hands spreading out to brush the tiles, my body contracting, my feet tucking in, my eyes all around me, that I remembered how terrifying such a place is. My fingers touched grout. My hands pressed down on the strangely warm tiles. What were they made of, exactly? How did they not break? Leak? If they leaked would they leak inwards or outwards? How heavy is water? Why was I not crushed? Everything was above me. The shimmering surface, the lane ropes, the legs – kicking and still – the light. All of it above me. And the bubbles that came from my mouth fled upwards. And my hair lifted upwards. Everything natural wanted out of there. I glanced at a nearby drain or filter cover, whatever it was – an ugly sinister thing where you could easily trap a finger or a toe. The brightness was awful, the clarity utterly deceptive. I could see everything, and yet I suddenly expected a tap on the shoulder, a face in front of mine, a hand on my ankle – unseen before I saw it. I was swimming in a flooded hospital ward, a submerged asylum, a sunken abattoir, a place so full of ghosts that they touched every inch of my skin with their half-cold own.

Perhaps the fear is about sound. Sounds there are so hideously distorted. It is an inverted silence – all unidentified roaring and the thump of your own heart. It's a muffling that suggests being buried alive; the prolonged, strangulated fade-out of dying.

Perhaps I watch too many films. Perhaps my fear isn't my own at all but has been gifted to me by Hollywood. I'm sure my mind is full of a lifetime of images of trouble underwater. Of murder in the swimming pool. Of course, now that I try I can't actually think of any. At all. Nothing specific. I can think of several celluloid underwater terrors at sea. But nothing in a swimming pool. I'm sure that they exist. They must. The relaxed swimmer, the pristine white, the lap of the water, the brightness. And then the underwater shot, the sudden odd angle, all sounds grotesquely altered, the light refracted, split and cutting, concentrated and threatening. The whiteness calling out for red. The sensual skin turned to vain vulnerability, the supporting water gone deep and thick and complicit. Everything suddenly stops.

My worries about dreams came back to me then, as my body came upright in the water and my feet sought out the tiles below me. For weeks I had puzzled over this. I think I've mentioned it. I had not been able to find a way of thinking about it that did not disturb and confuse me. It had started very simply over coffee one morning, as K and I sat in the kitchen with the radio on, not long out of bed. We talked about dreams. That isn't unusual, but that morning I remember that our conversation had been prompted by a story on the news. The security forces all over Europe were reported to be very concerned about the theft from an Italian laboratory of various poisons and toxins and that kind of thing. Vials of anthrax or botulinum or ricin or something. And of course, their concern was that the theft had been carried out by terrorists who would seek to use these toxins in an attack. As we listened, K looked up at me and frowned.

—That's very strange.

—What is? I asked.

—A lab, vials, all that.

—Oh, it'll just be another false alarm. It'll all turn up somewhere, or they'll arrest another cell because of it. It's the stuff that doesn't make the news that worries me.

—No, that's not what I mean. I mean it's strange because I dreamed about it. Or something very like it. I think.

I said nothing. K often relates dreams to me. I'm used to it. It's a regular thing. I don't really like it – I never have. Something in me clams up slightly when someone, anyone – not just K – tells me their dreams. I seem to have an instinctual resistance to it. I sipped my coffee, and my mind focused more on the radio than on K.

—I was in a hospital, I think. All white and clean, and it had that disinfectant sort of smell.

—You can smell in your dreams?

—Apparently. In this one anyway. I was looking for someone. I'd come to visit someone, I'm not sure who.

Keith Ridgway

The place seemed deserted, there was no one around at all and there wasn't a sound. It was all very creepy.

K smiled a little and squinted, trying to remember the details.

—Then this little boy appeared out of nowhere, wearing pale blue pyjamas, a real cute little kid, sleepy-eyed, straight out of a television ad for cough bottle or fabric conditioner or something, the only thing missing was the clutched teddy bear. And I asked him, could he tell me where I could find the Research Centre. I was very specific. And the boy told me that I would have to go and see Dr Harkin for my tests. And he took me by the hand, very solemnly, and led me down the corridor. The next thing I know is that I'm in a garden, outside the same building, and the little boy is gone, and there's an elderly man leaning out of a window, on the same level as me, talking to me, and I know that this is Dr Harkin, and he gives me this long elaborate spiel about my tests not being very good, and that I may have to have my *insides recounted*, that there may have been some error in the counting.

K laughed at this point. Although I was hearing the account, and remembering it obviously, I had the definite sensation of *not wanting* to hear about the content of the dream, of wishing that K would shut up, that the recollection was profoundly *uninteresting* to me, at the very least.

—He told me to come in, and I had to find my way out of the garden into his surgery, but I couldn't seem to find a door into the building. In the garden there were several people strolling and sitting around, and as I searched for the way back into the building, I realised that they, and I, were all naked. That didn't seem to bother me, and nor did the fact that I couldn't find a way back into the building.

50

Then the door was right there in front of me – obvious – but I couldn't get in because it was cordoned off by the police. I approached a policeman and asked him, could I go in. He said no. He said that there had been a robbery and that all the diseases had been stolen. He said, *Everyone is a suspect*. Then he looked me up and down and said, *The naked people are obviously not suspects as they have no pockets in which to hide the vials*. And that was it. That's all I remember. I am not a suspect.

—Good for you.

—Yes.

—Of course, all that means is that while you were dreaming about little boys and doctors and being nude in the garden, the radio alarm clock went off, and the news came on, and you heard the report about the Italian thing and you incorporated it into your dream.

K considered this and nodded, impressed.

—Very possibly.

I put my feet flat on the bottom of the swimming pool and pushed off. There was a rushing sensation, not unpleasant, although I could feel some kind of discomfort in my right ear, brought on by pressure no doubt. I reached out my hands for the surface and looked along the line of my arms. There was a horrible confusion of noise – a combination of my progress through the water, and changing pressures in my ears, and the general sonorous bellowing of underwater ambience. Well, that's what I thought.

As I said, K telling me a dream was not an unusual thing, and given the fact that its similarity to the news report had been explained, it didn't really stay in my mind. Other people's dreams never do. I imagine that if you had asked me later that day, even an hour or so later, what K had dreamed of the night before, I would have been hard pressed to tell you. The only reason I now remember it so well is that, two nights later, I had the very same dream myself.

It was not exactly the same. The hospital I went to was not deserted, it was busy, and it was the same hospital in which my mother had a minor operation last year. In fact, in my dream it was my mother I was looking for, not the Research Centre. But, like K, I couldn't find my way, until a small boy in pale blue pyjamas appeared and took me to see Dr Harkin. I too stood in a garden while the doctor spoke through a window. I'm not sure what he said to me, but it seemed to be about my own health rather than my mother's. Like K, I could not find the door back into the building. Unlike K, I remained fully clothed. My garden was deserted. When I did eventually find the door, my re-entry was blocked not by a policeman but by the same small boy, except this time he was naked. He told me that someone had stolen the diseases. At that point I became aware that my pockets were filled with vials. I woke up.

Unsurprisingly, I think, I found this dream quite disturbing. I remember when I awoke from it that I awoke completely – I was immediately fully conscious and alert, and every detail of the dream remained as vivid as reality. I knew that I had had a dream that had left a huge impression on me, but for those first few moments I was not sure why. I lay there in bed, staring at the ceiling, going through it several times, confirming to myself that I remembered everything – that there were no parts of it which had evaded me. It was after dawn – the room was filled with a soft grey light – but the alarm had not woken me, the dream had. I turned to look at the alarm clock, and despite the fact that the radio alarm clock sits at K's side of the bed and that therefore, by turning my head, I saw K directly for the first time since waking up, I honestly believe that it wasn't seeing K that made me realise the significance of the dream, but rather the actual physical movement of my head which somehow realigned my thoughts, so that I recognised that what I had just dreamed was, largely speaking, not my dream at all. It belonged to K. The time on the clock was 06:13.

I couldn't get back to sleep that morning. It didn't even occur to me to try in fact. I got up, as quietly as I could, and I went into my office and sat at my desk and wrote out, quickly, the details of my dream. I also drew rough sketches of what I had seen, recreating, as faithfully as I could, the boy in the blue pyjamas as he led me towards Dr Harkin; Dr Harkin himself, leaning from the window as he talked to me about my health; the garden, from several different angles, with its paths and flower beds and the small fountain at its centre; and finally the door back into the building, and my way blocked by the boy. All of this I did in a kind of daze, determined that I would record it all before it left my mind, as it inevitably would. Strangely, it never has left my mind. But perhaps the simple act of putting it all down on paper ensured that.

When K finally got up – astonished to find me at my desk so early – I made some coffee, and while we drank it I recounted the dream. As I related each detail in turn I watched K's face for the signs of recognition, surprise, even shock. But there was no such reaction. There was nothing. Nothing at all but a sleepy shrug. I was dumbfounded.

—Does none of that ring a bell?

—Ring a bell? No. Should it?

—Are you serious? Have you forgotten?

—Forgotten what?

—Just the other day, at this exact time, you sat there, where you're sitting now, just like that, drinking coffee, in your dressing gown, and you told me the same dream.

K considered me, bewildered.

—I did?

—Yes you did! Jesus! I don't believe you've forgotten.

—I can't, well . . . I do remember telling you about a dream . . . I do remember that. But I don't . . . Really? Tell me what you dreamed again.

So I did. I went through the details once more. K was silent, but this time I was sure that there was some recognition, that I was not mad, that something odd had indeed happened.

—God. That's a bit creepy. I *do* remember. It seems very like my dream. Yes. The doctor at the window. The little boy. The policeman.

—There was no policeman in mine though.

—No. But still.

We went through the details of K's dream and the details of mine, and we sought out the similarities and the differences. The differences were all fairly plain, obvious, matters of stark contrast, such as the atmosphere in the hospital at the beginning and, of course, the different endings. But the similarities – or more than that, the identicals – of everything else struck us both as peculiar in the extreme. We stared at each other, baffled, at a loss to explain it. What did it mean? Then I went to my desk and got the sketches I had made. K went through them one by one, examining each for several seconds before commenting.

—No. This isn't the boy I dreamed of. Mine was a bit

chubby. He had curly hair, freckles. Yours is a bit, what, blond and blue-eyed?

—Yes. He was thin too. A bit spectral, I suppose.

—Well. Who's this? Is this the doctor? Mine had no beard. Mine had glasses and no beard. And you have yours wearing a doctor's jacket, is it? I can't remember what mine was wearing. I suppose he would have been. I can't remember. The window looks about right. The brickwork on the wall looks right. I think I remember ivy though. Or do I? Ivy, or high bushes or something.

—Look at the garden ones.

K looked at them, and immediately frowned.

—No. Mine was completely different. Yours is all neat and tidy. I didn't have paths, or a fountain. It was just a lawn, with bushes around the edges, maybe some in the middle, not well kept, high grass. I wouldn't have recognised this at all.

The final sketch was the door back into the building. Again, this was different.

—You have the boy there again. And he's naked. Well. I was naked in mine, and there was a policeman. And you have the door open, but in mine it was closed, although it looks like the same door, to tell you the truth. Same arched thing, heavy wooden old-fashioned thing like a church door. There was police tape in front of mine. He wouldn't let me in.

K put down my sketches and smiled at me.

—Also, in my dream I was innocent. In yours you're guilty. Guilty of theft as well, you notice. Theft of my dream.

—Seems that way.

—Are you freaked out?

—A little.

—Well, I would have been as well if the sketches had matched my dream. But they don't. So. You didn't dream what I dreamed. You had my dream in your head and you dreamed *about* it. And you didn't know what anything looked like so you made it up. I wouldn't worry about it. It probably means you're jealous of my life or something.

K regarded it as a peculiar but really quite explicable coincidence, and I remember that although we did at that stage laugh about it a little bit, and the conversation veered off into mutual teasing, I was still troubled by it, and remained so. But my thoughts were at that stage limited to what had happened to us, nothing more.

Before K left for work that morning, we had moved the conversation on to the original source for the first dream – the news report about the break-in at the laboratory in Italy.

—It just goes to show, said K, that the most infectious thing of all is not anthrax or the plague or whatever, it's paranoia, and they've already released that. It's in all our conversations, in our private thoughts and our worries and our secret fears and our horror stories. And now it's in our dreams. It's contagious.

That final word stayed with me. For the rest of that day I got no work done. Contagious. If it was as easy as it seemed for one person's dreams to infect another's, then surely it must have happened to me before? I tried to remember dreams. I found that I could remember very few. One horrible nightmare from my childhood stood out, as did one extremely erotic dream from some months previously. But of my recent dreams I could remember very little. There were a few peculiar, isolated images – a coach on a winding, perilous mountain road; a bridge made entirely of broken glass; a black river; a tangle of snakes knotted together in a laundry basket; sheets of yellow paper blowing down a hillside. But I could recall no contexts, no stories, no sense of where I was or if I was there at all, nothing that I could reasonably think of as a proper dream, such as the one I had stolen from K. I knew, though, that I had dreamed many such dreams. It was simply that I had forgotten them. It made me wonder whether there was something about dreams which did not allow them to be easily remembered. Did they contain some sort of self-destruct mechanism? It was hard to remember them when you first woke up; harder still, as K had demonstrated, just a few days later; almost impossible, as I now found, after any length of time more than that. Perhaps there was a reason for it.

I remembered too how something inside me recoils from hearing someone else's dream. My mind shies away from it in the same way that my body shies away from a height or a dog. Perhaps there was a reason for that too, and perhaps they were the same reason.

I moved through the water and the muffled, riotous noise, towards the surface and the moving light. My feet kicked.

There would be nothing at all to worry about if dreams were unimportant. But I don't know that they're unimportant. I mean, they may well be unimportant, and if they are then I'm being stupid, and if you believe they're unimportant then this is going to make you very impatient. But the fact is – and I've done a little research – nobody really knows what dreams are. The scientists and the doctors and the psychiatrists have their various theories of course, but they are various, and no one really agrees about anything. So, imagine for a moment that dreams *are* important. Imagine that in some fundamental way they enable us to function. It's not unreasonable, is it? Maybe dreams are the way our mind makes sense of itself. Maybe it's in our dreams that we arrive at conclusions and make decisions which in our waking life take on the nature of givens, of truths, which we do not seek to explain. Maybe dreams are the way we develop our conscience, our morality, our personality. Maybe that's how, and where, we allocate priorities and sort through aspects of ourselves and arrive at an understanding of how best to proceed. Maybe dreams make us wiser and better and more human. Maybe they make us ourselves.

And imagine as well that what we remember of dreams is just the smallest part of what has gone on while we slept. It is highlights, and it is remembered as images and sounds and emotions and sensations because that is the language that our waking mind uses, while in fact, in dreams, the language is very different – something strange and irreducible, inexpressible in words or signs. So, dreams tumble through us, and only small pieces of them are remembered, and then only in translation as it were, recalled in a way that *allows* them to be recalled.

When I realised that I had dreamed K's dream, I realised too that this could not have been the first time that this had happened. It may have been the first time I had noticed it, but K has been recalling dreams over breakfast for years. And K is not of course the only person who tells me about their dreams. Rachel often does it, though I suspect she makes a lot of hers up, and another friend of mine, David, tells me regularly about his – complicated things that seemed to go on for ever. In the average week I will hear of strange images, unlikely circumstances, embarrassing situations, mysterious words and gestures and signs – all taken from the dreams of others. And all

of this is fed into my subconscious and stays there somewhere, along with all the other things I hear and see in
the course of my life. Inevitably, some of it will resurface
in my own dreams. It goes into the mix. It is improbable
to think that it wouldn't. And I have the clear evidence
of K's dream to prove it.

When I first thought this through, it took a little while
for me to work out the implications. But what nagged at
me was the sensation I have whenever someone tells me
their dream. I feel, as I've said, a definite reticence, almost
distaste. As if I know innately that hearing the details of
someone else's dream is bad for me. And of course, I eventually realised, if dreams really are evidence of a nocturnal,
deeply unconscious process by which we become ourselves,
then taking the translated highlights of one person's dreams
and inserting them into the dreams of another might well
be bad for all concerned. It might well be very damaging.
For what are we processing then? Certainly nothing that
is entirely our own. We're working on the detritus of a
different consciousness. Someone else's stuff. We're taking
in orphan manifestations of another inner life. We're dealing
in interference, static, muddied waters, a polluted stream,
a mess of mixed metaphors, a heap of confusion. There
are false reports in the dispatches. In among your bad day
at work, your difficult relationship with your mother, father,
husband, wife, your financial problems and the threat of
terrorism, is the bicycle ride along the cliff edge that your
daughter dreamed of last Thursday; and the man with the
sombrero who followed your work colleague around a
cathedral in a dream she had last night and told you about
this morning. How will these be processed? Will they be
dismissed? Will they be confused with your own reality? Are
they translations of very specific subconscious conclusions

or switches or trips, which, when redreamed by you, will affect, alter or stall your own sleeping deliberations? Is that why we find it difficult to remember dreams? Because our minds are naturally wary of contagion? Is that why I feel so uncomfortable hearing someone else's dream? Because I know it is infecting my own?

I voiced my theory to K. It would be wrong to say that the response was entirely dismissive. But my impression was that K was amused by it, thought it an entertaining conceit, a nicely ridiculous notion, and did not for a moment take it seriously.

—Dreams are not for sharing then?

—Well, no, they're not. I don't think so.

—Because they interfere with other dreams?

—Yes. I mean, I'm trying to think of an example. Imagine waking up in the middle of surgery and offering to help the surgeon.

—Yes?

—Well, it wouldn't be good, would it?

—Why? Was I dreaming?

—No, surgery is the dreaming, is the process you go through while asleep, while dreaming, and then, in the middle of that, you interfere, or someone else interferes, in the process. It's not a good example.

—No.

—OK, have you ever used one of those online translation services? You enter a web page in French or German or whatever and it gives you an instant rough translation?

—Yeah.

—OK, well, imagine that what you remember from a dream is like one of those translations. You know it's not accurate, sometimes the inaccuracies are quite funny, but it'll do, it gives you a rough idea.

—OK.

—Then imagine that you pass that translation on to someone else who then translates it again. Their translation will not only be an additional step away from the original, but it won't even be their original that it's one more step away from, it's someone else's.

—Why do they translate it again though?

—It's an example.

—You need to work on your examples.

—But don't you get it? Dreams are like your own personal, bear with me, your own personal essence.

—Oh dear.

—And telling other people about them risks, I don't know. You exhale your essence and they inhale it and then their essence is compromised by your essence.

—Jesus.

—Well, it's not an easy thing to get your head around.

—No. I get it. There is too much telling of dreams going on. Too much exhaling of essences. We need a reduction in global levels of essence. We need a new Kyoto Accord, except for dreams. Less dreams in the atmosphere. The Americans will want a derogation, you know. What with Hollywood and all. I mean, the American Dream for God's sake. You can't tell them to stop exhaling that.

—And that's another thing. The use of the word 'dream' in all kinds of stupid ways. Hollywood ways. Aspirational. My dream house; my dream job; my dream girlfriend, boyfriend. These are not dreams. Or, dreams are not these. Dreams are not good things. Or, they're not fluffy harmless diversionary things. They're the motors of self-awareness. They construct our individuality. If we share them we cease to be ourselves. We merge into a banal gloop of similarities. We get stuck. As human beings, we get stuck at this aggressive, self-obsessed, materialistic stage of our development.

K looked at me for quite a long time without saying anything, half smiling, but trying to work out as well, I think, how much of this I actually believed.

—Motors of self-awareness?

—Well, why not?

—OK. I won't tell you my dreams any more.

My concern about dreams did not diminish over the next number of weeks, but I didn't mention it again. I realised that it was a difficult idea to voice, and I realise it still. But it has preyed upon me considerably. I have had to stop people, a couple of times, as they began to tell me about a dream. I'm relieved when I wake and can remember nothing. I become agitated and nervous when details do get through. And all the time, my mind struggles with the notion of a polluted pool of dreams from which we are all drinking, oblivious, trapping ourselves in a dead end of shared, second-hand signs.

All this talk of dreaming. I rose through the water, fingers first, propelling myself towards the unmediated light, towards breathing. With the things that had been going through my mind you would think that breaking the surface and re-emerging into the air, into the direct sound of the world, would have seemed like waking from a dream, like coming from an unreal place into a real one. But it was not like that. Something had happened. In the tiny space of time during which I had been underwater, something had happened.

The first indication of it was sound. I had thought that the roaring in my ears, the drumming and the crashing and the jumble of noise that I had been hearing, was the water – the water going past me; my disturbance of it; the filling of my ears and my nose; the press of it against my head and my body; the echo of my inner spaces, suddenly surrounded. But as my head cleared the surface and I drew my first breath, the roaring continued. And it was more, it immediately seemed to me, than a matter of water. I had surfaced facing down the pool towards the shallow end. I caught a blur of the small girl, and her father, whom I'd seen earlier. She was climbing out of the pool, and her father seemed to be almost pushing her, while his head was turned towards me, or rather, past me, towards the deep end, with an expression which suggested some not inconsiderable alarm.

I spun round. The lifeguard's chair was empty. Something was wrong with my eyes. I could barely see. I blinked hard, I pulled my goggles on to the top of my head and blinked again. The air seemed filled with dust, thin and brown and falling, swirling, and with things in it. The lifeguard was underneath his chair, crouching, his arms over his head. I leaned back, kicked a couple of times, moving away. My eyes travelled upwards. Roof tiles were falling, peeling from above the pool like a layer of wallpaper that has come unglued, and they were disintegrating into chunks of debris, falling on to the poolside and the water below. Metal rods, aluminium brackets, plaster, cables, plastic, pipes – all of it was coming apart. The noise was of material wrenching itself away from its moorings and falling and hitting. The ceiling was collapsing. The pool barely a metre from my feet was a storm of wreckage. I floated, treading water, then gave another couple of kicks. It seemed that the collapse had started by the back wall and was moving forward, very like a wave, exposing a dark network of frames and girders and stanchions and gathered cabling with angles and junctions and crossroads. The collapse was moving towards me, one section's failure prompting an adjacent cracking, a line of catastrophic gravity making its way from the deep end like rain. I noticed suddenly, I don't know what drew my eye, the middle-aged woman who had been swimming lengths, sprawled over the edge of the pool at the side, two or three metres from the end, her upper body out of the water, her legs still in it, her arms covering her head. She seemed very still. There was rubble on her back. There was screaming, but I don't think it was coming from her. Off to the side, near the high-frosted windows, I saw a sudden firework spray of sparks. It occurred to me then that even if I managed to outswim the advancing shower of debris, I might well be electrocuted. I wondered, as I kicked my legs, why I was staying on my back, why I was not using my arms, why I was so curious, just then, about what death in a badly designed, badly built sports centre might be like.

I didn't find out, of course. I suppose I was in shock, of a kind. The kind that makes us watch what happens to us rather than do anything about it. I moved gently, lazily away from the line of pockmarked water which approached me, curtained by falls of dark objects of all sizes, and eruptions and splashes and noise. I was mesmerised. I could not bring myself to turn round, to break into the front crawl – the Australian crawl I believe it's sometimes called – to move any faster than the pace at which I now progressed – sufficient to keep me ahead of the danger, but no more. There were cries and shouts and screams. Somebody certainly shouted *Get out of the water*. But I could not turn. I believe that I required to know the exact nature of the danger more than I required to flee it. Or, knowing the exact nature of the danger – its speed and strength and direction and look – was preferable to being safer but knowing nothing about that which I was safe from. I required the information. At any moment anything directly over my head could have come loose. What I could see falling was certainly big enough and hard enough to daze me, even knock me out, had any of it hit my head. Given the chaos of the situation it's uncertain that anyone could have reached me before I'd drowned. I think I knew all of this. I think I was probably even thinking it all through at the time. I was fascinated by my own proximity to death. *Look at me, so near to dying, so unconcerned, what is it that makes me like I am?*

All progress, of thought as well as the collapsing ceiling, halted suddenly about a quarter of the way down the length of the pool. It seems there is a large steel girder there which acted as a bulwark. I was unharmed, if a little startled. I stayed on my back, my eyes on the ceiling, and kicked my way to the shallow end until I could stand and walk to the side. I had dived in and swum one length. In that short time the entire sports centre had burst into a noisy panic of activity and flight. There seemed now to be dozens of people, where previously there had been none. Tracksuited staff ran this way and that. Some of them helped the small girl and her father. A young man asked me if I was all right. I nodded. Attention was soon focused on the woman who lay, now fully out of the water, some distance away from me, at the other end of the pool. A huddle of concerned staff surrounded her. I heard a shout for a firstaid box. They gingerly picked pieces of the ceiling from her back and talked to her. Whether she replied or not I could not tell. After a very few moments I heard the approach of sirens. I was shivering. I walked slowly to the changing rooms.

There were two other slightly peculiar things about my trip to the swimming pool. As I stepped naked from the shower, groping for my towel, a police officer appeared suddenly in front of me, embarrassed, and a little flustered, and, not helping matters, standing between me and the hook from which my towel hung.

—Oh, I beg your pardon. Sorry. I'm just checking that everyone is all right.

—Well, I am. Not a scratch.

—Yes. Plainly. And there's no one else in here, is there?

—No, no one.

—You were actually in the pool, were you? Very lucky escape. Going to have to hurry you up, I'm afraid. We need to clear the building.

It was only later that I realised what the scene had reminded me of.

The other peculiar thing was entirely of my own creation. As I walked from the centre, through the hastily parked ambulances, police cars and two fire brigades, I switched on my phone. My intention was to call K and tell the story of my brush with death. But for some reason that I don't understand, I called Michael instead.

—The stain, I said. The stain on the fourth floor of this ghost building of yours.

—Oh yes?

—You said it was shaped like Australia.

—Yes I did.

—Was it?

—Was it what?

—Was it actually shaped like Australia?

—So I'm told.

—It's a distinctive shape.

—Yes it is. Where are you? Sounds like a riot.

Animals

—At the sports centre. I just had a swim. Are you sure that Australia wasn't just used as a throwaway thing? That really it was just a blob?

—No, no, it was definitely Australia-shaped. They all saw it. Tasmania and everything. Very definite. Very odd. Very creepy. Maybe the poltergeist is Australian?

—I thought the poltergeist was the previous building?

—Oh yes. I forgot. Why do you ask anyway?

—I was swimming, I said. And the roof fell in. And I couldn't bring myself to do the Australian crawl to escape almost certain death.

Michael laughed and told me he had to go and hung up.

I walked home slowly through the park, thinking about myself, and about dreaming, and about the shape of Australia. I forgot to call K.

The Spider

I didn't know what to think. There were too many things going on in my head, each of them clamouring for my attention, each of them asserting their own importance over all the others, each of them, in an attempt to occupy all of my thoughts, achieving nothing more than confusion. I'm not sure that I can accurately report what went through my mind for most of the subsequent hours, from my leaving the sports centre to the disastrous end of that day, and into the horrible night that followed. Or, I should say, I know *what* went through my mind during that time, but I have no idea what my mind *did* with it all – what kind of sense or senselessness I made of it, where it got me, how it affected or influenced or determined what happened later.

I do know, however, that when I got home from the sports centre, I

- drank a glass of water
- boiled the kettle
- buttered two slices of bread, sliced a tomato, cut some cheese and made a sandwich

- brewed a small pot of tea
- took off my trainers
- ate and drank while staring out the window at the clouds, lost, I think, in thought
- checked the answering machine – there were no messages
- switched on the computer and checked my email – there were no messages
- opened windows
- took some clothes from the washing machine and hung them on the clothes horse to dry
- took my camera from my bag

I had left my bag – the one I had taken into town with me to meet Michael – on a chair in the kitchen. At some point, as I was doing all those other things, it caught my eye, and I was reminded of the camera and what the camera contained. Or perhaps it would be more correct to say that the thoughts swirling around in my head suddenly reordered themselves, and the mouse came to the fore. Here was something of which I had a record. It would be possible for me to look again at the photographs and perhaps re-evaluate, or put into some perspective, at least one of the bewildering aspects of my day.

Of the things in my bag my camera was probably the easiest to locate. Certainly I have no memory at all of rummaging, of pushing things aside or taking them out, in order to find the camera. I have no memory of noticing anything else in the bag at all at that point. I must simply have opened the bag, put my hand on the camera and removed it. I have absolutely no memory of seeing the pen, or of thinking about the pen, or of even having any memory of the pen at all. I took the camera into the office, located the cable that connected it to the computer, plugged the one into the other and switched the camera on. I created a folder called MOUSE and transferred the pictures to it, disconnected the camera and opened up some picture-viewing software. I enjoy doing things with my computer. It calms me.

This, however, made me immediately uneasy. I shouldn't have done it. It was, I think now, very foolish to load the photographs on to the computer, and to think that examining them would be a good idea, and as soon as I looked at the first one I realised this, and stopped. For the truth was that however discomforting and odd the experience of seeing the dead mouse had been, it was still vivid and precise and *of import* in my mind. It was an experience, the memory and recollection of which moved me. I knew that it would never make much sense to anyone else – that it was incommunicably mine and my own. As soon as I caught the first glimpse of the first photograph on my computer screen I realised that I did not want my memories interfered with. I did not want the feeling I had experienced – and which echoed in me still, of sadness and resignation and knowledge – to be reduced by reproduction, to be trivialised into pixelated facsimiles and approximations of the *moment* which I had lived through.

I immediately closed the software. In the silence of the flat I sat still for a long while, my eyes on the blank screen, seeing not even the blankness. I didn't understand what had happened to me when I saw the mouse. But I knew that something had certainly happened. When I brought to mind his small corpse stretched in the gutter, I felt a kind of silence, a calm, which rose up in me like a pool of still water. There was a serenity and peacefulness in the recollection, and an exquisite melancholy. But I didn't know why. I felt as if, almost fondly, I was remembering a moment of painful understanding, a kind of breakthrough. As if, as I had stared down that morning at the dead mouse, some veil had lifted from the world, or from myself, or both, and that I had acquired a kind of wisdom. What the wisdom *was* though, I had no idea. What understanding I had reached seemed somehow to evade me. I felt that I had learned a secret and had promptly forgotten it – though its shape and its significance were there, on the tip of my tongue, as it were, or the tip of my consciousness, if only I could grasp them and not fumble. *This is life. This is death.* Something like that. *This is stone. This is flesh. This is the path of man. This is the goal of man.* No, not really, that didn't register. *This is the path and the end of the path. This is the road and the end of the road.* I couldn't get it. I could only contrive. *This road is human, this death is human too. This mouse is dead. This road is where he died. But the road is human. Not mousey* . . . I moaned in frustration. It was hopeless, gone.

I went to the bathroom to splash my face. I decided not to speak about the mouse. Not to anyone. I decided to keep it entirely to myself. It could not be shared without being diminished. To try and reconstruct it for someone else would mean dismantling it in my own mind first – taking it apart with the risk of not being able to put it back together, especially if the pieces had been damaged by the laughter, ridicule or simple incomprehension of others. As it was, K would probably ask me, as K already knew that it had happened, and knew too that it had affected me to some extent, though certainly not to what extent. There would be questions. I thought though, given what else had happened in the course of the day, that it would be relatively easy to swamp any talk of the mouse with news of Rachel and Michael and dogs and rain and the haunted building and the collapsing ceiling of the sports centre's swimming pool.

In the bathroom I paused and listened for a moment before opening the frosted window an inch or two to confirm that it was raining again, if lightly this time. I felt suddenly tired, and also quite dissolute – the day was almost over and I had done no work at all. I turned on the cold-water tap and washed my hands. Then I bowed my head, cupped my hands under the running water and gently splashed my face with my eyes closed. I did this three or four times, enjoying the cooling, refreshing sensation. I turned off the tap and reached for the towel which hung from the towel rail on the radiator to my right. I moved my head towards the towel at the same time, I think, so that when my hands were on the towel my face was pretty much just above it, just a couple of inches away, and I grabbed the towel and pressed it into my face – into my closed eyes and cheeks and nose and mouth. The first action was one of simple pressing, as the trapped water tickled me. Followed then, quickly I suppose, by a gentle rubbing, massaging. I straightened my body and turned at the same time to face the mirror once again. As I looked at my reflec-tion – as it was revealed to me by the opening of my eyes and the lowering of the towel, first of all past my cheeks and nose and then my mouth and chin – I knew that there was something wrong. There were gradations, however. As my eyes saw my eyes, everything was fine. As they saw my upper cheeks and my nose, there was nothing unusual. But as the towel came away from my lower cheeks I noticed first a small black mark on my left cheek, adjacent to the nostril. As I instinctively leaned in towards the mirror to better see what this might be, the towel, held by my hands, continued downwards, revealing above my mouth a stuttering continuation of this black mark into larger blobs and beads and scatterings, like an ink blot on my skin. As I peered, seeing that the trail continued on to my lips, and indeed between them, and as my eyes and my involuntary tongue confirmed that these blackish reddish bluish things were not marks or traces but were actually *material* of some description – debris – and as my independent, quick-moving tongue trapped one part of this detritus against the test surface of a tooth to discover a hard stringy grittiness, so my hands took the towel away from my neck and my eyes looked down, to confirm almost instantly what I had begun to suspect: that what littered my skin and had fallen or crawled into my mouth was the sundered parts of a large black spider, whose bulky twitching carcass was smeared across the white towel I held in my hands like the entrails of road kill dragged across the snow.

There are moments, now that I am an adult, during which my childish habit of bursting into tears reactivates itself, but silently, and drily, and without access to the comforts that a child can claim. A certain paralysis accompanies these episodes, and I was brought to a standstill there in front of the mirror: my eyes trying to lose themselves somewhere between the dismembered creature dying on my towel and its severed limbs still clinging to my face, and my tongue frozen by direct order somewhere mid-mouth, attempting an instant sensory amnesia, and failing. I could taste it, and the taste clawed at me, catching, like the surface of a stone and my own blood, mixed.

When I was very young my mother collected me from school one summer's day and took me home and deposited me inside the front door with her bags of shopping, and left me there while she went up the road on some motherly business.

—Put everything away for me, all right, pet? There's bits for the fridge and bits for the cupboard. What goes on shelves you can't reach you leave on the counter. You can have a glass of milk but no biscuit.

I was delighted with the responsibility. Alone in the house with a task to perform. I'm not sure that it was the first time I had been left alone – in fact, I doubt very much that it would have been. But it is the first that I remember, mainly because I spent most of it cowering in terror at the bottom of the stairs with the groceries sitting where my mother had left them, warming gently in the sun.

Some weeks previously, on a visit to relatives who lived in a seaside town, I had gone with the other children to buy ice-cream from a passing van. Wandering happily back to the house with my cone I had felt a mild, ticklish itchiness on my scalp, at the crown, and had idly sent my free hand to scratch it. There followed a blur of violent, tiny movement felt chiefly by my fingers, and a burst of pain sufficient for me to drop my ice-cream cone and cry out. It took me a while to realise what had happened. In fact, I think it was one of the other children who spotted the dying bumble bee on the ground beside the mess of vanilla and chocolate, while I concentrated in growing distress on the alarming swelling of my thumb. My mother comforted me that day, and eased the pain, and sent for another ice cream, and restored some goodness to the world. So it was her return that I awaited, in strangled sobs of terror on the floor of our hall, to where I had collapsed, immovable and lost to despair, upon seeing, patrolling the hall like a hissing yellow eye, a large ill-tempered wasp. It seemed to me that my mother took for ever to come home. I'm sure that it was only a matter of minutes, but in that time I lay stock-still, swallowing my tears, focused on the potential for pain, torturing myself with the anticipation of agony, while at the same time hating myself for my weakness, and my cowardice, and my unsuitability for this world. When she returned she was astonished. As was I at the fact that her simple approach allowed me to stand, and open the front door, and step out on to the porch to meet her – one of a dozen strategies which I immediately knew I might have employed earlier, had I been a brave or clever child. My suppressed anguish rose horribly and tore from me a flooded bellow of indignation. She scolded me for leaving the groceries in the hall. But I excoriated her for leaving me alone in the house, at my age.

Together, at her insistence, we hunted the vicious insect from our home, an adventure involving much screeching, giggling and running away, and which cured me of the more crippling aspects of my phobia. Nevertheless, since those days I have never much cared for small flying or crawling things. If they appear in the flat it is K's task to deal with them. If K is not around then they are not dealt with.

I threw the towel into the bath. I bent over the sink and spat, several times, while turning the tap on again and cupping my hands and bringing them to my mouth, sucking in water, swirling and rolling it, spitting, and again, and splashing at my face, wiping at the left side furiously, and spitting again, and retching, retching violently, and coughing, and hitting handfuls of water against my cheeks and into my mouth over and over, and moaning, wailing, while all the children I have ever been howled in my memory like a persecuted nation.

It was horrible. I thought I would vomit, though I didn't. How could something like this happen? How had I not seen a big black spider on a white towel? How had he not seen me? Though the thought of a spider's eyes smeared across my lips made me retch once more. He had been sleeping perhaps, if they do that. Or he had been dangling in mid-air above the towel rail, anchored on the underside of the cabinet, and I had caught him with my head, or with the lifted towel. I cursed and gagged and checked my reflection. Unbelievably, some sort of limb or antenna or mandible or whatever the hell they are made of, still clung to my chin like a cable. Furiously, I repeated the entire frenzy of cleansing, and shouted obscenely at the innocent sink like someone wrongly convicted.

Eventually, I seemed to be free of remains. With a great deal of trepidation I picked up the towel from the bath and carried it at the end of a long arm to the kitchen bin, into which I stuffed it while my stomach turned. I tied off the refuse sack and carried it, again at arm's length, to the front door, where I left it for K to get rid of later. Then I ran the taps in the bath for a long time, and took a fresh towel from the cupboard and shook it out violently, snapping it in the air. I took off my clothes and put all of them into the laundry basket before spending a good fifteen minutes in the shower, with the water as hot as I could bear it. When I had dried myself on the thoroughly examined towel I felt that I wanted to lie down, to rest. I was exhausted. There had been so much, and I was beginning to feel, much to my annoyance, tearful. But my mind was full of spider parts, and I was afraid of dreaming.

K

It is quite difficult for me now, even at this little distance, to explain what happened next. It shouldn't be difficult – after all, everything that happened next happened because of me. I made it happen. This is an account of what I did, and if anyone can explain it, it should be me who can explain it. Perhaps, though, there is no explanation. I hope that doesn't sound like a refusal of responsibility. I take full responsibility. But as far as an explanation goes, I'm not sure that even at the time I had any sense that things were proceeding rationally or logically; that the decisions I made and the things I did were exactly as they should be, that no matter how discomforting they were, they could not be any different. I really don't think there was any such sense, and if there was, I have lost it now. I have lost the trail back.

I have a temper. People don't see it that often, but they do see it. It builds over time, and I'm sure that it's a symptom of my general lack of anger-management skills, although perhaps *annoyance-management* is a better term. I silently accumulate my dissatisfactions with the world, until eventually, a bit like somebody collecting points on a supermarket loyalty card, I cash them all in on something pathetic and start all over again. In fact, it's often the case that my eventual burst of temper is directed at someone or some situation which doesn't actually annoy me at all. It's like spending your loyalty points on a barbecue set or a ticket to a film you don't want to see; or worse, spending six months' worth of them on the measly discount they earn you off the ridiculously expensive weekly shopping bill. This is fairly common, I think. I'm sure there's a term for it. I mean, supermarkets aren't stupid. So after weeks of swallowing setbacks in my work, and the financial slaps in the face which I suffer from those who claim to *love* what I do; after weeks of silently putting up with the various snags and anxieties that living in a city like this involves; of absorbing the tensions and worries and exasperation of living with another person, and of having to remotely manage relationships with my mother and father and the rest of my family, I will snap over a mislaid paperback or a lost sock or somebody stepping in ahead of me in a bus queue. When my temper does break, it is usually short and loud and rather hysterical and leaves me feeling exhausted and embarrassed.

I was annoyed with Michael for not understanding the significance of Australia. I was annoyed at myself for not understanding why I was annoyed with Michael. I was annoyed with Rachel for inventing a missing brother and travelling to Poland to exploit the fantasies of a lonely expatriate. I was annoyed with K for infecting my dreams. I was annoyed with all humanity for discussing dreams at all. I was annoyed at the council for nearly killing me. I was annoyed at the dead spider for his messy death. I was annoyed at myself for causing that annoyance. But instead of doing something sensible to vent all of these irksome aggravations, instead of trying to calm myself with silence or an interval of stillness, I sat in front of the television and watched a children's programme about mushrooms. What they are, how to cook them, how they taste, what the poisonous ones look like. But a spider appeared in the middle of it, crawling innocently over upturned soil, and I felt ill and switched it off.

I toyed with the idea of going out, but it was raining, and I knew that K would soon be home. I thought briefly about telephoning my mother. But the bee sting was in my mind, and our chasing of the wasp, and I was embarrassed at the idea that I wanted comfort. I paced the flat. I looked out all of our windows. I turned the radio on and turned it off again. At my desk I ran my eye over a series of drawings I have been working on for an anthology of children's poetry. Or poetry for children, I suppose. To be honest, I hate doing this kind of work. I find it difficult and frustrating to have to work from text, from someone else's imagination as it were, and doubly so when the text is intended for children, who are the most unimaginative of creatures. That's not quite what I mean. I mean that they are *very* imaginative, of course, but that their imaginations are fairly predictable, and that their only acceptable translation into the adult world seems to be by way of cuteness. It's not the children's fault. And when some adult has the bright, peculiar idea of writing for them, cuteness tends to be the language used. And cuteness is something I cannot abide. I suppose that's why I get these sort of commissions – because I am the last person you would think of asking to illustrate a book for children. And because publishers are daring in a very predictable way, and learn their originality from each other, I'm forever being asked to illustrate books for children. I do the odd one, for the money, although the money is no good at all.

Poetry is very difficult to illustrate. It's frankly boring to have to read through endless childish nonsense looking for an arresting image, something that fires in my mind in a way that will work. Usually I find nothing at all that isn't a parody of the poet's intentions. So I tend to fix upon random things that are described in detail, and render them as faithfully as I can. Inevitably, one little poetic child traipses after another, encountering fearsome poetic animals and comically baffling grown-ups, and triumphing, always, in the end. A review of a book of stories for early teenagers that I did a couple of years ago said that my drawings were 'surprisingly gentle and tender'. My friends found this amusing.

As I looked at these drawings again it struck me how stale and tedious they were. Even before they had been coloured they looked pink and blue. None of them seemed fully original, as if I had copied them from somewhere else. I often have this worry of course – that the images I come up with are not mine at all but are simply part of a communal library of stock images which we all accumulate over time, fed to us by advertising and television and by everything we see in between. Even when something seems to come to me completely out of the blue – something I'm particularly proud of – I spend a not inconsiderable amount of time waiting nervously for someone to recognise it as something pre-existing. Something already drawn, already said, already imagined. It was at this point that I remembered the quick sketch I had made that morning – just before I found the mouse in fact. It had been of a giant daffodil running through a field pulling the heads off children. I was sure now that I thought of it, that it wasn't an original. I had seen it somewhere and it had stayed in my mind and had popped up that morning, probably because the children's poetry book was bothering me, and I was feeling mean about childhood.

I wandered through to the kitchen to get my sketch-book from my bag. The rain had eased off. I glanced through the window, which looks out on to the street at the front of our building, and saw a hooded teenager, perhaps one of the ones I'd seen that morning, swagger past on the far side with a bag of shopping from Eric's. Eric has these electric-blue plastic bags that always smell of vanilla. The boy's trainers shone and travelled in the gloom like a child's luminous mobile.

I carry lots of things in my shoulder bag, and often not the same things. There's a pocket at the front which holds my phone. That was empty – I'd taken my phone out to take to the sports centre. Now it was sitting on the hall table. But the rest of the bag was pretty full. Inevitably, I spend a lot of time rooting around in there looking for things. With my hand blindly feeling its way. When I had taken my camera out of my bag, however, I had not had to rummage. And this time too, when I opened the bag, which was now lying on its side on the table top, my sketchbook was there in front of me and all I had to do was reach in and pluck it out. As I did so, at some point in the process of doing so, either while or after, or possibly even before, I saw the pen. And at first, it didn't register. It didn't strike me. I might as well not have seen it at all. I didn't even think, *Oh, there's my pen*. It was only with my hand on the sketchbook, withdrawing it from the bag, that I realised – and I think it caused me to snatch a little – that I realised, with a mixture of puzzlement and disgust, that yes, there was my pen – the same pen with which I had poked the carcass of a dead mouse. The pen that had touched that dead grey sack on the street and had disturbed its innards, rattled them, made them move, and had come away damp. I tilted the bag so that the pen rolled out on to the table. With it rolled the half-eaten apple, another sight not exactly helpful in settling my stomach. I stared at the pen. It had been the cap end I'd used. Or had it been the butt end? No, I'd held the butt end and poked with the cap end. It was grubby and malign, and although I didn't lean in close enough to see, I knew that something had clung to it, that it was stained with the grime of putre-faction. It looked compromised – like a weapon recovered from a crime scene.

I didn't understand then, nor do I understand now, how it got back into the bag. I had laid it on the ground because I didn't want to keep it after I'd done what I'd done with it. I had even seen it in the photograph – the first and only photograph I'd glanced at. There the pen had been, as clear as could be, on the ground beside the corpse like a measure. I had moved it for that very reason – that it had made the scene seem staged. I had picked it up and . . . and what? Why hadn't I just moved it out of shot? Flung it up the street or on to the pavement? Kicked it out on to the roadway? Some automatic part of me had rebagged it. Obviously. Without thinking, I had repeated something I've done probably a thousand times. I put the pen back in the bag. Even though it was the last thing I wanted. Distracted, I had done what I knew how to do. I put the pen back in the bag.

Some of that passed through my mind at the time, but not all of it. I felt some mild annoyance at myself for not having managed to throw the thing away, and felt a small residue of disgust. But really, since then I'd had a spider crushed to death across my face, so the discovery of the pen was not as discomforting as it might otherwise have been. I decided to throw it in the bin, but didn't. I had tied up the refuse sack containing the towel and the dead spider and put it in the hall, and hadn't yet replaced it. I would have to rummage around in the press under the sink for a new bag, and I had my sketchbook in my hand, and my mind just then was on work, for a change, and I left it, knowing though that I should come back to it, and soon, before K came home, because the apple needed to be got rid of too – it was evidence that I had only half succeeded in my undertaking to eat it all in the course of the day. K has been trying to get me to eat more fruit. This has simply nothing to do with anything. It's just there, in the bag as it were, this insistence that I eat an entire apple or orange or banana every day. Which is a good policy of course, it's just one that I find difficult to follow, I don't know why. I find it childish.

Back at my desk, I examined the sketch of the giant daffodil and the decapitated children. It wasn't bad, for such a quick thing. I'm getting pretty good, I think, at suggesting movement, economically, without the clutter of tiny lines and spirals of a conventional wake that I've previously used. Maybe I've picked up something from Michael and his buildings – something about line and angle. Although it also helped that I'd given my daffodil a little pair of furious legs, and strangely bulbous feet. I'd also given him arms, hands and long sharp fingers which immediately called to mind the monster in the jumper from those films about nightmares. The daffodil's face was what worried me the most though. It was a conventional, full-eyed growling thing applied directly to the flower, and I immediately thought of early-twentieth-century *Punch*, making some kind of unsubtle point about a politician. I went on to the Internet and started searching through various image databases. I'm forever doing this. Some of them I have to pay a subscription to. I'm aware that it's a confidence problem. I'm aware of that.

I heard K come in while I was looking through an archive of classic *New Yorker* cartoons, beginning to suspect that I'd stumbled upon a Thurber. I made a dash for the kitchen to get rid of the apple. This should have been a fairly hopeless endeavour right from the start, as the front door to our flat leads straight into a hallway around which all the other rooms are arranged. K should have seen me. But as I rapidly crossed the hall I heard a shout of greeting and saw, fleetingly, K's shadow disappear into the bathroom. In the kitchen I opened the press beneath the sink, found the roll of refuse sacks, tore one off, and was smugly pushing it into our stainless-steel pedal bin when I heard K's voice, almost at my shoulder.

—You didn't eat the apple.

Startled, I spun round to see K in the doorway, eyeing the fruit and holding a clump of toilet paper to a runny nose.

—Jesus, I breathed.

—What?

—Don't creep up on me.

K smiled at this, but it was quickly lost in the contortions of a vigorous blowing of the nose.

—I ate half of it.

—Well, half isn't all of it, is it?

—Don't nag me.

—I'm not nagging you.

—I did pretty well, I thought, eating half of it.

—So why did you only eat half of it?

84

—I only wanted half of it.

—You could finish it now.

—It's gone off.

—Off?

—Well, look at it. It's all brown and dried out and horrible.

K went to the table and picked up the apple and seemed to agree with me, but still said, while putting it in the bin:

—You're such a baby.

It was light-hearted of course. It was casual banter. But I didn't like it. Perhaps because I felt like a bit of a baby, not just over the apple, but over everything else as well. I went a little grumpy. K asked about my day and I replied simply, sullenly, that it had been a bad one.

—Well, Jesus, mine's been an absolute nightmare. We've got next quarter's budget figures, or quarter after that actually – figures that none of us understand, given that someone somewhere has decided to completely change the way the quarterlies are drawn up, so that the first thing I think when I look at it is *Jesus – when did we decide to axe the voucher redemption scheme*, but of course it isn't axed, it's relocated, *reallocated* actually, under a new supplementary sub-heading or some similar *device*, and I have to spend most of the day having the whole thing explained to me by two spotty teenagers from treasury and I'm still not entirely convinced that we haven't been fleeced.

I should have told K about the sports centre at least. I mean, I could have died. Of all the things that had happened it was the most conventionally newsworthy. But I was angry, or annoyed, that K hadn't asked why *my* day had been a bad one, and I was determined not to mention anything about it until that question came.

Actually, I'm not at all sure that what I've just said is true. It seems to me that it probably is – it makes sense to me, it's the kind of stupid thing I would do. But in fact, I have no actual memory of deciding not to tell K about the collapsing roof at the sports centre. The only things I remember thinking about at the time, as K told me the details of what sounded to me like a fairly standard day, were the spider and the mouse. And I was thinking, specifically, that I didn't want to mention the spider because it was a disgusting story and might very well disgust K; and that I didn't want to talk about the mouse because that was special, that was mine, and I was still trying to work it out.

—I'm in the middle of something.

—Well, get back to it then.

We exchanged a perfunctory hug and kiss and I went back to my desk. K said something about having to make a phone call, and showed no inclination to ask me anything at all. I never even looked at the pen.

Our flat is a nice flat, or we think so anyway. On the second floor, it looks out over what is usually a very quiet street at the front; and at the back, where our bedroom is, there are variously disordered gardens, a tiny laneway, and the backs of the houses of the next street along. Three bedrooms, one now converted into my office (K calls it my studio), a decent-sized bathroom, a lovely kitchen, and a split-level sitting room with fine full-length south-facing windows. We bought it years ago, when it was really quite cheap, and though we have talked about selling it many times, and of moving, we can think of no real reason to. We like it here.

While I flicked through seemingly endless *New Yorker* cartoons on my screen, K wandered around the flat, talking on the telephone and sniffing – at one point wandering into my office and over towards my desk for no apparent reason, looking at me and wandering out again. The conversation was work-related, of course. K often spends a great deal of time on the telephone talking to various colleagues, especially in the early evenings, soon after returning from the office – as if none of them actually talk to each other during the course of the day. This used to annoy me a great deal, but I've grown accustomed to it, especially since we abandoned our landline in favour of our individual mobiles, meaning that I no longer have to field K's calls. The job is an extremely stressful one of course, but K seems to thrive on that, or, if not thrive exactly, then certainly not to suffer very much because of it. K, I should tell you, is an adviser to a mid-ranking minister in the current government. Not a civil servant, but a political appointee – one of those people whom everyone distrusts and envies and holds in contempt, in roughly equal measure. K is very good at it, and there was talk late last year of a move to a much more senior minister's office. For some elaborate machiavellian reason which I can't quite now remember, K decided to stay put. For the time being.

I wondered, as I searched in vain through the online libraries of cartoons and illustrations, whether I wouldn't be wiser not to do this kind of thing every time I had some doubt. I worried that I might simply be filling my head with even more imagery which might at some future point resurface, masquerading as my own. I was going through them so quickly that my memory of them was bound to be subliminal, dangerously potential. I should probably just stop.

I was examining, on a whim, one of Heinrich Kley's oddly nauseating cartoons featuring centaurs and flouncy ladies, when I became aware of K standing in the doorway. What happened next was quick, sudden, but came to me and passed through me very slowly, and not in a fluid manner, but in jerky, progressive stages – not in slow motion in other words, but in separate frames, like my own Zapruder film. I still have it.

1. K in the doorway, still speaking on the phone – not holding it but clutching it between head and shoulder, and at the same time writing in a notebook.
2. The Kley on the screen in front of me. Shapes formed from scribbles, like a machine made of tissue.
3. Thought: what is K writing with?
4. K in the doorway, holding the pen and notebook in the right hand, pressing the hang-up button on the phone with the thumb of the left. I can't see the pen.
5. K's phone disappears into a pocket. For an instant I don't know what I'm looking at. A frame is obscured. There is a smile. K's eyes are on my own. The notebook transferred to the left hand, the pen on its own in the right.
6. Thought: it may be a different pen.
7. K walking towards me, saying something.
8. It's the pen. My pen. The dead mouse pen. But the cap is off. The cap is off and is stuck on the other end, on the butt end.
9. K lifts the pen, says something to me. I don't hear it.
10. K in the middle of the room, looking at the notebook, the pen rising. K's mouth is open, but I can hear nothing at all in the world, because even though I know it's going to happen there seems nothing I am able to do to stop it, and before I know anything else, the final frame of this film freezes in front of me.

11. The pen, the pen that has death all over it, is in K's
    mouth, like the last trailed limb of a great and ancient
    spider, crawling down K's throat.

—What's wrong?

I said nothing. By which I mean that the very notion of
speech seemed at that moment to be so utterly impossible
that it did not even occur to me to try. By which I mean
that the notion of speech as a possibility was entirely absent.
It would have made as much sense for me to think about
saying something at that moment as it would for the Kley
creatures on my screen to think about stepping off it and
into the world to put a stop to everything.

—What's wrong with you?

K was asking this through the pen, over it, and the smile
which lingered suggested that whatever was on my face,
while being sufficiently odd to prompt the question, was
also sufficiently odd for K to assume that it was faked –
a joke. The pen was pointing at me. Its nib was like a
bone that had poked through flesh. It jiggled up and down,
and yet no hand was near it. Which could only mean that
the cap of this pen which had prodded a corpse and had
come away weeping, and which was now attached to the
butt end inside K's mouth, was being manipulated by the
fleshy surface of K's tongue. In my own mouth I could
taste a sudden small version of all the world's soiled matter,
its rotting ruins, its smeared, festering debris.

I did two quick things. The first was to stand and slap
the pen from K's mouth, clumsily but forcefully, taking as
much care as I could not to make contact with K, only with
the pen, but nevertheless, inevitably, causing the pen to rattle
off K's teeth uncomfortably, even painfully. There was a
confused cry, a kind of yelp. The second thing I did, as I felt

a sickness rise inside me, was to turn to the window, which I opened one-handed, violently, (my other hand, having briefly touched the pen – even if it was the *clean* end of the pen – was now hanging useless, quarantined, at my side), lean through it and, with a horrid, disgusting, noisome belch, vomit. I kept my eyes closed and imagined a stream of black spider pieces flowing from my mouth to the ground below like a load of carcasses tipped from a slaughterhouse lorry. This continued for several long, disordered minutes.

I lose the detail here. As if the clarity of what had gone before has somehow forced a disintegration in my recall of what followed. There are scenes of shuffled options. There are a few possibilities. As the vomiting eased I became aware of K's hand on my back, and K's confused and concerned voice trying to determine whether I was all right. I believe I shouted at this point, something along the lines of *No I'm not bloody all right* and *Get your hands off me*. This was followed by a laugh, clear and distinct, from somewhere ahead, which was immediately joined by others. I looked up to see several hooded boys looking back at me from across the street. I may have shouted at them too, I'm not sure. Certainly they shouted at me, and continued to laugh in a forced, artificial, pointless kind of way. Everyone is owned. Set up.

Eventually I pulled myself back inside, and knocked my knee against the brass cat that sits by my desk, I think, and brushed past the protesting K to the bathroom, I think, where I once more scrubbed at my face, and my hand, and certainly this is the case, felt a rage at the repetition. I was angry now. Maybe that's why the details elude me; why the sequence is folded and some of it obscured, and the code of it difficult for me to decipher. I was angry. I simply could not believe that such a series of stupidities had gathered to such an absurd point. I felt humiliated and disgusted and battered. I railed at K for picking up the pen, I shouted about infantile behaviour, about everything having to be bloody tasted, like a bloody child, about the stupidity of not looking, not examining something before you put it in your mouth; how, in any case, it was one of my sketch pens and K had had no bloody business using it in the first place and were there no bloody pens in government? And eventually, because beneath my anger was a level of disgust that even then I found dangerously specific, personally focused, I ordered K to the bathroom sink to wash and spit and rinse, and wash and spit and rinse again while I shouted out the facts of the pen's contamination, becoming more angry by the second as I realised that my mouse, my encounter with the mouse, my *discovery* of something related to the mouse – all of that, all of that mystery and significance – was now to be reduced to a nauseating anecdote about a dirty pen. And it was, I told myself, entirely and overwhelmingly K's fault.

That is what happened. I see my arm going up and coming down, again, to make the point, again, and I see K in the bathroom, arms and hands and legs in the bathroom, and I see, again, my hands, and the tiles and the enamel, and the colour of gold or orange or red or something from the shape of the light and the rubbing of skin, and both of us crammed in the bathroom and the air speckled with rage and disorder and the bloody noise of it all.

K was not of course silent. I cannot remember what was said exactly. I can't remember. There was concern. Confusion and bafflement. Rather than offence or anger. There was fear.

Fear, I think. Perhaps fear. From not understanding. I can't remember a lot of it, to tell you the truth.

In retrospect of course I can see that K would have been more than justified in reacting very badly to what had happened – blaming me, for instance, quite rightly, for having left the pen on the kitchen table in the first place; accusing me, with good reason, of being ridiculously unfair, and of dramatically exaggerating the seriousness of what had happened. But I think K was calm, or as calm as I and the situation allowed, and did not shout or flail about or struggle or in any other way rise to my level of hysteria. I have no memory . . .

It was as if I was alone, at the end of the shouting. I don't recall. As if I had somehow . . . I cannot and will not blame K. This was me, and me alone. Me alone.

In any case, I left. As I've said, I cannot really remember the exact sequence of events, or what was said. There is a confusion in me still about all of it, even now, a week later, and after so much else. Perhaps that *else* has interfered. Perhaps the first thing never stays the first thing, never remains just that. Subsequent things subtract from it. Or add to it. Or alter it completely.

I left. I packed a bag and I left. And I remember how pale K was. And I remember the bathroom and how it seemed the scene of something terrible, and how pale K was, how pale. I'm sure I said I would return. In a quietness that was uniform, I'm sure I said I would return. But I have not been back since.

It was about a week ago. Friday. I took an umbrella because there had been rain, on and off.

I have not been back since.

David

I need to tell you what has happened since. I need to lay out the details and the facts. I need to line them up and go through them, one by one: each day following each previous day, down, in collapse. The terminally weighted sequences of hours. The minutes that pack them, that stretch them to splitting. The seconds that sabotage the minutes like rocks in pockets, dragging them back into ancient, unmeasured moments in which all things happen now, and that's all that happens. I'm drowned and I'm drowning, and you're reading my bloody mouthfuls like an augur. My entrails, my remainders. This is what's left. This is what it amounts to. And I'm handing it over. This lump of skin, this lump of skin.

I am monstrously tired.

I am not a stupid person. Seriously. I *know* that I am not a stupid person. How do I know it? Well, I am educated, I am well read, I have an interest in and knowledge of politics and history and culture. And I am aware of the privilege of these benefits. And aware that they are – of course they are – as inessential and accidental

93

as uneducated ignorance. So, I am not stupid because I am aware of myself. I am aware of myself as a person certainly, a physical person with an uncomplicated variation of the standard set of physical characteristics and abilities; and I am aware of my circumstances and how they differ from the circumstances of others, in ways which are sometimes to my disadvantage but mostly not; and I am aware of myself as being, while certainly distinctive and separate, something of a constructed personality – made from the assorted materials of my upbringing, education, family life, cultural influences, social circle, economic means. And I am aware of myself as being at a specific place in my own progression, a place arrived at through the accumulation of my own choices over the years, and I am concurrently aware of the essentially chaotic nature of choice and consequence – aware that I could just as easily be other than I am, or anyway that I could be in another place, doing something else, with somebody else, and yet still be recognisably myself. And I am not stupid, finally, because of my ability to recognise that all of this is contingent upon my ability to formulate it and your ability to accept my formulations. I am aware, in other words, that this is just talk, and that notions of self, and self-awareness, and stupidity and intelligence, might be all that we share. We talk to each other to prove that we're not stupid, to make clear to ourselves that we know what's going on here, we know the score, we see the way this is all put together. And while we talk the sun goes down and a billion cold stars nail the lie that we tell ourselves. We know nothing. I know nothing. And that's what makes me intelligent – the fact that I know that I know nothing, and that knowing it negates it and that knowing that it is negated is nothing worth knowing. We live in a world of words. And everything you imagine is not what you see.

I am in a ridiculously comfortable room in a ridiculously expensive hotel in the middle of my ridiculous life. I need to sleep for a while.

Fear. Fear is a mechanical experience, something you feel in yourself like machinery, like implements and devices, like apparatus. So you hear talk of ratchets and grinding and cold steel. It's a human industry. Man produces fear like Argentina produces beef.

I was terrified for most of the time. I have been terrified for most of the week. I have been terrified almost continually since I walked out. As far as I know. Fear alters time, slows it and speeds it and dashes past it in cold, sweating sleeps, and halts it entirely at significant moments, all the nuts and bolts of it shuddering with the strain. So it doesn't much feel like a week. It feels like a year and it feels like an hour. My body is a factory on time and a half, double time, overtime, short time, long time, bundled time, overlapping shifts, twenty-four-hour bonus shifts, shifts that shift the sequence.

What I have to tell you: *leaving; the park; the fear; going to David's; the fear; David; the knife; the fear; the argument; leaving David's; the café; Catherine Anderson; the fear; the bathroom; the fear; the hotel; the fear; the fear; the fear; Anna; faking it; Anthony Edgar; BOX; the fear; the hotel; the fear; THE FEAR; the leaving; the posters.*

Jesus Christ. I mean, it doesn't look like much, does it? Fear collapses everything though. It's so much worse than it looks.

*

I slept badly in David's place. I think I must have *stayed still* for about fourteen hours over Friday night and into Saturday morning, my eyes prised open by horrors, wrapped up in David's spare duvet on his little camp bed, dreaming, when I did sporadically lose consciousness, about absolutely nothing, sweating in alternating thirst and hunger and pain – pain which seemed to travel around my major organs like something looking for a way out. Even when I heard David up and about I lay for a long time waiting, staring at the strangeness of David's walls, which are covered almost entirely by things he has made up.

He was very kind to me. He is kindness itself. He made me breakfast and didn't ask many questions. But every time he came back into a room I was in, and every time he finished a telephone conversation, and every time he came back from outside, I stared at him, waiting for the catastrophe, waiting for his kindness to reform as disbelief and fear and disgust and hatred. But he never really questioned me about K. He left it. Thinking, I suppose, that if I wanted to talk about it I would. He is accustomed, by now, to how these things work. The domestics. The ruptures and the rows. He didn't realise . . . He didn't know quite what this was.

His partner walked out on him about a year ago, quite abruptly, after David's obsession with his work became too much. It was a mess really. An intense implosion of something that had seemed, perhaps because it was so unlikely, very solid. K and I had found it quite awkward, as we are friends with both David and Mark, and for a while we seemed to move between the two of them like an incompetent delegation. Mark has now moved abroad.

(I'm making a mess of my list already. I'm getting ahead of myself. But I really don't think I can tell you much more about what happened on the Friday, after I walked out. At least, not at the moment. Most of it is still confused in any case – a ragged and shredded fabric on which there are a few odd patches of clarity. And I don't quite know what to do with clarity just now. It seems false and improper. Suffice it to say, for the moment, that I ended up in David's, much to my surprise, after a time spent in the local park, an encounter with a policeman, and a long consideration of death. I had actually decided to go home at some point in the middle of all that, but it didn't happen. I was diverted by fear. I was assaulted and overthrown by fear. Fear staged a coup. An idea had occurred to me in the course of my chat with the policeman, an idea which may already have occurred to you. If it hasn't yet then it will, shortly. I'm fairly sure of that. So let's let it be for a while.

(When I say death, I mean death generally, as well as particularly. I mean all death, as well as my own death, or the deaths of those close to me. I don't mean, when I say 'a long consideration of death', that I stood on a bridge and looked into the water.)

(And when I say an encounter with a policeman, I mean a friendly encounter with a policeman, who was very kind actually, and offered me some assistance, and a little bit of inadvertent insight, and a cigarette.))

David had obviously not been expecting anybody to call on a Friday night. When he opened the door to me I thought I caught the faintest, tiniest flicker of disappointment that I was not Mark, come back to him. As if such a thing might be possible. But maybe I'm just projecting, or whatever it's called, and it wasn't that at all. Whatever it was, it was almost immediately replaced by a confused concern. My leg was bleeding quite badly, and I was limping, and I think my hands and face were quite grimy, and I was bathed in sweat and the bag slung over my shoulder was damp, dripping actually, and there was, I found out later when I took it off, a rip in my jacket, at the shoulder, and I was pale and probably shivering a little, and my eyes, which are not my best feature, were most likely, by that stage, too far back in my head to convince anyone that I was seeing anything in this world at all.

—Oh my God, what's happened?

—I had a . . . I left . . . I banged . . . can I come in?

—Of course, Jesus, come in, you look awful.

Etc.

David is a tall, thin, bespectacled young man – a good deal younger than either K or myself – who we met originally at a horrible dinner party hosted by a colleague of K's who had tried to impress his guests by employing a couple of waiters. The waiters were fakes – Mark (who was the host's younger brother) and Mark's boyfriend David. Their service had been disastrously bad, much to Mark's brother's annoyance and K's amusement, and K and I ended up abandoning the fatuous dinner-table conversation for the refuge of the much friendlier kitchen, where we drank wine with these 'waiters', established that we lived very close to one another, and became friends.

David and Mark were always more manageable as David and Mark than they ever were as either just David or just Mark, if you see what I mean. It's not something that you would wish on any couple really. Mark was, is, very funny – unrelentingly so – full of mischief and gossip and jokiness, with a tendency never to ask you anything about yourself, and to immediately forget anything you might manage to mention. 'Full of life' is the expression they use. Which after a while can become very wearing. And David, while possessed of a dry wit, is a much more serious person, wrapped up in his work, considerate and kind and patient – almost priestly in his solicitude and earnestness. And almost endlessly curious about other people and what they think and what they feel and what they believe. Which can also be wearing. Together, they formed a balanced whole, and were usually perfect company, each counteracting the excesses of the other, smoothing out the jagged discomfort of time spent with just one of them. What had ever made them a couple, though, I have never really understood. It had been a little while since I'd seen David, or even talked to him.

I told him what had brought me to him, in the state I was in, more or less. I may have glossed over certain things, I can't remember. I can't have told him everything, that's certain. I would have held back on my latest thoughts. Anyway, it didn't take long. I left things out. And the things I left in I downplayed, I don't know why, perhaps because I felt that most of it sounded ridiculous. It made me seem a fool and I didn't want to seem any more of a fool. Anyway, the main point of the story as I told it to David, was that I had walked out on K, and on hearing this David became briefly less solicitous, as if I had trespassed on his territory, or had shown myself capable of some of the same cruelty as Mark.

—Why? he asked me, not unreasonably, but quite sharply.

I was unable, obviously, to answer. I floundered, said something about a misunderstanding, that I needed some time away, that it wasn't fatal, terminal, decisive, that it was a temporary thing, almost an experiment, or not an experiment, but more of a stepping out than a walking away, and that anyway, I had turned my phone back on and K had not called. But, I added quickly, realising that this was a troublesome fact, K's not calling meant nothing, other than that I was probably, mostly, just being stupid, and that K was mad at me, and it was probably as well for me to stay away for a little while, and if David didn't mind could I possibly stay the night? and anyway, how was he? I hadn't seen him in ages, and we should catch up, and he could afford to take a night off from his work for once – it was Friday for God's sake – and I didn't really want to talk about K – I was angry at K, but that was all, it wasn't fatal, and anyway, if he didn't mind, I didn't really want to talk about it too much at all, and did he have any drink? He did not have any drink. I must have looked dangerously forlorn at this news, because he immediately promised to go and get some.

Before that, though, he became nurse for while. I suppose I did need some of that. He took my bag from me, helped me out of my jacket – frowning at my confusion over the rip – and insisted that he have a look at the cut. I tried to pull up the leg of my trousers, but that simply wasn't working, so I had to take them off, which I did, in the bathroom, while David ran the hot-water tap in the sink and took a clean towel from the shelf and wondered out loud about whether he had plasters and bandages and the like. I have no idea to be honest whether David has any kind of sexual interest in me or not. I think probably not. In any case, he showed no sign of it as I perched on the edge of the bath in my underwear and he knelt in front of me and cleaned my wound.

—The cut isn't too bad. It's right on the bone though. Must hurt like hell.

—Oh. I don't know. Yes, I suppose it does.

—There's a lot of bruising. It'll be black and blue by morning. Were you running?

—Was I running? I don't know. I must have been. I thought I wasn't. It was dark though – hard to tell.

—Do you want to take a bath?

—Why?

—Well, you can if you want to. There's plenty of hot water.

—Do I need a bath?

—What?

—Am I dirty?

David looked at me as if I was mad. Or foolish. Or as if I was a child. Actually, I don't know what made me think that he might ever have had any kind of sexual interest in me whatsoever. I don't know why I even mentioned it. He plainly does not.

—No. Don't be silly. No. You're just shivering a little and maybe a nice hot bath would be good for you. If you want. While I get the wine.

So he ran a hot bath, and left plasters and a bandage for me, and another, bigger towel, and his dressing gown, and while he went to the shops to get wine I lay quietly sweating in his bathtub, scanning the walls for spiders and finding none, but taking no comfort whatsoever, from anything.

It's very quiet where I am. I imagine that it's been quiet for some time, but I have only noticed it now, since I turned off the television. I watched the rolling news while I ate an omelette. There's really nothing happening in the world. I really couldn't tell you what the top stories are. I was surprised that they were able to bring me an omelette, at this hour. It's very late. Or very early, I suppose, depending on which way you're facing. I cannot sleep. I tried after I finished writing the last part, the part that ends with the leaving of K, but my mind was racing on, covering the shaky ground that leads to the solid wall of what happened this morning, or yesterday morning, which provoked me into setting all of this down in the first place. I lay in the deep soft bed but it was neither deep enough nor soft enough to get me away from myself. Maybe it was too soon after eating. Maybe I should try again now.

It's so quiet that it makes me a little uneasy. It's the kind of quiet that presages some tumult. The sudden stillness in the forest. You know what I mean. The birds go silent. The deer look up. The fox stops. The badger and the stoat cease their frolicking. The pony opens an eye. The squirrels prick up their ears. The goat cocks his head. I'm a city person, completely. I actually don't know what goes on in forests at all.

I have drawn nothing for a week. Not a single thing. I think that's unprecedented. I think it's possibly the first full week of my entire life, since I was about five years old, that I have not sketched or scribbled something. For the first few days it simply wasn't in my mind – I was at David's and didn't get any sketchbooks or anything back until late on Saturday, and then there was the whole Paddorn disaster; and on Sunday there was . . . well, there was utter madness. I'll get to that. The list. See above. But since Monday evening, after I'd been in the BOX building and seen the stain and felt a dim urge to draw it (it's all on the list), I have consciously, or half consciously, chosen not to draw anything at all. All that's on hold now. In abeyance. Since Monday night. Since then I have barely left this hotel room. I cannot resume, I cannot take up my life again. Everything has a brittle shell, a fragile structure, as if frozen, and I am terrified to do anything, to take a step or move from this place, or attempt to trace the delicate shape of anything, in case everything breaks. I tried to. Yesterday. I tried to leave here. And the whole world, frankly, tipped sideways. I'm not doing that again. Now, somehow, I feel that if I write it all down, set it out, if I talk it through, that my breath will thaw it and the world will be firm again, and able to bear my weight, and I can walk back to what I had, and where I was, and that everything will be all right.

My hotel room is beautiful. That's the wrong word. It is comfortable. It is quiet and warm, and its basics and its gadgets all work perfectly. It is made of dark woods and deep carpets and fat square pillows, and the bed is supremely comfortable. It's like a nest. It costs a lot of money. This is my fourth, or fifth, night here. I was supposed to leave today. Yesterday rather. And I did leave yesterday. But I came back. For reasons which still amaze me, I had to come back. I had to return to the hotel. Which I did about fourteen hours ago. I have a lot to get through, a lot to tell you about, and here I am telling you about my hotel, which isn't even on the list. Oh, it is. But not here. I need to speed things up a bit. I should order some coffee. Maybe you should too. A silver pot of coffee and a jug of warm milk. Here, they send you a plate of biscuits even when you don't ask.

I spent Friday night and Saturday night in David's, and left on Sunday after he became upset when I criticised his novel, or the idea of his novel, which, it seems to me, is stupid, although that isn't actually the word I used – far from it – the words I used were 'contradictory' and 'para-doxical' and 'illogical' and 'self-defeating' and, possibly, 'pointless'. Actually, I did say 'pointless'. Certainly I did. Because it is.

He came back from the shops with four bottles of wine, which alerted me to the possibility of self-indulgence on my part, of taking things too far into myself, or out of myself – in any case, of *taking* things.

I am older than David, and I am not unaware of the fact that he looks up to me somewhat, that he feels I possess a greater wisdom than he does, that I know more about life; and although I am an illustrator and he is a writer, he believes that we share a creative sensibility (which we certainly do not), and also that I have achieved a certain level of success of which he is (healthily) envious, and he often quizzes me about all of that, looking for clues, hints, tricks and insights that he can use for himself. He often asks me about my ambitions for my art, and usually I have to make something up. I inevitably forget what I have told him, and when, the next time he asks, he gets a different answer, he doesn't see in this evidence of duplicity or vacancy on my part, but of a *fascinating development of thought*. He mistakes my ambivalence for depth; my apathy for humility. He is forever attempting to get me into conversations about the very *nature* of art, or, more recently, the nature of love (I think he believes the two are fairly interchangeable) and the business of being in the world and how to negotiate it. And I could see him, as he came back with the wine, trying to repress the sense of excitement he felt at the idea that I had turned to him in this desperate hour; the hope this had given him that after a couple of years of skating around the issues, we might now, finally, be on the cusp of saying something *essential* to each other.

I didn't want to say anything essential. Not to David. But there he was, with four bottles of wine and all that expectation. And there I was, red from the bath, with my shin wrapped and throbbing, in David's pale blue dressing gown, with such a volume of thought in my head that the urge to talk was almost overwhelming. It was not that there was anything *specific* that I wanted to say of course. I wanted just to talk – to put some kind of shape on the mess. I wanted to put the things that had happened into sentences so that I could hear how they sounded. I wanted to try and build something out of the clutter, and then stand back and see what it looked like – if it looked like anything. But I didn't want an audience. My God. And I certainly didn't want an audience of David. I was terrified of what I would say. I was suspicious of my own thoughts and of how they were related to the reality of what might have just happened. And suspicious too of David's capacity for listening. And I was convinced that out of these suspect elements some false and minor and irritating and point-less *truth* would be arrived at – or I should say *invented* – by David's idiotic, adolescent, sentimental compassion, and by my apparent ability to give David, without ever really intending to, whatever *material* David wants, or needs, in order to reach the compassionate conclusions that he would have reached anyway. Except that without me feeding him his lines he might have reached them in less *validating*, less convoluted language. And I knew, as he smiled at me kindly and asked me how I felt, and whether the bath had been all right; as he opened a bottle of Italian red and made a friendly, gentle, wholly appro-priate and disarming joke about there being, at last, after all this time, a naked man in his flat – I knew that I would, if I didn't stop myself, tell David everything, and more, and speculate with him and theorise and be *honest* and *open* and converse in *essentials*, just so that he would stop pointing his compassionate puppy eyes at me so bloody expectantly.

The maps. I forgot to tell you about the maps.

—This one, I said, knowing that if there was any way of deflecting David, it was his work. – Is this, what, a city? Which city is this?

—That's Delvern. It's the oldest Padrain city. That's how it looked about two hundred years after it was founded.

It was hanging over his desk, which was a cheap plain wood self-assembly thing slotted into an alcove, piled high with ring binders and notebooks and loose pages covered in David's dense, black, tiny handwriting. And I really do mean tiny. Some of his notebooks run to what looks like a hundred pages or more, and he has filled them, covered them, with what must be a dozen full-length novels' worth of text. It seems never to stop. His writing is so small that I have to practically run my nose along the page, and I swear that when I do I can smell the ticklish ink – a dizzying sort of thing – which combines with the squinting to make me feel that I am peering from a huge distance at what David has written. As if his work is located in the past, or not just *on* the pages but somehow within them. You have to climb inside his notebooks to read them, in the same way that you have to climb inside a car in order for it to take you anywhere. Of course I understand virtually nothing of any of it. You would perhaps have to start at the beginning, and I'm not sure that there is one. David, in fact, claims not to have actually started at all yet.

—At that stage it wasn't very impressive, I suppose. Striking of course, given the setting, but there was no interesting architecture to speak of. It was still a settlement rather than a city really. The major building works – the things that make it the architectural centre of Paddorn – weren't started for about another hundred years. But I like the look of it at this time. The way the contours of the streets follow the coast and the mountains. Later, a lot of it got levelled out and straightened. And the amazing buildings like the Padrain Council and the Public Liptim were put in. And the Kollomander of course. Which is actually built on this outcrop of rock here. It was a real warren at this point. Dangerous, squalid, interesting.

I should explain that Paddorn does not actually exist. In case you were wondering whether you'd missed out on a nice location for a weekend break. Paddorn is a fictional place. David has invented it.

—I've completed the chronology I was having so much trouble with.

—Oh? Well, that's good.

—It's the period that leads up to the Secondary Council. From the Great Western War and the settlement, up to the Secondary Council. It's a relatively long period of peace. About seventy years. You know, in comparison to what went before, and certainly to what follows the collapse of the Council and the assassination of Graydle.

His maps are pretty terrible. They're rudimentary, childish little things, with random shapes and squiggles denoting various geographical features or human interventions. Is human the right word? I'm not sure. He has no concept of scale, so that in some cases different maps of the same area are simply impossible. His maps of towns and cities, such as the one he was showing me now, look suspiciously to me as if they're traced. Delvern is probably a suburb of Buenos Aires. But if his maps are bad, his drawings of buildings are just plain awful. For a long time I've been terrified that he will ask me to help him out with this stuff. To just draw a couple of things for him – a town hall maybe, or a particular mountain range seen from the east at sunset, or a view of the harbour at Whatdyacallit. But he's never asked.

—Of?

—Graydle. He was the Phin of Delvern at the time. Do you want to talk about other stuff?

—No. The King of Delvern . . .

—Not King, *Phin*. It's like a president. Though of course the office is very different to our understanding of a presidency. There were no elections as such. Well, I mean there were elections, but the electorate was always fairly limited to the religious classes and the wealthy, depending on the times, on what was fashionable and who was in charge of it. There was only ever one attempt at a democracy as we'd understand it on Paddorn. It was among the earliest Padrain settlers in Aylthrew. It was a disaster. As was the whole attempted settlement at Aylthrew anyway.

—Why?

—Mostly geographical reasons. Nature. Both of the place and of the Padrain. They were completely cut off by the mountains. A very harsh sea. Bad land. It provided the foundation of the Padrain's mythologising of course. That's extremely important. Their notion of Paddorn as theirs, and the Weldern Mountains as the holiest of places. Right high up in the Welderns they somehow built the so-called 'Holy City', which became known as Threw, although the real name has been kept secret.

I'm not sure now whether this conversation took place on the Friday night or on the Saturday. I actually can't remember. I know that on the Friday I certainly stopped myself talking about what had happened to me. And I know of course that at various points over the Friday, Saturday and Sunday Paddorn was discussed in great detail. But I can't remember now if we started all that on the

Friday night. There's a possibility that we didn't. That David simply sat with me and we watched television or something. Or we ate. Or I ate. David cooked for me. He had already eaten, after coming in from work. He works as an office administrator for a large charity. I'm not sure that he makes a very good living from it. The flat is rented, from a relative as far as I can remember. One of the reasons Mark left the country was that he couldn't afford a place on his own. He was always a barman, or a waiter, or something or other, for about six months at a time, one place after another, gay bars and clubs mostly. Now he does that somewhere else where living is cheaper.

David showed me another map, pointing at a dot in the centre of some concentric lines that were supposed to denote great height. Contour lines. There were no altitude figures given, and I couldn't help noticing that the lines were all closed, and circular, which would have made for a mountain range that looked something like this –

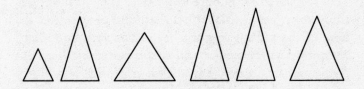

in which all of the mountains were independent of each other and were of a completely regular triangular shape. Well, conical then. I've given you the head-on view. Also, the city he was pointing out to me, called Threw, was placed between two sets of circles. *Between* two mountains in other words, at sea level, and not where it was supposed to be – up in the snowy peaks. For a second I thought that this was some kind of elaborate but strangely pointless joke – that in order for Threw to be 'high up', someone would indeed have had to have thrown it. But one glance at David's earnest, concentrated face convinced me that he was entirely serious.

—It's not really called Threw then?

—Well, it is. It's *known* as Threw. But the real name, the holy name, has been kept secret.

—You mean you haven't thought of it yet?

—No. I don't mean that.

—So what is it then?

—It's kept secret by the five Weldern priests. Originally they were all based at Threw, but there was an attack on the city by a schismatic group of early disaffected Padrain in the first years of the settlement. Four of the priests were killed, and the secret of the name, along with various other secrets held by the priests, was almost lost. Since then two of the priests have stayed at Threw, with one each in Delvern, Padrain Possel and Har Kyle. That has lasted for hundreds of years. They have various ritual roles, ceremonial roles, that kind of thing. At the time I'll be writing about, they're not very important. Paddorn is fairly secular and sophisticated by then. But previously they would have had a great deal of political power. One of them, Pyotor Lensible, actually ruled all of Paddorn, briefly, including the Westorn Lands.

—Jesus Christ.

—What?

—Nothing.

David isn't mad. Some of our friends think that he's mad. Michael, for example, won't go near him. Rachel says she likes him and claims to be interested in what he's doing, but it's clear that she also thinks he's entirely insane.

Another friend, who teaches gender studies and literature, is fascinated by him because he fits perfectly into the stereotypical male adolescent escapist obsessive category, except for the fact that he's gay, reads Proust and Cervantes and Joyce, listens to choral music rather than heavy metal, and is really quite a nice, sweet guy, with impeccable personal hygiene.

—So what's the secret name of the Holy City?

—I don't know. It's a secret.

—But you made the whole thing up. You made up the mountains and the city there at the foot . . . in the peaks there, of the mountains. You made up the priests and the wars and the whole history of the whole entire planet, which you also made up. You made up all the names. You made up 'Threw'. You made up the fact that there's *another* name. You made up the fact that it's secret. *You* did. So what is it?

—I'm not telling you.

David is not a fantasy novelist. If you suggest to him that he is a fantasy novelist he will be horrified. He'll admit to novelist, when pressed, but will remind you that he hasn't actually written a novel yet. He's *getting ready*.

David, I should make clear, is no thriller writer or entertainer or creator of diversions. David is a serious author. He's ambitious, but not for sales. He's not aiming at John Grisham or Nick Hornby, or even at Ian McEwan or Toni Morrison or John Updike. He's aiming way past those guys – towards Tolstoy and Joyce and Proust. He's aiming mostly, if I understand him correctly, towards Cervantes. There are about twenty different editions of *Don Quixote* lying around his home, as well as countless commentaries and critical volumes and biographies and what have you. There is a lot of Homer too, and various other Greeks and

Romans. And Milton. And some Dante, and André Gide, about whom I know nothing. There is a large amount of politics and history. There isn't much from the last twenty-five years or so. There is no *Harry Potter*. There are no hobbits. Fantasy plays no part in the work of a serious author – so says David, who is, as you'll have noticed, the creator of Delvern, the Westorn Lands and the Priests of the Weldern Mountains.

Mark told us, years ago, how it all started – with the simple decision to write a novel in an imaginary city. Actually, at first it wasn't even that – it was just an unnamed city. And the reason he didn't want to name it was simply that the novel was to be largely about politics – about politicians and power, about the human interactions that take place within the architecture of political organisation and discourse and that kind of thing. And David didn't want to clutter up his writing with correlations to the real political landscape of any particular, recognisable place. He wanted his story to be unfettered by the limitations of those systems that are familiar to us in Europe or the United States, or in historical systems such as the Soviet Union or the French monarchy or fascist dictatorships or what have you. He wanted his narrative to occupy a kind of sterile, sealed space, where he could allow characters and ideas to flourish and conflict and realign and change and develop, without the constraint of accuracy.

So David began making things up. Which is what novelists do, I suppose. David, though, began making *everything* up. If he was making up a city, why not make up a country? And if a country, why not other countries with which it has to deal and trade and contend? And if he was making up countries then he might as well make up their geography as well, given that natural resources and populations and territorial boundaries are bound to play a large part in the affairs of these countries. And such things will also contribute to distinctive religious and cultural practices, which he might as well make up too. And while he's doing that, obviously he has to provide a historical context for all of this or it means nothing.

When he talks about it, and he talks about it a lot, there often seems to be a great weariness to him, as if he's aware of the task he's given himself, is scared by the immensity of it, but is unable to stop. He can't turn back. He's as tired and as conscientious as God, to whom it must have seemed like a good idea at the time too.

—In the Holy City there is a temple. Inside the temple there are three rooms. Three chambers. Two of the chambers are the ceremonial halls of the Weldern priests, the two who live at Threw. In the third chamber there is a sealed inner room. Inside the sealed room is a container. A kind of canister. Inside the canister is the source of the universe. The substance out of which all things are created. The story goes that if the canister is ever opened this universe will be destroyed – pushed out of the way by a new one, an empty one.

—I like that. That's kind of exciting. Are you going to get someone to open it?

—It's myth. Threw, at the time I'll be writing about, is a tourist trap. There are stalls all over the place with little jack-in-the-box canisters that terrify children.

I didn't dream at all in David's place. I barely slept. I shook and sweated and stared. He fed me on the Friday night with pasta and a simple tomato sauce. At some point he played some music that he wanted me to hear. He seemed disappointed that I wasn't immediately moved by it. He had the radio on all the time. News stations or chat shows. Never music. When he wanted music he would put on a CD. At one point, maybe on Saturday night, there was an embarrassing moment when I was sitting at the kitchen table, having just returned from the shops, and David, not realising I was back, walked naked into the room, in search of some clean clothes. He laughed and blushed and got me to throw things at him while he crouched behind the door.

On Saturday morning, or afternoon, when I awoke, I switched on my telephone while still lying on David's little camp bed. I held it in my hands and stared at its gentle lights for some time, watching them dim and go out, waiting for them to reanimate and startle me with incoming. Which they duly did, plucking stupid, brutal shards of notes out of the machine's inner armoury. In the quiet they sounded louder than an air-raid claxon. There was a voice message from Michael. Something about the sports centre. How he'd thought that I'd been joking but then he'd seen it on the news and my God was I all right and I should sue the architects as well as everybody else, and he had no plans, and did K and I want to go out that night? There was a text message from my mother, reminding me that my father's birthday is . . . well, it's tomorrow now. I'll have to call him. I've left it far too late to send him anything. Not even a card. I will call him tomorrow. A simple happy birthday call. No news, no, nothing major. There was a text from the assistant editor of a monthly magazine for whom I've done some work in the past, including a couple of covers. She wanted to know had I got her email. I suspect that she wanted some last-minute stuff, as they should have gone to press sometime this week. I never got back to her. I haven't checked my email. I should really.

Perhaps somewhere in the hotel there is some kind of Internet access. There's bound to be.

From K, there was nothing.

The cold, still notion, that had dissipated in me while I fought with sleep, reformed itself, became as solid as a tumour and the fear flooded me again.

I held down the 2 key on my phone, the quick-dial for K. I was put straight through to voicemail. K's phone was switched off. Or something. K's phone was switched off or dead. It was switched off or it was out of range. It was switched off or it was beyond the range of usable air, buried somewhere in the incommunicable silence of a blind spot. It was just switched off. K had switched it off while sleeping, while angry, while annoyed, while depressed, while inconsolable, while gone, while out of my range. K's voice chirped at me, from a previous time, ghosted from the cheerful distance, *Hello, I can't take your call right now* . . . and I pressed another button and the silence came crashing down like a lid. What should I have said? *Hi it's me sorry about all that I'm at David's hope you're still . . . hope you're . . .*

I lay in the light of David's front room, staring up at the misshapen cities and mountains and lakes of Paddorn. Where did they come from, the Padrain? How did they get there? If they were settlers where did they come from? Somewhere with canisters. On one map a line of red Xs split the western third of Paddorn from the rest. I know that at several points in the very long history of the place, David has had some despotic monster emerge out of these 'Westorn Lands' to wreak havoc among his own people first, and then to attack and occupy various parts of the settled, colonised, civilised place where David focuses most of his attention. These Tamerlanes and Stalins seem to serve some kind of reorganising purpose in David's grand scheme of things, as if they are devices for clearing large logjams, for unclogging the forward momentum when it gets bogged down in process and too many layers, when it becomes too complicated and falters. Violence brings simplicity. There rises an army in the west.

David smiled at me when I walked into the kitchen, and told me that he'd heard my phone, and so he'd made some breakfast, even though he'd eaten hours earlier, and had been working at the kitchen table, and hadn't wanted to disturb me, he'd just crept into the room and got some of his notebooks, and had been working ever since, until he'd heard my phone. I must have slept more than I'd realised then, if he had been in the room.

—I heard your phone.

—Yes. You said.

He rolled his eyes at me.

—Well? Have you heard anything?

—Oh. No. Actually, no. Sorry. I'm still, still, what do they say? I'm still in the doghouse. I think.

—Well, you should call.

—I did call.

—Ah.

—No answer.

I looked, I imagined, still sleepy, my face lined with pillow scars, my hair in a state. He didn't pursue it. Maybe I looked sad.

—Did you sleep all right?

—Like a baby. I was exhausted.

—I washed your jeans.

He nodded to a clothes horse that stood in the corner of the kitchen, where, sure enough, my jeans hung drying, along with the shirt I'd been wearing. On my plate was a fried egg, two sausages, three pieces of bacon, half a grilled tomato, two slices of toast and a little glass pot of marmalade. David had made a fresh pot of coffee. There was a morning newspaper on the table. The sun shone over his shoulder. On the Sunday, the next day, the breakfast was much simpler. Coffee and a couple of croissants, and the marmalade again. The Sunday papers. And on the Sunday we ate together, and I said the things I said, and he asked me to leave. But on the Saturday David just watched me, and chatted. About Paddorn, I think. If I were him, I'd be a little embarrassed about it, I think. But he'll talk about it to anyone.

—It's not a planet.

—What?

—Paddorn. You said it was a planet. It's not a planet. It's an island.

—An island?

—Yes.

—On Earth?

He mended my jacket too. At some point. Didn't do a bad job. Sewed up the shoulder. You'd barely notice it now.

—What?

—On Planet Earth? Here somewhere?

—Well, yes, here, somewhere, I suppose.

—Should it not be a planet?

—Why should it be a planet?

—Well. If the idea is to make *everything* up, then surely you have to make up a new planet?

—Why?

—Well, what's the point in making a point of making absolutely everything up then? You say you can't use anything at all that you actually know, you have to invent everything, so then it's sort of cheating to use Planet Earth. You know. What if somebody flies over Paddorn in a helicopter?

—You're being far too literal.

—I am?

Sometimes I think that maybe he is mad. That something in his head has not quite closed off. That he is an escapist, to a profound, disturbed degree. I've talked to Rachel about it. She worries that David will spend his entire life reclusively, obsessively doing preparatory work for art that never actually comes into being. I think that idea fills her with horror, whereas I think it's kind of romantic. She sees only sadness in what David is doing. She doesn't see it as at all valuable in itself. It has to be communicated. It has to be shared in some way. By being offered to an audience. I know she's talked to him, tentatively, about putting some of his stuff on display. I think her idea was to collate some of his notebooks into nicely bound volumes and stick them in a gallery under a glass case, with a new page turned every day. She didn't mention the maps. David's handwriting is very nice, I must admit, if difficult to see, but I really don't think Rachel was thinking straight. Neither did David. He thought the whole idea was ridiculous.

—Oh. Well, how did they get to the *island* then?

—The Padrain came from a previous place, from which they were exiled.

—What place?

—To the east.

—France?

—No. I don't know.

—Do you not need to know?

—Not really.

—Does where they come from not explain more about them – the kind of people they are? Does it not provide more context?

—It would only be imported context. The whole point is to avoid that. So it doesn't really matter.

—But they are human then?

—Of course they're human.

—From somewhere actual in the world?

—Well, yes, I suppose so.

—You've just shipwrecked them on an imaginary island?

—In a sense.

He was leaning against the kitchen counter, with his arms folded, looking down at me, half smiling, younger than I am.

—You know, there are various, um, precedents for that kind of thing.

—I know.

I should just tell you about the argument. While we're here, talking about the place anyway. Because it did all more or less hinge on this idea of precedents. I'm jumping around my list a little, I know. But actually to go through it as it happened is no more straightforward, and it sort of proves my point anyway, which is that it's impossible to tell you certain things without having first told you other certain things. Which may, on the face of it, look like David's point, but David is actually seeking to conduct a kind of zero-gravity experiment, whereas I am in the process of falling down. David doesn't want to refer to this world at all but rather to create a new one and refer to that, as if something profound or good can come from weightlessness, when in fact it's not weightless at all, it's a clutter of rubble like cheap tacky scrap metal, like the bits and pieces of his broken-down world. It's the apparatus of fear disassembled and reorganised to look simpler, cleaner. But it just looks sillier. And the fear remains.

The argument started on the Saturday night maybe. I had gone to the shops, come back with more wine, he had walked naked into the kitchen and I had blushed as much as he did, and perhaps that was part of it. I have no idea. And we had started, later, to talk a little about the whole idea of context, when I asked him whether his readers were not going to have a terrible amount to learn before they could understand his novel, and he had expressed his view that the very point was that he didn't want his readers to have any of their assumptions left unchallenged, that his novel would exist outside of any context they could comfortably supply for it, that it would demand of them that they drop their inherited beliefs and their learned thinking and start again, and I had protested that you can't get people to unknow what they know. And perhaps as a defence David had asked me something about K. About whether I loved K. We'd had some wine. He asked me whether I loved K, which I thought was pretty low, in the sense that he was on the back foot about his inherited beliefs thing, and I was starting to ask him about where he thought he'd got his from, and apropos of nothing he swerved the conversation in a completely different direction, asking me bluntly whether I loved K, and I said, *What's that got to do with anything, don't change the subject*, and I think I must have looked a little taken aback, and I suspect now actually, now that I think of it, I suspect now that David had sort of forgotten why I was there, and was reaching for an example of inherited beliefs and thought that love might be such an example, and had asked me whether I loved K in the full and reasonable explanation that I would say *Yes, of course I love K* without giving it a moment's thought, and then he would have launched into some half-arsed exploration of the nature of love and what was it, and was it not just a cultural artefact, and why did we call it love and not affection or not lust or not loyalty or some other such train of thought – trains upon which I have travelled with David before, and it's always a bit of a close call as to whether they derail before they reach a station, or, having reached a station, whether that was the station that David had intended to get to. But. The point is that I now see that he was probably using an innocent rhetorical device and had forgotten, somehow, that the only reason I was drinking red wine with him in his living room on a Saturday night was that I had walked out on K, and that therefore any question about my love or otherwise for K was bound to be one which, just at that moment, might prove somewhat difficult for me, no matter what the answer. The answer was yes. Of course it was yes. Is yes. But I hesitated, and I think I probably looked a little shocked, and I probably paled slightly. And all of that made me angry. Annoyed. And as soon as that happened of course David remembered why I was there and became flustered, and forgot about his theory of inherited beliefs, and the conversation, which had been lively and animated, faltered and fell, and we were left in a simmering silence, which was broken after about thirty terrible seconds by the kind of thing that only happens because it's supposed to happen at times like these – a phone rang.

I knew immediately that it wasn't mine – it was a different ring tone – but I think David wasn't sure for a moment, and gawped at me. And I was thinking – there was a chance it might be K. So I was gawping back. It turned out, when David answered, to be a man he knew, and he left the room to talk, but I could clearly hear him apologising that he couldn't meet with this man, because he had a friend over – *no, just a friend* – and he'd call later in the week.

—Why don't you go out?

—Because I don't want to.

—I'd be fine here on my own. Go out for God's sake.

—No, really, I don't want to. He's a bit . . .

—A bit what?

—Odd.

—*He's* odd?

—Oh, thanks.

—You're the one with the new planet.

—It's not a planet.

—Well, it should be. What ocean is it in? Pacific? Atlantic? Is it Atlantis?

—No, of course not.

—Is it, you know, northern hemisphere? Or southern? Is it Middle Earth? Are there orcs? Are there signing trees? Do you have any peculiar animals on Paddorn? Do you have cattle? Do you have sheep? Do they talk?

—Oh forget it.

That kind of thing.

On the Sunday morning we got up at about the same time and shared breakfast and afterwards, while I was washing the dishes and David was standing beside me, I started talking, soberly, about the flaws, as I saw them, in David's approach to his novel, giving, as I saw it at the time, a much more reasonable and thorough analysis of where he was going wrong, without recourse to petty or childish trivialisations, such as I had employed the night before. I see now of course that I was doing precisely the wrong thing. That David would have much preferred that the entire subject be dropped, that he'd had enough of it, and for me to start on it again seemed like a deliberate and crass attempt to undermine him and, more importantly, his work.

I'd tried to call K again the night before. Twice. No answer. So I had thrashed uncomfortably in David's camp bed, the street lights picking out the pointed peaks of the Welderns on the wall, and I had, silently and completely and comprehensively, destroyed David's created world and any reason he thought he might have had for creating it. By morning I could remember very few of my insights. I tried calling K again. The dead phone. The silence. The pieces scattered. But I could remember enough to have a go at it as I washed the dishes in David's sink.

He had his arms crossed and then uncrossed, and crossed again, as his fists clenched and unclenched over his elbows and under his elbows, his hands, first one then the other, going to his chin, rubbing his chin, or his eyes, or brushing his nose, then collapsing again, into a cross-armed slouch, then his back going sideways left and sideways right against the kitchen countertop, as if he was trying to cut himself slowly in half at the waist, as if that would be something sort of worth doing, and his feet were pushing him up and then letting him down, and he crossed his legs at the ankles a couple of times and dropped a shoulder, in disbelief, and his eyes took his head everywhere, to look at parts of his kitchen I'm sure he'd never seen before, as his mouth dropped and his head shook, and the whole question-mark shape of him seemed to hover between a sigh and sudden violence, as if he was unsure whether rage or resignation was his role in life.

—It's not simply that the whole idea is in itself flawed.

I mean the whole idea of trying to create something out of nothing. It's not just that that's a ridiculous, cowardly response to this world, it's the fact that even on its own terms, what you're doing makes absolutely no sense. It's not consistent. It breaks its own rules. It has no inner logic. It's actually pathetic how detailed you've made it and how you've missed the most obvious things of all.

—Like?

—Like what language do they speak?

He just stared at me, and his arms went through their semaphore of miserable self-defence and bluster, as if he could magic me away from him with the shape his body made – as if he could make himself a sign.

—What language are you writing it in? What language do the Padrain speak? Padrainese? No? Some French? Italian? German? No. It's English, isn't it? They speak your English. They speak our language. What kind of weird creation is it that doesn't create its own way of talking?

—It's translated.

—What?

—It's all translated from their language. From Pallaf, which is the language of the Padrain, and Tillmo, which is the Westorn tongue.

He squirmed then, which I probably provoked, with my stare.

—Translated. You translate it, do you? From the original sources?

—Well, no, obviously not, that would be just . . .

He stalled. All his arms stopped their wrapping and their punching and his head turned down. He looked serious and lost. I should have felt sorry for him then.

—Just what? Just what? Just stupid is what that would just be, David. I mean. You invent the people. And you invent where they live. And you invent what happens to them. You create it all out of nothing. So that it can be pure and free of any polluted ideas, any shadow of contingency. But it can't be, David. It can't be. It is contingent on your language, or your little life, or your ability to draw the maps for it, on the fact that you can't really do mountains. You can't do shaded elevation, David. You do it all wrong, you don't have the patience for it. So you don't do it very much. So Padrain is flat. Except for the Holy City, of course, which seems to house all the things you haven't thought of. It's like a little canister of displaced complexity, that is. Anything not quite working for you? Refer to the Holy City. Some sort of confusion over the way things work around here? Holy City. And you know nothing about ships. So this island, this island with all its coastal towns is a place where no one seems to have a boat.

—They do have boats.

—What do they look like?

—I don't know. Ships. Boats.

—What's the history of the Padrain shipping industry? How did it start? What approach do they take? Is it sail-powered? Oars? Do they have slaves? Are they steam-boats? Actually, have they come up with the combustion engine yet? Or are you inventing new energy sources while you're at it? And, it occurred to me last night – are there queers on Padrain? What's the gay scene like? And what colour are people?

—Don't –

—It's all nonsense, David. You have this lovely idea that imagination is pure, that it's the primary source, and if you draw directly from it, and only from it, that you'll create something that is essentially true – true in all its facets.

Without compromise. Without contingency. But what you're not seeing is that your imagination is just as polluted as the reality you're attempting to bypass. You're formed by *this* world, David. You're made here. You can't not be. You can't start from scratch. All you get if you do that it a self-indulgent, crippled, half-place. It doesn't work. As complicated as you make it, it's still a sandcastle. You're wasting your time. You have a wonderful talent for writing and you're wasting it. You're like a beetle fallen on its back. You could spend the entire rest of your life describing the clouds.

I don't know if I said that exactly. Something like that. He said, very quietly, with his arms folded and his chin down and his eyes very solidly on me:

—What a stupid thing to say. What a stupid, ignorant, arrogant thing to say.

Which was when I knew that I had overstepped the mark. I stopped what I was doing and looked at him. He was furious. I dried my hands on the tea towel.

—You are wonderfully talented, David. You write beautifully, you really do.

—I'd like you to leave please.

—What?

—Just get your things together and go.

—Go? David?

—Just get your stuff and go please. Your jacket is on a hanger in the hot press. Sorry but I can't have you here any more. You have to go.

—Oh David, for God's sake, I was just chatting. David! It's not important. Well, obviously it's important, your work is important, but I was just talking off the top of my head. I wasn't saying anything that really matters.

—I'm not discussing it. I want you to go. Now.

And he went to his room and closed the door. I couldn't

126

Animals

believe it. I believe it now of course. I believe it now, certainly. But I didn't believe it then. I was doing that horrible thing we do when something takes us so stupidly by surprise – that half-laughing, mouth-open bewilderment that makes the anger directed at us all the more intense because of how bloody stupid we look.

—David. Please. I'm sorry. Talk to me.

—Fuck off.

David never curses. He rarely curses. Even this time he had to be behind a door before he could say it. But he'd said it. And it brought home to me instantly how I'd miscalculated. Or, more accurately, how I'd failed to calculate at all.

I stand by what I said, but I shouldn't have said it. I should have left it unsaid. But I had used him, and wished him harm, and I had planned, if necessary, to kill him, and I had seen him naked, and all of those things perhaps conspired, I think now, to get me out of there. I looked at his closed bedroom door for a moment, and my face crumpled, and I felt everything crumple, and I gathered my crumpled clothes and other belongings, including the crumpled extras that David had himself retrieved for me from my flat, and I left, unshowered, unhappy and with a tangle of confusion upon my head like a hat.

Kill him. Yes, I'd planned to kill him. It wasn't on the list. Or was it? While he went to the flat. I sent him to my flat. To pick up some stuff. And to see. I left it aside. Purposely. There's not a lot to it and I'll tell you it now. List or no list. It was while I was contemplating killing David that I stumbled upon the notion of language being the loose brick in his tottering construction. So it's all rather neat, as it turns out.

Saturday.

127

—David. Could you do me a huge favour?

—Sure.

—There's some stuff I really need from the flat. Some bits of clothes, the charger for my phone. A couple of sketchbooks. That kind of thing. Could you go over there when you get a chance?

—Why don't you go?

—I really don't want to see K. Not just at the moment.

He nodded, considered me. He's quite handsome. He has very beautiful eyes. They settled on me and I could see his concern in them. I could see his unease at not knowing exactly what was going on – at not knowing how serious it was. I could see that he was afraid of assuming that it was as bad as his break- up with Mark. And I could see that he was afraid of assuming that nothing could ever be that bad, and in so doing somehow letting both myself and K down. Most of all I could see that he was worried about me. He wanted everything to be all right.

—You're not going to tell me what really happened, are you?

—I'm not sure what to tell you, David. It's not that I'm keeping anything from you. Not really. Not as such. It's just that I'm still trying to work it out for myself.

This was the truth of course, I think, wasn't it? It must have sounded like it. He nodded and sighed loudly and walked over to me and gave me an awkward half-hug, with me still sitting and him standing. Then he wandered out of the kitchen.

—Make a list, he called back. —You know, write it down, there's pen and paper on the sideboard. What you want me to get and where I can find it. I'll call K.

—What?

128

I stood up and went after him. He was patting the pockets of his jacket which hung in the small hall.

—You're going to call K?

—Well, I want to warn him I'm coming over. Maybe it won't be convenient.

He was right of course. It was sensible, polite. It was sensible. Half of my mind told the other half to shut up.

—I've been calling him. The phone is . . . He's not . . . He's switched the phone off . . .

—I'm not getting into it though, OK? I'll tell K that you're here and that you're fine, but that's it, I'm not getting into anything else. There'll be no messages passed back and forth. If you want to talk to each other you'll just have to talk to each other. I know what this is like. Me and Mark were terrible for that kind of thing. So I'm just not doing it.

—He might be out or something.

—Well, you can give me your key. Where is my phone?

I waited outside his bedroom. I expected him to call from in there, and stood close to the door, trying to hear. But then the door opened suddenly.

—Oh. Don't eavesdrop.

—I wasn't.

—Yes you were. You can listen, you know.

He called from the living room, sitting on the camp bed, and when he started talking into his phone, when he started to say hello, I felt my heart shift in my chest, as if something crushing it had been lifted, and I think I drew a sharp breath because he looked at me quizzically, and my chest and shoulders seemed to lift and I felt that I wanted to take the phone from his hands, but it became clear, immediately, that he was talking not to K, but to K's voicemail.

He tried to make the message bright, even cheerful, but I could see from the look on his face that he was not feeling anything other than discomfort. Poor David. My chest and my shoulders settled and went cold, and I could not breathe until it was over, and the weight on my heart, that I had forgotten, was eased back down again, and I knew fear.

As soon as David had left, the fear took over. I went to the living-room windows and lifted a corner of the blind and watched him walk to the corner, the empty bag swinging at his hip. He seemed to check his reflection in the window of a parked car, or perhaps there was simply something on the passenger seat that caught his eye. Then he waved across the road and exchanged some words with a woman going the other way. Then he was gone.

In my mind I followed him on his route. I imagined him walking now past the shops on the main road. I wondered if he'd go in to get a newspaper or something. He'd already got a newspaper. Something else then. A bottle of water. Chewing gum. Probably not. I imagined him reaching the pedestrian crossing at the intersection. If the road was busy and he'd been unlucky with timings, he might stand there for a few minutes. I didn't know how long. I looked at his desk. I flicked through a few pages of his tiny black writing in a loose leaf folder. Pages of solid text. It was illegible to me, standing. It was rows of constrained dark shapes on white, arranged in blocks, and the spaces between words joined and formed shapes on the page like worms or blasted arrows or dry paths through mud. And the rows themselves, when I looked at them, seemed like the parallel trails of a miniature army, an army of ants, say, or even smaller – an army of micro-organisms, organic killers, going left to right, left to right, each of them intricate, weaving, intelligently creating a signal like a wave, but none of them deviating from the line, none of them changing direction, none of them disobeying orders, breaking rank, suing for peace, stopping. None of them stopping. And I thought that the whole thing looked like it might be code. I thought that the code might be decipherable. That I might be able, if I looked at it in the right way, to learn something. I thought that the marks might even be a language. My mind worked its way through all these possibilities and the wildest, most ridiculous one turned out to be the dull truth. It *was* language. It was words on the page. In English. The Padrain spoke English.

In my mind I caught up with David as he passed the sports centre. Maybe he'd wonder why it was closed. Would there still be police there? Fire brigade people? There would be something. He'd note it, ponder, walk on. He would cross the road to the park. Through the small gate. Where I had been. Along the paths where I had been. Calmly through the trees and past the playground and through the park where I had been. Walking lightly, maybe trying K again, getting no answer. The gate into my street. I paced. I wandered through the small hall to the kitchen. I ran the hot tap. Filled the sink with soapy water. He would be at our building now, looking up at the windows. I put my breakfast things in the sink. Maybe David didn't walk as fast as I imagined he did. Maybe he walked faster. I didn't know where he was. I went into his bedroom. I'm not sure I'd ever been in there before. His bed was made. The room was neat, tidy. There were some bookshelves, a chest of drawers, a wardrobe. There was a laundry basket. There were pairs of shoes by the window. There were the kinds of things that K and I have in our bedroom. He would be there now. He might be there now. He could be.

Standing in my home. Staring. Staring at the floor and the walls, calling out, Hello, K? Are you there? It's me. It's David. And there would be no answer. The scene. The state of the place. What was he seeing? What was he staring at? Why was he stalled? Why was I stalled? On David's bedside table there was a framed picture of himself and Mark, arm in arm, younger than they are now, with everything still alive.

In the kitchen I took a carving knife and tested it in my hands and tried to put it in my waistband but stopped before I cut myself and hid it instead in the sleeve of my jumper and I waited for David to come back, and I hoped that I wouldn't have to kill him, but knowing that if I had to I would, and knowing too that I could not cut up his body. I simply could not cut up his body. Which was a source first of relief, and then of dread.

You have no idea what's going on, do you? I should have stuck to the list.

The Park

Friday. It was Friday when I left. Friday of last week. When I left. There was a taste of vomit still in my mouth, and in my head a sort of howling, as of agitated air, as if I had no thoughts, just an absence of thoughts, like a ruined place after a storm. But I had thoughts of course.

For a while I think the boys in the hoods followed me, laughing and calling out, doing what they do, what you'd expect of them, flashing their brands in the half-light, adopting voices from elsewhere, but I really didn't care about them. I don't know where exactly I went. I know at some point I turned off my phone, not wanting to hear K calling me. I'm not sure now if it rang and then I turned it off, or whether I just turned it off. Pre-emptively. And at some point I noticed that it was raining, and had been for some time, so I put up my umbrella, only for the rain to stop again almost immediately. I found myself, eventually, in the park which is right at the end of our street, but I'm certain that I didn't go straight there – I walked the long way round, by the main road which circles its south side, and entered by the main gate. Perhaps I went even further afield and then came back to it. In any case, all of a sudden it was almost dark, and there I was – on a park bench in the light drizzle, with my bag beside me.

My thoughts were disordered, naturally. I can't really remember now what I was thinking. I suspect that a large part of it was embarrassment. I felt a little like someone waking in the morning after a terribly drunken night – I shakily reconstructed events with a sense of dread. What I could remember was bad enough, but it was what I couldn't remember that really worried me. So my embarrassment was large, but it was stalked by a creeping, desperate confusion, and from time to time the two things seemed to break into a run, and chase each other, panicked.

One of my difficulties was in the allocation of priorities, in both my consideration of what had happened up to that point, and in my vague notions of what I should do next. For a while I could not work out, could not remember, my motivation for leaving. I felt that there was no reason for it. I mean this literally. I thought I had just upped and left, that I had simply walked out, that nothing had preceded it, that it was a single thing, and that I had made some kind of awful mistake, like someone who finds themselves on the wrong train. At the same time I knew that there *was* a reason and it had escaped me, and this fact appalled me to such an extent that I stood and paced in front of my bench for some time, alarmed at the catch in my thinking that had snagged my recollection and had ripped it so disastrously. For what seemed like a horrible black hour or more I ran blindly through the stranger mazes of my mind, and the chase seemed helpless.

Eventually, from the unbidden memories of childhood afternoons and adolescent nights, and the accumulated

clutter of all that absurd business of my own history, I
dredged up the truth of things, if it's true, which even now
I think it may be. I remembered the mouse and the pen,
and the pen in the mouth, and the mouse in the mouth,
and the death in the body of the person I loved. Love.
Have loved. Love. And while I struggled to allocate the
correct value to all of the elements, and had continuing
problems with the ways in which each thing was connected
to each other thing, I began to know again what I had
known.

The park is not big, but it's possible to be in its middle,
where I was, and not really be conscious of the world
outside it. It was almost dark by now, though the rain had
stopped and the sky seemed to have cleared, and it was
pleasant, if a little cold. There was no one around, and I
took advantage of that to say things to myself, out loud,
and to use gestures and movements of my body which I
never would have dreamed of employing had I been
observed. It's rare to find a private place in the city. I
debated with myself. I argued it through. I tried to see my
actions from all angles, to examine my thoughts as objectively as possible, and then to think them again as subjec-
tively as I could, to test them, to test everything, to reassure
myself that I was not acting irrationally, that I was not
being stupid or melodramatic or ridiculous. That I was
not mad. It won't surprise you, I suppose, to learn that
after a good couple of hours of this I decided, firmly, to
go home, apologise to K, and hoped that I had not caused
irrevocable damage to our relationship. Because it seemed
to me, fully, that while I could not explain or completely
understand what had happened, I had been a fool.

I felt it would have been wrong of me, though, to dis-
own my feelings and actions entirely, and it was not my

135

intention to abandon them as some kind of aberrant episode. I had left, as I saw it then, for two main reasons.

1. Out of simple disgust at the sight of the pen in K's mouth. Behind this there is, or could be, I've no doubt, a lot of pseudo-psychology about my fear of illness or fear of death, even a possible previously unexpressed fear of the generally corporeal, which would imply, as these things seem to, inevitably, some level of self-loathing. But I'm not about to get into that. Because frankly, it would be just another blind chase, of little use to anyone.

2. Because my mouse had ceased to be just my mouse. He had become something else, something much less. My memory of him had been soiled, in a way that I knew would be ongoing, and which would eventually undermine my own sense of the dignity and import of his death. It would affect and infect me and wear me down, and no matter how much I tried to maintain my grip on the memory of how I had felt when I discovered his body, of the strange and exhilarating way it had *impressed* me, that grip would be loosened by the vulgar idiocy of what had happened afterwards, and its endless replaying in my mind, and its ineluctable recounting by K, who is a naturally garrulous person, and cannot resist telling a good story no matter how it reflects on either of us.

I imagine that you're sceptical. I imagine that you think there's more to it than I'm telling you. You probably feel that my dramatic walkout, my exit, requires a better explanation than *things were a bit yucky and I was besotted by a dead mouse.* You're awaiting, I'm sure, some exegesis of our personal history and the development of our relationship. You need more detail. You need evidence. You want to understand. You're like David.

I was sceptical too, as I picked up my bag and made my way towards home, determined that as well as begging K's forgiveness I would also set out my reasoning as honestly as I could, and that we would have to deal with it. I was sceptical. My mind was flecked with doubt, suspicious that there was more to it than that, that something else was going on, and I wasn't seeing it. But I was tired, and cold. I had enough, I thought, to return with. And in any case, if my understanding was partial then perhaps K could complete it. If that was where the full truth lay, somewhere in the folds and layers of our life together, then I was going in the right direction.

Of course, I never got there.

What is understanding? Really, what is it? What is it but a conspiracy of convenience? What is it but a cease-fire called on one square metre of an endless, limitless battlefield? If I were to tell you that K and I had spent a year or more arguing with each other, resenting each other's presence, feeling an unutterable sense of having reached a conclusion, would that satisfy you? If on the other hand I said that K and I had never been happier, that despite difficulties we had become, over the previous year, increasingly aware of our importance – our essential importance – to each other, would that help or hinder? Understanding is an agreement we make with ourselves and others not to ask any more questions. It saves us time and embarrassment and it's as invented as the wristwatch and the microwave oven. Once you understand that, you understand everything. In fact, once you understand *anything*, you understand everything. That's my understanding.

I was locked in the park.

Even as I approached the small gate that leads on to our street, even before I got to it, I realised *it's after dark, the gate is going to be locked*, and sure enough when it came into view it was closed over, and when I reached it and pushed it and pulled it, it was shut fast and immovable and far too high and spiked to be vaulted. From where I stood with my hands on the bars I could see down my own street, could make out the shape of my own building, could see how close I was to comfort.

I knew that they left the main gate open for longer, so I made my hurried way along the black paths, past groves of oily trees and the strangely sensual abandoned playing fields, feeling in the pit of my stomach the old childhood terror of being lost in a dark place, and the much more adult fear of making a fool of myself, again. When I got there I had a brief moment of hope, but it was a trick of angles and street lighting and other generally malign contrivances, and I was left forlornly standing with, I imagine, the shadows of the railings on my body, like the stripes of an idiot uniform. My mouth, I'm sure, gaped.

I still can't believe that there are people in charge of these places who simply ignore the fact that there is someone still in there when they shut them, or fail to notice that there is someone still in there, or do not make some kind of inspection of the place, or sound some kind of warning for those who've lingered a little too long, lost in thought or some other thicket. I mean, what is the point of having a park in an urban area when it becomes a trap for the distracted? There may, I suppose, have been some alarm that was sounded, but if there was I didn't hear it, and in any case, what about the deaf? And I do not recall seeing any notices, anywhere, warning me about a closing time. I'm sure they're there of course, tacked to some rotting board in some obscure corner, but I've never seen them. And yes, I did *know* that the park closes at some point, roughly when darkness falls, but that is only because I live down the road and I have come to know it over time. What about tourists? And anyway, I had forgotten, or if not forgotten precisely then momentarily put aside all useful knowledge while I dealt with personal business. Is that not what parks are for? To provide people with a place to wander and think and forget about timetables and deadlines and the stultifying structures of the streets and the buildings and the traffic and the noise and the clamour?

I pressed my face to the wrought-iron gate, which is elaborately curled at its top, with some sort of golden crest displaying its face to the street and its hollow grey inner topography to me. I could not hope to climb it. I wondered about waiting for a passer-by. But there are not many pedestrians on that road after dark. There is nowhere really for them to be walking to, other than the park. And in any case, what could one have done? Nothing, except perhaps add to my humiliation. There was no sign, need-less to say, of any kind of official presence. There was a noticeboard, and I did look at it, hoping that there might be a phone number to be called in this very circumstance, perhaps appended to a list of opening and closing times. There was an injunction about dog shit and an invitation to worship at a local evangelical church, and that was all.

There is one other gate, which comes out opposite the sports centre, and I set off for it in the vain hope that it might have been left open. The park was properly dark now, and with no lighting along the pavements I moved quite slowly, picking my way uneasily, navigating through the shadows by applying my memory to their shape, and

creating a usable if inaccurate idea of where I was. Some
of them looked like people, but none of them were. I
stopped from time to time, to listen to the path behind
me, not knowing if I had heard something or was simply
doing what one is supposed to do in such situations. If I
was not *actually* being followed then my fear – my expectation – that I *might* be followed was following me, and
my mind wrestled with many such tortured formations,
dismissing and embracing them in turn. Having stopped,
and turned to listen, and having allowed the silence to
build to the point of reassurance, it was then of course
impossible to prevent it from going past that point into
the knowledge that the turning round again to continue
had become the real moment of danger. There would be
a figure looming up in front of me, a knife in the dark,
eyes, something like that.

It was then, fully aware of the silliness of my own imagination, half laughing at myself, that I saw the dog again.
The dog that had followed the rain, earlier in the day. I'm
going to say definitely that I saw him, rather than that I
dreamed him up, because even if I did dream him up, I
still saw him. Whether he was there or not, I don't really
know. But I saw him. I had cleared a small copse that
crowds the main path near the centre of the park, and I
had gone quite fearfully through there, sure at one point
that there were three men to my right, who stopped talking
as I approached, and who watched me pass, as still as tree
trunks. So that by the time I had once again made the
clear ground on the other side, I was relieved and a little
giddy, convinced that I was seeing nothing more than trees
and bushes and litter bins and benches and the other unlit,
innocent, harmless clutter of the place. And then, ahead
of me to my left, at the edge of the path, I thought I saw

two reddish pinpricks of light, at knee height, quite close together. I didn't pause or hesitate. I continued to walk at the same pace, but my eyes now were fixed on what I told myself could not possibly be, how ridiculous, another pair of eyes looking back at me. A shape emerged behind the red dots, very like a dog, and some internal steering system pushed me to the right of the path, but at the same pace, and as I drew level the eyes – because now I thought that *yes, those are eyes* – swivelled to watch me, and I could hear, low but distinct, the heavy breath, and could see – *Jesus* – the pale tongue and the glinting teeth and the black coat, and all the gathered power of an animal intelligence, considering me, smelling me, letting me go by and letting me go, as my head twisted painfully to watch him just in case, ready to break into a hopeless run should he decide on a whim to tear me to pieces.

There is no point in me rationalising it into a dog-shaped bush with, I don't know, two vaguely reflective berries attached. That just seems to me as unlikely as the dog. Either there was nothing there at all and it was a hallucination, or it was the big black dog from earlier in the day. And whichever of those it was, I think it's fairly remarkable. The possibility remains, and I can't rule it out, that the dog has always been a hallucination, that each time I've seen him I have been seeing nothing more than the physical manifestation of my own fear of the real world – by which I mean the natural world, by which I mean those parts of the world that are not created and controlled by us. By mankind. The next time I saw the dog, which was on the Monday, I saw him from a car. He was standing at the side of a street, staring at me, and by the time I thought of pointing him out to my companion of the time, Anthony George Edgar, we were turning the corner and it was too late. The next time I saw him, yesterday, it was again from a car, a taxi this time, and I was on my way back from the flat, having cut short my return home because of the posters, and I was mad then, I admit it, with rage and a horrible hatred, and I didn't really trust anything I saw, so filled was I with disbelief at the world and the people in it, and the way in which I had been so betrayed by K.

I'm getting ahead of myself. Again. I just wanted to make the point here, that I know what you're thinking. And you may well be right.

After I saw him in the park I was dazed for a while, too terrified to look behind me, increasing my pace and calculating the distance I had to go before screaming might be audible, and I was conscious of every noise, and most of them were mine, and I was angry at myself for being so obvious, so awkward, so out of my depth, and at some point, it was bound to happen, I took a wrong turning, inept and incompetent, and realised it only when an unidentifiable rustling at an alarmingly close proximity provoked me into a sudden run, which was brought to an agonising and almost immediate halt when I collided with a children's roundabout. The umbrella went flying. My bag fell to the ground. I uttered an anguished oath. I felt the world close down to the size of my own body, and for a short moment nothing else existed, and I might have been invisible for all I know, lost to whatever eyes were watching me, while I wandered like David in a world all of my own making, inventing religions to soothe me. He must be the loneliest man imaginable. David, I mean. I can see that now.

The pain decreased and the hooting started. Or I started to hear the hooting. Owls or pigeons or foxes or badgers

142

– I really have no idea. The pain decreased, limiting itself first to my lower body, and then to my leg. Only my leg wandered in the Welderns, looking for Threw. The rest of me clamped down in silence, suddenly aware that I was surrounded by living things. Clinging to a children's roundabout, crippled and trapped, some instinct that I have no knowledge of insisted that I chew off the damaged limb. I felt sick. A nausea, the same as the one that had so convulsed me in front of K and the pen, grabbed me again, around the waist, like the jaws of a rancid predator with all the time in the world.

At least it gave me a fix on my location – the roundabout, I mean. I was off course to a shocking, perplexing degree, my radar berserk. I have no idea what the noise had been that had scared me initially. Wind, probably, through leaves. It didn't really matter, given that it had now been replaced by a whole cacophony of tapping, squeaking, rustling, hooting, humming, groaning, slurping, the snap of a twig, the certain flapping of wings, hissing and farting and the squelch of one thing feeding on another. I think I actually must have screamed with the pain, when I first hit. Because my throat was sore. Although how I noticed that over the pain in my leg I have no idea. Perhaps it is a false memory.

The damage was mid shin, right leg, and it felt as though the bone had shattered, which it hadn't. But I could not walk. I felt that I could not walk, never mind run, and that there was, in any case, no point in walking or running, or in going any further. What was the point in going further? What was the point of anything at all? No matter how far you travel, I told myself, your destination is the same. At least where I was, where I found myself, with the swings and the climbing frame and the peculiar see-saw, I was in a human place. Under siege perhaps, but under siege in a human place.

I abandoned my bag and my umbrella and clambered, pathetically, up on top of the roundabout and saw the animals everywhere. The dark was alive with forms, with life, with the idea of living things. With thought. Some kind of baboon thrashed through the undergrowth. A screaming grounded bird broke twigs beneath its talons. Cockroaches galloped and scurried on the playground concrete. A flight of ants peppered the dim sky. I felt the certain presence of rats, gathered into a hunting party, sniggering, surrounding me, sniffing the wound, arguing about who would get the leg and who would get the genitals and who would get the face. A pack of cats infested a tree at my back. The see-saw was perfectly balanced with a blooded fox on one side and its weight in spiders on the other. In the branches over my head bats dangled and clicked, reaching out their blind black embraces and their burned claws towards my cowering head, their radar perfect. The slugs and the worms and the breathless snails writhed their way towards the smell of my skin.

None of this is true.

We know nothing about the world. We live on manufactured surfaces, inside boxes, with everything brought to us, and we learn the language of our fathers and we learn a way of functioning and we proceed and nod at each other and we are warmed by the sun and we swim in safe water and we cannot understand earthquakes or volcanoes or thunderstorms or what the weather will be like tomorrow, and we believe that we are above it all, that the world is ours, that we are rooted by our history and our stories and our cities, but really we know nothing here, we have forgotten what the world is, we have forgotten the terror and the threat, we think we are solid, but we could be flung to the ground in a second, by any one of a million sudden things, by any possible horror, and we talk in a maze of created meanings, we give each other God and we give each other science and we give each other comfort, and we think we are ancient but we are new, and we think that we are safe but we're not, and we think we're special but we are surrounded, and we think we're in control but we are surrounded, and we think we are alone but we are surrounded – by animals.

I perched on top of the roundabout and decided to wait for dawn.

When I was a child, on sunny days, I used to take a bucket of water and a paintbrush and paint pictures on the flagstones at the front of our house, and I would delight in the disappearance of the things I had created and I would race to maintain them, dancing around bent at the waist like a chess prodigy winning twelve games at once. Sometimes little insects drowned beneath my flourishes. I did not intend that, and occasionally I would pause over the wretched flopping of a ladybird or an ant, and feel a little guilty.

I didn't wait for dawn, obviously. I stayed there probably about twenty minutes. Half an hour. Not much more than that. By then I was sufficiently calm, sufficiently in control, to make my way to the third gate. My panic, and it certainly was a panic, dissipated fairly quickly once I had not been set upon by wild beasts in the first few minutes. I don't think it entirely unreasonable for me to have been made so nervous. After the day I had endured, to be stranded in such a dark, unnatural place would be enough to unnerve most people, I think. Most of you would probably have imagined yourselves chased by murderers or rapists or ghosts or some such. The fact that I felt persecuted by a particularly grotesque menagerie is no more than a reflection of my work, my drawing, which, as I may have mentioned, tends to be preoccupied with such creatures, I don't know why. K says it's because I can't draw faces.

When I had come more or less to my senses, I sat still for a while, massaging my shin, which felt damp – although I assumed at the time that this was sweat, as I was fairly drenched. I talked to myself in an attempt to calm down, and looked around me, and got used to the dark shapes and where they were placed, and set everything out and named it – that is a tree; that is the little rose garden; that is the climbing frame; that is the drinking fountain, etc. Simple, pleasant things made ominous by the dark. No more than that. Human things unlit. Some rustling certainly, the sounds of birds, but generally speaking the place was probably quieter than it would be during the day. I put the dog out of my mind.

Eventually I slid from the roundabout and stood. Gingerly. I tested my leg. I took a couple of steps and retrieved my umbrella. It was impossible, I told myself, that any creature could have made a home in it so soon. I plucked my bag from the ground and shook it by the strap and then by the handle, and slapped it a couple of times and did some coughing and may even have sighed a loud *Oh dear* and generally I blustered and carried on, and my mind ascertained all possibilities and attempted to cling to the best of them. I tried to give the illusion of being uninjured and unconcerned, mostly to myself. I had worked out which way it was that I needed to go, and I set off there now, in a lopsided gait, as loudly as I could, muttering and clacking my umbrella on the ground.

I had to pass through a narrow gap, between two hedges that circled the playground. It was dark. In the distance I could see the glow of a street and a couple of distinct lights. But in front of me I could see virtually nothing other than shapes, and variations on pitch. It was a narrow gap, you understand. No more than the span of my arms. I have short arms. My bag was slung across my shoulders. I gripped its handle with my right hand. The umbrella in my left. My left. From where, as I passed through this pinch of darkness, something loomed up at me. Or flew at me. I don't know which it was. Some presence or force or person. Some breathing thing, some danger. It came at me, out of the darkness, out of the hideous living dark, and I don't know what it was.

I reeled backwards and to my right. Back and to the right. To face what was coming. And at the same time my left arm, extended and strengthened by the umbrella, flew upwards and out, up and out, to connect with whatever it was that bore down on me. My feet stepped back, my arm flew up, my umbrella left it, I lost my balance, I fell, painfully, on to my backside, and whatever it was that had attacked me, was gone. Through me, possibly. Maybe I'm possessed.

The truth of the matter is probably that I was startled by a gust of wind, and in my agitated state, mistook it for an assault of some peculiar evil thing, and as a result panicked, flung my umbrella into the night sky and fell on my undignified arse. But you never know. Maybe I am possessed. Maybe some nocturnal spirit entered me in the park that night, and that's why I'm here now, at dawn, or midnight, or whatever unsocial hour this is, trying to exorcise myself with a pen and black ink, for all the world as mad as David is, as consumed, as ridiculous, as idiotic.

My umbrella really took off. I couldn't see it anywhere. I consoled myself with the thought that it might have impaled a rat in the bushes. But that also made me worry about revenge, and I did not linger. I picked myself up, brushed myself down and limped towards the light.

By the time I got to the gate by the sports centre I was more cheerful, greatly heartened by the wash of the street lights and the resumption of the human noises of cars, and tinny music from a block of flats, and voices somewhere unseen, in the distance, laughing and shouting; and by the smell of made things. The organic fume of the park faded slightly.

The gate was closed of course, and for a moment I lapsed back into a stuttering despair. Then I noticed a possible method of escape. Close to the railings on the right of the gate was a litter bin, or what turned out to be, on closer inspection, a depository for dog-shit. People who own dogs will be familiar with this. You take your dog for a walk in the park, where you keep him on a leash and usually on the paths, and when he shits, you stick your hand in a plastic bag and pick up the hot hill of excrement and deftly, you hope, turn the bag inside out and carry it to this dog-shit bin and place it there. The reason for this is people's shoes, and children, as I understand it, who will pick up almost anything. It must, I've often thought, be a puzzle to the dogs, and quite a disturbing procedure for them to witness. It's long been one of the main reasons why I've been against getting a dog, much to K's annoyance. Anyway, I thought that I could probably get up on top of this thing, and from there reach the top of the railings, which were unspiked, and hopefully haul myself up, swing myself over and drop to the other side.

By now of course, after everything else, you expect me to tell you that I crashed through the top of the bin into a vat of canine excrement; or that I ripped my clothes to shreds on the low branches of the overhanging tree; or that I broke a leg, twisted an ankle, lost an arm or was otherwise mangled by the exercise. But no. I took my time, I planned each move before I executed it, I measured and calculated and made no assumptions about my own athleticism, strength or suppleness, and took account at all times of my damaged leg. The only thing I got even slightly wrong was when I threw my bag over ahead of me (something which was, I thought, quite courageous) and it landed in a puddle. But everything else went smoothly, and I caused myself no further injury, which was just as well, as my shin was agony. Landing was a jolt, but I was out. I was clear, safe, back in the world. I picked up my bag and sighed deeply, felt a choke of emotion in my throat and turned to face the long walk home. Which was when I noticed that watching me from across the street, with a look on his face approaching mischievousness, was a policeman.

My first thought was that I should run. It seems stupid now of course. But now is now, and here I am resting on plumped-up pillows in a warm robe, fresh after a hot bath, with a gin and tonic from the minibar. From here everything seems stupid. I should have thought *What's a policeman doing standing on his own at the side of a quiet road in the middle of the evening?* I should have simply nodded and turned and walked away calmly. I think now that he probably would have let me go. But instead I felt a warm loaf of guilt rise in my stomach and I stood where I was and stared at him, and my options seemed limited to running or standing – I never thought of walking – and I simply looked at him, with probably one of the guiltiest faces ever turned towards a police officer, thinking *I can't run, not with my leg in this much pain, I'd only kill myself.* My guilt of course was about K, and walking out, and making such a mess of things, and so on, none of which is punishable by law, but perhaps part of me felt that it should be, and that to turn myself in would be restorative and right and the first step back towards something better. I wonder what I would have done if he had not, eventually, walked over to me. I worry that I might have tried to turn myself in, a hobbling lunatic, insisting on my guilt for something, anything; for anything at all that would get me punished.

—Are you all right?

He had obviously sized me up pretty accurately. As no threat. As a somewhat pitiful idiot, incapable of the basics required for civilised living, prone to accidents and errors and wrong turnings, too timid to flee, too confused to talk, battered by collision, triumphant only over railings.

—Yes.

—Locked in, were you?

—Yes.

—Happens a couple of times a week, you know. Usually people call us. Can't manage the climb – old dears, little kids, that kind of thing. This is about the only place where it's climbable. But there's actually a gap in the railings on Cross Street. It's almost another gate. Over by the pond. Of course, that's no use to you now.

—No.

—Have you cut your leg?

I looked down at my shin and sure enough there was a large dark stain on my trousers.

—Apparently, yes. Why don't they put up signs?

—They do. There.

He pointed over my shoulder, at a small wooden notice attached to the railings beside the gate. It stated clearly that the park opened at 7 a.m. and was shut at sundown.

—Looks nasty, that.

He meant my shin.

—Yes.

—Fall over, did you?

—No, I . . . I walked into something. It's all right.

—You'd want to have that looked at.

—I'm sure it's fine.

—Tetanus jab, if you haven't had one in a while. Know a man who cut his finger on a rusty boiler pipe. He lost the arm. Live locally?

—Well, the other side of the park. I'll have to . . .

—Bit of a walk. Will you be all right? If you want to hang on a few minutes there'll be a patrol car by, they can give you a lift.

I had visions of a police car pulling up in front of the flat, of K staring out the window.

—No, I'll be fine thanks.

—They're coming along anyway. End of my shift, you see.

He jerked his head back towards the sports centre.

—Terrible business, he said.

—What?

—Oh. The swimming pool there. A ceiling fell in earlier today. A woman died.

A swimsuit of navy and sky blue. A woman died.

—What?

—A forty-four-year-old lady, from Cooper Street there. Killed. They think her heart gave out, because her injuries . . . Are you all right?

—She was . . .

She was swimming slow, steady lengths. She wore a white cap. Her legs were still in the water, her upper body out of it. Her legs, though, were still in the water. I was still in the water.

—Did you know her?

I imagine that if you had asked me then, what had just happened in the park, I wouldn't have been able to tell you. *What park? What are you talking about? Park? Don't be ridiculous.*

—No. No, I didn't know her.

He was looking at me with a new curiosity. I tried to be careful. But all I could see before me was the body of the woman, half in the water, half out of the water. Her backside is what I was looking at. Her rump. Dead. I could not gather myself. I could not be careful. I sank to the ground. Leaned back and let the railings take me and slid to the ground. Maybe that's when I ripped the shoulder of my jacket. Who knows? David fixed it for me. I sat on the ground with my back to the railings, and I stared at the policeman's knees.

—You seem quite taken aback, sir.

Her shape. I found myself concentrating on her shape – the shape of her as I saw it, like an uprooted tree, her legs disappearing into the water, her torso collapsed on the tiles. I could not fathom her presence, how it had returned to me, as if I were looking at her now, and yet the details were obscure and some of them were impossible. Her head for example, with blood on the nape of her neck, and a wound by her collarbone that seemed to grasp at the air. And I could see her fingers terribly stretched. But I could not have seen any of those things.

—Well. Yes. I am. I was . . . You see, I was . . .

I was a witness, obviously. I should have told him that I'd been there. That I'd been in the water, that I'd no idea that she was dead. But I was silenced. I couldn't tell him. I didn't dare. The fear started here. I'm pretty sure. The fear climbed into me as I pressed my back against the railings. The fear climbed into me and stayed. And for a while I didn't notice it was there. I thought I was shocked. Saddened. I thought, like the policeman, that it was some form of third-party grief. But it wasn't that at all.

Her fingers stretched as if to reach me. I backed away from her.

—You were . . . ?

—Why are you here? What are you guarding?

—Well, it's a potential crime scene. Negligence. To say the least. Unsafe structure open to the public. That kind of thing. The law is complicated, but we treat it as a crime scene. For the moment. And a crime scene gets guarded. There's a colleague in the building as well. You all right, sir?

I stood over a dying body and I stared at the wounds. They grasped at the air and the fingers grasped at me and I backed away and left. I did not remain. My head filled with it like a pool. I could see nothing else for a while. Not the policeman, not the street, not my bunched-up legs or my bloody trousers or anything real. I felt a cold coat on my shoulders, and my sensations were severed from my thoughts. There was a dying body in front of me, and I could smell the blood and hear the breath, and hear too the drowning words that seemed to mention me, in passing, seemed to have my name among them, and I could not understand what I was remembering, or seeing, or feeling or experiencing, or where it had come from or how it had reached me – this bloody death, the fingers and the cut lips, the jerking feet and the collarbone cracked like a cup handle. Where was I getting this from? The pleading and my walking away. The carpet. The lip of the bathtub and the mess of the towels. The roof coming down.

—Sir?

—Sorry . . . I'm just . . .

I was obviously behaving in such a way as to generate some interest. And something told me that would be disastrous. Something suddenly kicked me in my ruined shin. *Shut up*, it barked. And then, *Say something, you fool, say something innocent.*

—It's just that I swim there. You know. I go there regularly. I'm just a little . . . Well, I'm just shocked really.

He sighed.

—Ah. OK. That's all right. I can well understand it, sir. Always a shock when something like this happens in places we think are safe.

—You sound relieved.

—No, sir. Well. Actually, when you seemed to be so affected, sir, I was just remembering a time a few years ago when I was at the scene of an RTA, a car crash, and I was just clearing the area, and a woman asked me what had happened, and I told her, being a bit blasé about it, I suppose, to be fair, that a man in a small green Fiat had just been crushed to death by an overturned lorry. She became hysterical. Turned out she was the man's wife.

He whistled to himself in disbelief.

—You should let my colleagues in the patrol car drop you home. They'll be along any minute. They're late.

I stared at his knees. I felt the railings at my back and thought about where I had been and why I had been there. I reconstructed what I could. It was the terrible calmness with which I realised it that confirmed for me that it must

154

be true. I felt certainty. The story about the crushed man simplified it for me.

—I suppose, I said to him, —that you could easily tell someone about something like that and inadvertently remind them of something similar that might have happened to a loved one in the past. You know. That she could, the wife of the crushed man, just as easily have been the daughter of a man crushed years before.

—Yes. I suppose so, sir.

I coughed and sat up. I made to stand, and the policeman held out his hand, which I grasped and used to support myself. I had killed K.

—Beg your pardon, sir. Have you lost someone previously in a similar circumstance?

—No. No I haven't. I was just thinking . . .

—Well, I'm glad of it. I should probably be more careful what I say. I'll get myself in trouble. Fancy a cigarette, sir?

He had pulled a packet from his trouser pocket and was proffering one.

—I don't smoke.

—I'm off duty now, officially. My colleagues are late. No surprise there.

He lit the cigarette with a lighter, and inhaled deeply. I watched him very carefully now. I must, I was sure, have done it very quickly. I felt that I had used a knife. Or possibly something heavy, like the iron. It must have happened in the kitchen then, where those weapons are kept. And yet I was sure that it had happened in my office, immediately after I had seen the pen in K's mouth. I tried to think of things there that I could have used. Beside my desk there is a small bronze cat. It was a gift from K's sister, who likes cats, though neither K nor I can stand them much. The thing sits beside my desk on a pile of old sketches that I did last year, a peculiar bunch, studies of fire extinguishers. It's about eight inches tall. Kitsch Egyptian. It weighs perhaps a couple of pounds. Its base is rectangular. The cat's head and upper body makes a good handle. One blow, very hard, trying to knock away the pen. Slightly misaimed. Hitting the collarbone, the side of the face. Would that have been enough to kill? Maybe the pen hadn't moved. Maybe I'd taken a second go at it. Maybe I had wanted to hammer out the mouth. Hammer the death out of K's mouth.

It startled me to learn that I was unsure. I could not understand how I could not know, for certain, whether I had killed K or not. It worried me. It worries me still. Something had happened to my mind. Something bad. There was a fracture in the path that I had followed. So that when I turned and looked behind me, I could not see where I had been or what I had done there. All I saw was darkness and shadows on it, and the suggestion of possibly this and the suggestion of possibly that. But I had spent so much time in the silence of the park trying to remember. And I had not fully succeeded. And now this news of a death seemed to register with me in a way that suggested much more than a woman in a swimming pool, much more than a coincidence of placement, much more than an innocent chat with a smoking policeman. It rang in me like a ricochet. As if I was a canister with a pebble inside me. What had I done? What had I done, exactly?

I hobbled away from him, declining his repeated offers of a lift in the patrol car. Of which there was in any case no sign.

You see now, don't you, why I sent David back to the flat? You see what I was thinking there? I'm not sure what I intended to do really. I don't think I could have brought myself to kill David. But I might have used the knife on myself if, for example, he had returned with some policemen, or with K's blood on his hands, trembling, tearful with the news. I might have slit my own throat. Or had a go at it. My. David came back with a couple of bags full of books and knick-knacks and this and that, and when I asked whether K had been there he said simply that there had been no sign of K at all but the place was a mess and he hadn't been able to find my camera.

So I didn't kill K.

Unless of course I disposed of the body somehow. By cutting it up. Putting bits of it in bins around the neigh-bourhood. Or in the park, for example. A park full of animal noises and human remains.

But I didn't.

Slugs

The sky was low. It hung like sacks of black ink over the city, and I thought that if it burst we would be drowned and discoloured equally, and the stubby buildings stained indelible, like useless thumbs stuck in the air. What a mess. What a collapsing, stupid, pitiful mess.

I felt sick. I felt a terrible clarity of sickness, as if I'd been drawn sick by some malign illustrator of this Sunday morning set-up – sick man walks through cold empty streets, green-faced, shuffle-legged, all his pale damp skin barely holding him up. I blew my nose and discovered blood on the tissue. Is that a haemorrhage in there somewhere? A tumour behind the eyes? I don't know. In my stomach there was a dull persistent ache close both to hunger and a full bowel, but it was something else entirely – a kind of nausea of tedium, a miserable self-disgust, and I was full of it. My feet were weary, and they dragged – either I dragged them or they dragged me, I don't know. I could not have decided. I had no energy for anything. Not for decisions or directions or despair. I walked. That's all I did. I walked and things went by me.

158

I think now, sitting here in this expensive rosewood glow (I have no idea what kind of wood it is), that I was still lucky then. Just at that particular moment, having left David's, walking through a Sunday of calm predictable blankness, despite my sickness and my inability to act or think or to think about acting, or to know what I was thinking (or doing for that matter, as I later discovered) – despite all this it was a lucky moment. No, of course it wasn't. But I was still capable then, if only I'd known it, of turning things around. I think I was. I feel that it would not have been, at that point, too late, probably. I may be wrong. But I believe that, had I known what to do just then, Sunday morning, under the ink of heaven, everything unwritten, I might have been capable of a positive action and it might have proved the end of things. The resumption of things. The return. If only my automatic feet had taken me home. If only the clutter of maps in my head had thrown up a route of reversal; a way of retracing my steps to the street where I lived, to the home I still had, possibly.

But there was nothing in me other than a sickness. Or an absence of wellness. I was distended, malformed, incapable. All the streets ran at me and touched my clothes and ran away again. I didn't know where I was. I doubled back on myself, hesitated, went forward in one direction until there was no point going in another, and then went in another. The sky swung at me and I was smeared across the temple and the cheeks by a black spittle of undrawn pictures. Nothing was in me. Everything pressed against me from outside. From elsewhere. The ruins of things suggested themselves. A rewind of events coiled up in my head like razor wire. I kept on seeing the crumbling ceiling of the sports centre. I kept on seeing the impossibly dead body of K, limb cut from limb with a kitchen knife, draped severally over the side of the bath and the hall table. David's innocent, returning face, having seen no such thing. I kept on seeing the dog that came after the rain. I kept on seeing the slaughter of a million spiders and the wars of the Second Council and the seas of Crease Bay turned red from the hordes of Westorn dead.

I became mad.

Then, somewhere, I was outside a little café that I didn't recognise, called Arthur's, and I was thinking that I should eat. I was thinking that I should be out from under the glare of the gunmetal clouds, where I could sit with a cup of tea and try to make myself understand something. I had slept well, and dreamlessly, the night before, relieved no doubt that I was not a murderer. Or most likely not a murderer. But I was exhausted. So exhausted that my suspicion was that I had in fact been dreaming all the time. I wondered vaguely, as you do, whether I was still dreaming, but that thought never wakes us from anything, does it? It just walks with us lazily for a few steps and then falls away.

Arthur's seemed full. Its windows were steamed opaque. A couple entered clutching newspapers, and the clatter of crockery escaped. Would fresh air not be better for me, for a while, rather than the fumes of other people? I could not decide. I stood at the edge of the pavement opposite the door. I wondered if there really was an Arthur, or whether, like Eric's, the name was older than those who used it, something meaning someone else, but orphaned and then taken on again by others. I suddenly remembered the woman I had seen in Eric's on the Friday morning, buying a mousetrap, and almost immediately I found myself looking into the roadway by the kerb, as if I might find a mouse there, my mouse, as if there might be that kind of repetition in the world, as if there might be a second chance. There was no mouse. Of course there was no mouse. Why would there be a mouse? There was a crushed beer can and a little pile of ashes and butts, where someone had emptied a car ashtray. But there was no mouse. Dead mice are not a regular thing in the gutters. But for some reason I felt that there *must* be a mouse. Somewhere. I just wasn't seeing it. I paced up and down for a minute, and craned my neck, and peered for a while at a strange misshapen organic mass that could have been, I supposed, a dead mouse in the later stages of decomposition, but was more likely to be a piece of rotting fruit. I stepped into the roadway to look at things from there. I walked a little way east and a little way west of Arthur's, searching for the corpse of a mouse, like someone looking for a lost wallet. There was no mouse anywhere. I felt a strong peculiar swell of disappointment.

Arthur's was surprisingly busy. It seemed strange to find all this activity so close to the empty streets. Most of the tables were occupied by couples or larger groups, sitting chatting or working their way through piles of newspapers, eating various types of breakfasts, drinking coffees and teas from white cups, looking young and healthy and prosperous. One couple huddled together in front of a laptop. I found a table beside the clouded window, and felt, on my own and with nothing to read, quite self-conscious, as if I had walked on to a stage. A woman stared at me with bemusement from an adjacent table. I probably looked homeless. Which of course I was, I suppose. I had two bags with me – the original overnight bag which I had taken myself, and David's holdall stuffed with bits and pieces including my sketchbooks and notebooks.

I rummaged around in there and considered taking out a pen and drawing some of the people. There was something so smug and calculatedly urban about them that they almost called out for caricature. But I found that I was far too concerned, for reasons which I did not understand, about what they might think of me to express in drawing what I thought of them.

I was annoyed.

At the bottom of the bag I found a science-fiction novel. I presumed it was David's. On the cover was an elaborate but remarkably stale rendition of an insect-like creature at the controls of some kind of spaceship. It looked as if it had been carelessly copied from H. R. Giger's designs for *Alien*. I broke the spine and laid the book flat on the table in front of me as a refuge, from where I stole occasional glances at my surroundings.

Actually, the novel wasn't David's at all. How could it be? I remembered after a while that a woman from one of the publishing houses that I've done some work for had sent it to me for some reason. I had started it and forgotten about it, and found now that I could not bring myself to read a word of it. There were far too many invented place names. It reminded me of David's cracked creations and my own stupidity. There were maps on the endpapers.

A woman brought me a menu and I ordered coffee and an orange juice and when she brought those I ordered a small fried breakfast by pointing to it on the laminated card, unable, for some reason, to speak. I had already eaten at David's, and really didn't want much more than the coffee, but I felt that I had to order a meal. It looked like the kind of place that might have a minimum charge. And she looked like the kind of waitress who would make a fuss. A benign fuss. She looked like she would coo at me and tell me that I needed some feeding up. Something like that. While I waited for my sausage and bacon and scrambled egg I wiped a sleeve across the window and wished that I'd stayed on the street.

Something odd happened at Arthur's that I want to mention. There was an incident. It was not a very serious thing in itself, and no one in the café really noticed it, I think, apart from the waitress. But it worried me, and taken with some of the other things that were happening to me, things that I've told you about and things that I have yet to tell you about, as well as the fact that the same thing happened again later in the week, fully, then I should really tell you about this now.

The waitress came and set my plate down in front of me, and by that time I was actually quite looking forward to it, and people had stopped looking at me, and I was more relaxed and quite pleased with what had arrived. Nice-looking bacon, some lovely toast, perfectly fluffy scrambled eggs. So I said *Thank you.* Except I didn't. I didn't say *Thank you.* I said *More ay a.* I intended to say *Thank you.* Those were the words that I formed and those were the words my brain sent to my mouth, but those were not the words which I spoke. *More ay a*, I said. Which is not anything that means anything to me. Embarrassed, I immediately said *I mean thank you*, except I didn't. I said *Push goosh a far liddle.* That is what I plainly heard myself say. I looked up at the waitress. She was smiling, if hesitantly, and I cut my losses and said nothing more, just nodded. She may have thought that I was foreign. It didn't seem to bother her that much.

It put me off my food really. I sat there with my head bowed testing out words on myself. *Thank you. Yes please. Breakfast is good. This bacon is very nice. These sausages are lovely, although the eggs could be a little warmer.* I had no problem with any of it. I read a little from the science-fiction novel.

Forward Charger III had been closed for nearly six years following the Grak attack. Hudson knew that there would be little there of use, but he hoped that there might be some power units they could salvage, even some weapons. If the Grak had left anything. He doubted it. The Grak were vicious, barbaric. They had slaughtered the entire population in less than seven hours.

People were starting to look at me again. I shut up. There were small, neat stainless-steel salt and pepper shakers on the table. Plain, like little canisters. I liked them. I shook salt on to my plate. I pushed aside the food and emptied the salt container completely and then slipped it into my pocket.

When I left I made a point, when I'd paid, of saying, clearly and distinctly, *Thank you very much*. Which was exactly what I did say, thankfully. My waitress looked a little startled, and the hubbub of the place seemed to diminish for a second, but I was relieved.

Before I'd left David's I had taken a mug from his kitchen. It was a stupid mug, white, not even clean. It said DAVID around its body in big red letters. It was tea-stained on the inside. I had put it in my bag.

I had a plan now, it seemed, after leaving the café. I couldn't remember creating it, but there it was. I needed to be somewhere still. From where I could take a little time to become calm. I was, I knew, slightly confused. In a state. If I could spend some time in a safe place, a place where I would not have to concentrate on anything other than myself, then I could start to think about going home. Rachel was away. I would go to Michael's. I called him. His phone was off. But I could spend some hours there, working things out, and then I could talk to K. Negotiate my return.

A state. By the time I got to Michael's I was sweating, and did not feel well. It was a muggy day. The sky was still oppressive. What I had eaten of my second breakfast had done me no good. I felt bloated and queasy. I felt post-operative, as if the meal had been an invasive procedure conducted under a light and sickly anaesthetic. Also, my temporary incapacity with language had disturbed me, and I was conscious that I had behaved badly with David. And hanging over that was the memory of the day before, and my stupid notion that I could do him some harm. And before that my even more stupid notion that I had killed K. And over all of it, my departure from everything – which I felt as a dull ache, an imprecise agony which I could not locate but which reverberated through me in terrible, suffocating waves.

Did I hurt you?

I wanted nothing more really than to lie down and close my eyes. Michael would understand. He understood everything. There was nothing that he could not accommodate. I was sure that he would, for example, allow me to lie on his bathroom floor, close to the friendliest of household appliances – those that empty and cleanse us. Where we can mumble to ourselves and never have it heard. Where we can be silent and never have it broken. Where we can rest and be recovered. Michael would let me in and he would provide a cold glass of water and access to the white tiles of his bathroom, and the taps and the handles. And

I could spend a day there, sleeping, shitting, vomiting, coming back.

I tried to call him again, and again I was connected immediately to his answering machine, which suggested to me that he was still in bed. Which was fine. He would answer the door, he would let me in. All the better if he was not finished sleeping and wanted to go back to bed. That would be ideal. It would give me time.

I dragged my bags through the streets. In my pocket I felt the salt canister press uncomfortably with each stride I took. What was that for? The day looked the same, but the air was different, warmer, staler, as if someone had breathed on the city. It felt thick and damp and I thought of mushroom soup and old bread. Nothing I thought of was good for me. I walked some steps with my eyes closed, and took then to seeing how far I could go blindly. But I stopped when I very nearly walked into a litter bin, opening my eyes within a foot of it. I remembered my shin, still sore. I went on with open eyes, looking at everything with great interest for a while, as if I really had been blind, and was astonished now at the level of detail available in the world. Everything has been put here, you know. Every single little thing – made and manufactured and placed by man.

I stopped suddenly as I turned into Michael's road, disturbed by two sudden thoughts, and a third, which was horrible, but which came slowly crawling after the others like the mangled survivor of a car crash that I had not noticed occurring. The two thoughts were these:

- I had stolen now, for no reason that I could think of, two items – one from David's home, and one from the café – and I did not understand why.

- Michael might have company – someone who might have stayed the night – which would make my presence difficult for him.

And the third thought, which startled me to such an extent that I dropped my bags:

- Michael lives miles from the neighbourhood which K and I share with David. He lives in a completely different part of the city, one which is unreachable except by bus or train. And yet, I had walked. I had simply walked from the café to his road. And it had taken a matter of minutes. How? How could it be explained?

I can't overemphasise the effect this third thought had on me. I felt it as an actual noise, like someone had clapped their hands inside my head – as an unbalancing actuality. It was as palpable as the wall with which I was now supporting myself. This was happening too often. Twice is too often. First, there had been the blankness surrounding my departure from my own home. And there had been the desperate, idiotic way in which I had tried to fill in that gap. Now there was this. Another gap. I simply could not have walked. Not in the time that had passed. What had I done now? Who had I killed this time? David? The waitress from Arthur's? And what was Arthur's after all? I had never seen it before. I didn't even know where it was now. I wasn't sure that I could find it again.

I slumped and I groaned. It was impossible that I could be so stupid. So unrelentingly stupid, all at once, after so many years of relative intelligence. And yet here I was, at a loss to know how I had travelled so far in such a short time. It was as if I had stepped through some ellipsis of the streets, going from one side of the city to the other in a single unlikely step.

And of course I hadn't. It took me probably a good five minutes of astonished gawping at the way I had come and at where I found myself to realise that I had taken a bus after leaving David's, and had then taken another, and that I had found Arthur's not in my own neighbourhood, but in Michael's, and that the reason I could not remember these things was that I knew them already, and I had more important things to be worrying about, and my mind was simply taking up the slack, proceeding automatically with the mundane operations of buses and directions and the like, and that this was evidence, if it was evidence of anything, of a great mental agility on my part – that I could delegate the nonsense of navigation to my subconscious. I should be relieved. I should be impressed. I should be proud of myself.

Slowly, gingerly, as if I might crumble or snap, I swallowed and picked up my bags and moved on down the street, paying attention to every step I took, to Michael's house.

Michael is one of the few people I know who lives in an actual house, rather than a flat. It's small, but it's beautiful. Or, at least, I have always thought of it as beautiful. But when I stood in front of it in my flustered state, it looked more ominous than welcoming. It is very narrow, squeezed between two looming five-storey apartment blocks, though not attached to either. It is flat-roofed. Its windows are small. Its brickwork is yellowish and stained and in need of repair. Worst of all, from my point of view, the upstairs windows' curtains and blinds all seemed to be open. Although when I thought of it I could not remember whether Michael's bedroom was at the front or the back of the house.

I rang the bell. It made an old-fashioned *ding-dong* noise which Michael probably thought was cute. There is a little garden, tiny really, and I turned and examined it. The grass was almost non-existent. A scrap of mud and cracked concrete was what it amounted to, with an anaemic shin-high hedge behind the old railings. The railings seemed to have been recently repainted. There was a tree, or the corpse of a tree, about my height, in the corner away from the house; and a border of nothing against the yellow wall. A large green plastic council wheelie bin stood on the foot-path.

I rang again. I put down my bags. I played with Arthur's salt shaker in my pocket. There was no one there.

I knocked. It hurt my knuckles. I pressed the doorbell and kept my finger on it for four whole *ding-dongs*. I called him on my phone.

Hard luck, caller. Leave me a message and I'll certainly get straight back to you.

I sat down on his doorstep like a child. I didn't know where to go. When I was very young my father once drove me to my school early on a Saturday morning for some kind of sports practice. Swimming maybe. He dropped me at the gate and promised to be back at midday to pick me up. The school was deserted. There was no sign of anyone. I panicked. I don't know why. I'm not sure why I thought it was such a terrible thing that I be on my own for a couple of hours, outside, in an environment that was familiar but altered by silence, and the absence of any human voice or footstep – of anything like me. But I did. I thought it was terrible. I sat in floods of tears in the middle of the playground for about twenty suicidal minutes before another boy turned up. He had made the same mistake, missed the cancellation notice as I had, and he laughed at me, and took me home on the bus. I was embarrassed of course, and afraid that he would tell my friends. But at the same time I could have hugged him. He told no one. He must have seen how much I trembled. Perhaps he trembled too. Perhaps I saved him as much as he saved me. But I don't think so. I doubt it. There's something . . . I shouldn't even *remember* things like that. They are so trivial. They are absolutely nothing. But I do. I remember them in the way that other people remember child abuse or car crashes or the death of their mother.

There's something wrong with me.

I stared at Michael's doorstep, and at the path, and at the trampled grass that was dying beside it, and at the thin ditch of rubbled clay by the wall of the house. And I thought again in tiredness and in blankness, like a kid that builds comfort out of details, and then scares himself with details, that all of these things had to be put there by someone. By human hands, man's fingers. I stared at the few square inches between my feet, of simple concrete and the cover of a drain. In all this vast city, of countless territory and endless spaces and places and dead ends and rundown nowheres where your eye would never linger for a second unless lost, there is no part that has not been *made* by someone. Some workman, at some point, in the course of an exact historic minute, poured that concrete and smoothed it. Someone put that drain cover there. Even the grass. Someone planted it, scattered it, rolled it, flattened it, did whatever it is they do to make grass grow among inventions. The street, the houses, the trees, the parks, all of it *placed*. Placed just so. Layer upon layer, over the course of years, over countless years, countless people have designed and planned and constructed and placed every square inch of it. There is nothing naturally occurring anywhere. You can probably unravel your entire life thinking such thoughts, waiting for your father to come back and get you.

A man was staring at me from the rolled-down window of a people carrier across the street. His lips were moving, like he was talking on a telephone. Hands-free, presumably. I coughed and drew my bags to me. What must I look like? Where would I go?

Home, I thought. *Go the hell home.*

The windows of the people carrier were black. Tinted deep black, they reflected a curved reversal of Michael's house. I stood and shuffled miserably. I felt no better. I was grubby and defeated. I would go home to K. And I would probably cry.

The man was wearing sunglasses, and he peered at me, and although I tried not to look back, he was simply too ridiculous to ignore. He had a drooping moustache that arced over his upper lip and fell to two points on his jawline. His head was shaved. He seemed to be dressed in a T-shirt and braces. He seemed to smile. Nod even. I expected him to say something as I passed, and I expected his voice to be that of a Mediterranean villain. A Sicilian, I thought, probably. He had the swarthy skin. But he said nothing.

And not only are all things placed by people, but so are all people. Constructions that we glance and categorise, with hardly a thought. They might as well be cartoon characters, for all the attention we pay them. Pre-summarised by what we know of the world, and how we carry that. And they do it to themselves. And I to myself, and you to you. What are you wearing? Why are you wearing it? What are you doing? Why are you doing it? What are you thinking? From where come your thoughts? What on earth makes you think that they're yours at all?

As I reached the corner, and wondered how angry K could conceivably be, I heard an engine start up, and knew without looking that the Sicilian in the blacked-out people carrier was coming after me. I thought about being alarmed. I considered fear. He might have a gun, a machete, a broad-blade knife, a heavy chain of spikes, a razor-sharp daisy-cutter lance emerging from his hubcaps. But I was too tired and too fed up and too weary of all the strangeness, and too aware of how much of it was my own creation, and in any case, I could not really take his moustache seriously. Not his moustache, driving that car. The categories were mismatched. That's where comedy lives. I'm sure it's been the death of millions.

He was moving at my pace, right by my side, though he had closed his window. I stopped. I stopped and turned and faced him. He stopped too. My own reflection looked back at me, squinting and buckled, as if I was something underwater preparing to shout at the sky.

—WHAT? What do you want?

My voice sounded ridiculous to me. Why on earth was I trying to assume a kind of brawling, half-drunk street slur? I went for it again, enunciating my vowels and consonants.

—What? WHAT – DO – YOU – WANT? Hello? HELLO?

I sounded like a terrible actor making a mess of an audition.

There was a whirr, and I expected to see myself disappear and the Sicilian to take my place, maybe pointing a snub-nosed Mauser at me (is that a dog? I mean a gun of course, but that may be a dog that hunts rodents or something), but instead it was the rear window that lowered.

The back seat. A face emerged, half smiling at me, and there was – or did I imagine it? – a breath of lovely calm, cool air. I knew the face. At first I didn't know how I knew it, but I was so certain that I did that I smiled, apologetically, as if sorry for shouting at a friend's car. I imagine that celebrities get that a lot. People thinking that they are friends. People being polite by mistake.

—I'm so sorry, dear. This must look like a kidnap attempt.

I stood up straight. I had never met her before.

—Which it isn't, obviously. Please forgive us. You were at the door of the house around the corner. Number 48. Weren't you, dear? Do you know who lives there?

It was Catherine Anderson. *The* Catherine Anderson. She was wearing what looked like a tracksuit. There is probably a different name for it. For the type of tracksuit that celebrities wear. It was a dark navy. She wore a baseball cap with a logo that was familiar but I can't remember now. She wore sunglasses that were like the windows of her people carrier in miniature. Her skin was a perfect honey colour, as if she was coated in something. She was very small, I thought. Not short, but slight. Thin. Or narrow – like Michael's house. She was very beautiful. She looked about eighteen.

—Yes, I . . . Hello . . . I'm . . . I'm a friend of Michael's.

—Well, I thought as much really. You looked like you might be. I'm his mother. I'm Catherine. How do you do?

—I know. Very well. Hello. Nice to meet you.

She looked me up and down a little. She took her time with it. I felt very grubby. Stale and peculiar. Dogs don't bring mice home and dump them on the kitchen floor. Cats do that. Snub-nosed mousers.

—What's your name, dear?

The question arises as to how much I should tell you about what happened between Catherine Anderson and myself. She is, after all, famous, and you will probably want to hear about her just because of that. That even the most boring of details about her will be entertaining to you simply because she is who she is. And that I should therefore not tell you anything at all, because to tell you would simply be pandering to that stupid fascination we all have for details about people who aren't supposed to have details, who are supposed to have only headlines and highlights and the big-picture perfection of famous and wealthy and glamorous lives. Add to that the fact that she will feel, I'm sure, that some of the things I could tell you would be breaches of confidence on my part. Not that she ever explicitly said that what happened between us was private – I mean, why would she? – but there were things that did happen, or things that I found out about, which should probably, for decency's sake, remain private. Things which should probably remain private even if they were not about Catherine Anderson at all, but about some utterly anonymous citizen instead, some private person completely unknown to the public at large. Even then, you might think, these are things that I shouldn't put down here. Some things are just beyond the pale. Because they are so completely *personal*. As I'm sure you'll agree as soon as you've heard them.

Because I am going to tell you. And not because it's Catherine Anderson. I could say that I'd tell you even if it was about someone you'd never heard of. But the fact is that what I'm going to tell you could only be true of a famous person – a wealthy, pampered, publicly adored, glamorous, beautiful person. And it's right as well for me to tell you this because it does directly affect, in some odd perpendicular way, what has happened to me. It tipped me off, if you like, about what was going on. What was breaking up.

—You look miserable, dear. You look completely exhausted. Was Michael expecting you?

—No, not exactly. Do you know where he is?

She smiled at me, very broadly. It was quite dazzling.

—Darling, I don't know a thing about him. Why else do you think I'm camped outside his wretched little house like a stalker?

She is charming, and of course I'm not immune to that kind of thing, or, for that matter, to the very notion of celebrity itself. Who is? No one is. Even when we hate them, the hate is generated by the same machinery that generates adoration, and machinery like that, when you see it up close, is pretty impressive. I felt a little frisson of excitement just to be talking to her, to somebody as famous as her. And, of course, I was conscious of my own excitement, and how idiotic it would appear to her if I were to reveal any of it. So I spent most of my time while I was in her company trying to downplay, in my own mind, the very idea that there was anything remotely impressive about being famous, and as a result I probably came across as a little bored, a bit distracted, not really very interested. And it struck me after a while that most people probably do this when they meet a celebrity, and that most celebrities must find it slightly odd – that people are so bored by them – and must therefore put in a little extra effort in an attempt to be interesting or entertaining or whatever it is that they feel they must be, and that such efforts are bound to make them appear slightly frantic, overeager, far too fond of themselves, with the result that people find them irritating, and when the encounter is over they feel that the celebrity they just met is a real overbearing pain is the arse, while the poor celebrity probably wonders why, if everyone is supposed to love them, no one seems to like them very much.

She asked me to join her in the car.

I think all she wanted, at first anyway, was information. She thought that I might be able to tell her things about Michael. I really didn't want to get into the car. Well, I did. But I didn't. I did because it seemed lovely in there – cool and calm and quiet and comfortable. And I did because of where it was – it was the inside of Catherine Anderson's car. But I didn't want to get in there because I had yet to shower that day, and I had been sweating, and I was carrying bags and was awkward and uncomfortable and didn't look at all at my best, and I was embarrassed about the fact that what she was doing was a little odd. I didn't really want to end up having a row with Michael. He would instantly conclude that I had been swayed by his mother's fame to take sides against him in some way. Michael would think me childish and simple and idiotic. He would be angry at me, convinced that I had slighted him; or that I had, through my star-struck naivety and general cluelessness, given away something about him which meant nothing to me but which would alter entirely his difficult relationship with his famous, beautiful mother.

—Come on, dear. I'll break the air conditioning if I leave the door open too long. And Itsy will be annoyed. Let's not annoy Itsy.

Itsy. He turned out to be Scottish, and his voice was a lovely lilting thing, with no edge. His shoulders though, they flexed and twitched and the back of his neck was like an animal part. He seemed possessed of terrible potential.

She used his name as a threat at various points. Not directly, you understand – always as if the threat was to her, and that if I didn't do something or other, I'd get her in trouble with Itsy. He *was* wearing a white T-shirt and braces. On his upper left arm was a tattoo of a snake, coiled around his bicep like a rope, its head hidden somewhere under the short sleeve.

As soon as I was in the car, piling my bags in the corner like a schoolboy, perching on the seat like a bird, she had Itsy take us back to the parking space opposite Michael's.

—It's humiliating. It really is. I mean, people do this to me. They stake me out. Press bastards. Photographer bastards. Weird bastards. They sit outside the apartment or outside the house, in their darkened cars, and they wait and they wait – all day, all night, all the next day – just waiting for me to make the smallest slightest teeniest move, and they pounce. Animals. And here I am, doing the same thing, outside my son's house. As if he was off-limits to his own mother. It's embarrassing to me. I'm aware of it. It makes me cringe.

I nodded. I didn't know what to say. She was looking idly out of the window towards Michael's house, which was on her side, and every so often she would swing her head all the way around to look at me. I wasn't sure what I was supposed to be saying, or doing. Why was she stalking Michael? That's what I wanted to ask, but it seemed so like the obvious question that I thought it must have already been answered and that I had missed it, and if I asked it now I would appear stupid.

She looked at me directly, as if waiting for something. I nodded again.

—So why am I doing it? That's what you want to know, isn't it?

—Well, yes. I was just going to say. Yes. Why are you doing it?

—Because he hasn't spoken to me in about two months. Because I haven't seen him in six. Well, I've *seen* him, but he hasn't seen *me* in about six months, and every time I call him he hangs up, and because the last thing he said to me, I swear, can you imagine anyone saying this? he said, *Why don't you just stop being my mother and carry on being you.*

She looked at me as if it was a devastating, terrible thing to have said. But I actually couldn't really see it. It sounded vaguely generous to me. I don't know what I did with my face. Catherine Anderson seemed to peer at me as if she wasn't sure whether I would be of any use to her at all.

—Does he have a girlfriend? At the moment?

—I don't know.

—Where does she live?

—Well, I don't know of any girlfriend actually. So I don't –

—No, of course. How do you know him? Have you known him long?

K and Michael met at university. They have been friends ever since. I told her some of that. She nodded. Then she announced that she had met K. She remembered it well. She described K to me, but the person she described was not K. She shrugged, as if it was possible that it was me who was mistaken rather than her.

—Michael so rarely brought people home, after that incident with the boy.

I didn't know what she was talking about.

—But there was that girl last year, wasn't there? The black girl, very pretty, they came down to the house one weekend. In the country. Michael hasn't been there since.

I really thought . . . She was allergic to the cats. Or the dogs. Or something or other. Spent a whole day sneezing before Michael found her some tablets. She was a bit quiet, watchful. I don't know what happened there, do you?

—That was Monica. I don't know what happened.

Actually, that wasn't entirely true. The relationship with Monica had ended in the same way that most of Michael's relationships have ended – with Michael becoming suddenly, and almost pathologically, *bored*. He seems to tire very quickly of people who love him. I should have told Catherine that. But I think she knew it anyway.

—I used to think Michael was queer of course. For years I thought he was queer. I think that may be part of the problem. Well, how was I to know that he wasn't? There was a thing with another boy, you see, when he was young. Really quite young. And I discovered them. My God. They were like two little baby mice, all naked and wrapped up together. It was *very* cute. I laughed, which was probably not the right thing, was it? But it just looked so sweet and innocent. They were terrified of course, though my God I don't know why; there were more queers around during Michael's childhood than there were women. And I went out of my way, *out* of my way, to make sure he understood that it wasn't a problem, that I loved him unconditionally, that I was proud of him and he could have his boyfriends over if he wanted to and I wouldn't mind, that he was my lovely son and there could never be a problem. I was the textbook perfect mother. Except it turns out that it *was* sweet and innocent – that for Michael it really was a bloody phase.

She stared at his front door and sighed. Her skin is

179

remarkable. She must have had work done, and when she turned away from me I found myself looking for the signs. But I could see none.

—Perhaps if I had scolded him, been mean, told him he was disgusting, perhaps he would have liked me more. He's embarrassed by me. He always has been. I don't know what it is about me that is so embarrassing, but there you are. Mind you, mind you . . .

She turned round to me again.

—Being camped outside his house hoping to be able to talk to him, hoping for a glimpse of him, it is embarrassing, isn't it? Mortifying. And you have no idea how hard I've tried to repair things between us. And he's been, oh, he's just been so stubborn. If only he'd offer me something. Some affection, some access, some way into his life, no matter how small. Then I wouldn't have to do this. Do you find him stubborn?

—Well. I don't know really.

—I'm sorry. I'm embarrassing you now. I don't even know you. But you look so trusting. I trust you. Michael doesn't tolerate rogues. Not as friends. I know that much about him. And you're no rogue, are you? I can see that. I don't know any of his friends though. He never introduces me.

She looked away again and I thought she was crying. I wondered if she was drunk. I could smell nothing but the lightest, most summery of perfumes. But I noticed that there was a little boxy cabinet set into the space in front of where we were sitting. Like a little hotel minibar. It looked exactly like the one that I have here in my room in fact. Perhaps a little smaller.

—He tells me nothing, you know. Nothing. He resents me. He seems to think that it's a terrible cheek of me to be his mother. It makes it more difficult for him to ignore me completely.

She wasn't crying. She sounded angry.

—I bought him that bloody house. Look at it. It's hideous. What were we thinking? Perhaps he did it on purpose. Forced me into buying him something ugly. I've been here for hours. Staring at it. He doesn't know this car. And he's never met Itsy. I saw him here on Thursday. Thursday night. He came home alone. Walked down the street carrying his briefcase and some shopping, and in he went. He picked up some litter beside his gate. Threw it in the bin. He yawned while he was rummaging for his keys. He had to put the shopping bag down to open the door. And in he went. Lights then. Coming on and going off. Itsy tried to talk me into calling on him. Ringing the doorbell. Is there a doorbell?

—Yes.

—What sound does it make?

—An old-fashioned ding-dong-type sound.

—Really?

—Yes. You know, *ding, dong.*

She smiled at me.

—That's the one we had in the old house. When he was a boy. Where he grew up. He used to love it. He'd race to the door from wherever he was. You'd hear ding-dong followed by the pounding of Michael's feet racing to the door from wherever he was, shouting *I'll get it, I'll get it.* Jesus Christ. What a stupid woman I am. When was the last time you saw him?

—Friday. We had lunch.

—You must tell me all about it. While we drive. I've had enough of it here. It's like looking at a gravestone. Itsy, drive us somewhere.

—Where?

—Anywhere.

—Anywhere it is.

It's a cliché really, isn't it, the idea of the very famous being very lonely? I began to think, as Itsy drove us aimlessly around the city, that Catherine Anderson was one of the loneliest people I'd ever met. Maybe that's why I told her more about the weird things that had happened to me on the Friday than I had intended to. I told her about the mouse. I told her about lunch with Michael. I told her about the scary dog. I told her about the swimming pool, and about talking to Michael briefly about the Australia-shaped stain. She listened, and as she did so she seemed to warm to me, as if I was more entertaining than she had expected. But she did not seem to understand any of it. Or seem much interested, except in the parts that related to her son. That's really all she asked questions about. What he ate. What he wore. What he had talked about. What he was working on. Whether he had a new phone. She went as far as checking the number I had stored for him, as if afraid that he might have changed it because of her. He hadn't. I told her about leaving K. She asked some questions about that. Mostly baffled, incredulous questions, most of which I could not answer. She said that it was all very sad – as if it was a finished thing, historical, about which nothing could now be done. She asked where I had stayed. So I told her a little about David. I didn't tell her what had happened because I thought that it would reflect badly on me. I invented a returning flatmate whose presence had made it impossible for me to stay on. Immediately, she offered me a bed.

—I insist. I really do. It's not as if I don't have the room.

And you were going to ask Michael could you stay with him. Weren't you? Well, he would expect me to make the offer. It's politeness. If you can reach him later then maybe you can go back to his place. But for the moment, I'll take you in. I will take you in. I insist on it.

I was unsure whether she was doing a favour for me or for Michael. I was unsure too about her tone of voice and some of the ways in which she said things. There was a lot of acting to it, a lot of inflecting, and what was probably, for the most part, irony and self-deprecation. The way she said *I will take you in*. She had made it sound half charitable and half predatory. She was playing. She was in complete control of her voice and its register and of all that it implied. There was truth hidden in it, but there was self-defence as well, and I couldn't quite pick up on where that started and where it ended.

I'm sure it's part of her skill. Her talent. To make you feel that the conversation she's having with you is the most important conversation she's had in months. I'm sure it can't have been the case that it actually *was* the most important conversation she'd had in months. Of course, it may be that everyone *assumes*, when they're talking to someone like Catherine Anderson, that any sincerity or profundity they glimpse is either faked entirely or manipulated in some way to make them feel special, and that they therefore dismiss it, don't rise to it, and for this reason people like Catherine Anderson never actually do get to have any genuinely heart-to-heart, important conversations. And that's why they tell everyone everything, as if privacy is a strange, old-fashioned concept that has no interest for them.

She told me about her work, or rather, about the complicated reasons for the fact that she was not doing much work; she told me, in fragments, about Michael, and in more detail about the scarce facts of their estrangement, and about her labyrinthine speculations that fleshed it out. Firstly, she had dismissed it all as a simple sulk. Then, in an explanation that I could barely follow, and felt that I shouldn't, it was something to do with Michael's deeply repressed erotic fascination with her. Then she had wondered about a misplaced loyalty to his imprisoned, disgraced father. But none of her theories satisfied her, and she turned to me every now and then for something new that I might be able to tell her about Michael. Some detail that would allow her to understand what was going on. I don't think I was able to help.

—We have both lost loved ones and we don't know why.

This was not true. I could see that. I couldn't believe that she couldn't see it as well. And yet she seemed to have missed the essential difference.

—Perhaps we can comfort each other a little. Perhaps we can offer each other that.

And she put her hand on my arm.

Perhaps the trouble is that no conversation, no encounter with a person like Catherine Anderson, can ever exist on only one level. It has undercurrents and subtexts and counter-narratives built in. It has her magazine history, her chat-show biography behind it. It has her fame and your non-fame threaded through it like a curious path that you feel you should stick to, and which rings alarm bells when you leave it and stray into the unscripted undergrowth, where the snakes and spiders loiter. I imagined, in the space of a tenth of a second, an elaborate scandal in which I might become mired: THE FAMOUS ACTRESS AND

HER SON'S FRIEND. I'm sure I've already read such a story somewhere. Perhaps the trouble with talking to someone like Catherine Anderson is that *all* possibilities seem entirely clichéd.

Her hand stayed on my forearm for about thirty seconds. She said nothing. She just smiled at me, and let me run through all the connotations of *comfort* that I could think of. Thirty seconds is quite a long time. It constitutes an awkward silence. But the only awkwardness was mine. I nodded my head, and shook it, and made a couple of hesitant noises, and reddened, and eventually smiled crookedly back and turned to look out the window.

—There is comfort in understanding. Isn't there? We understand each other, I think.

And her hand gave me the lightest of squeezes and was gone.

Catherine Anderson is not lonely. She is famous. They look quite alike, but they're two different things. The lonely don't have anyone else in their lives. The famous have everyone else in their lives, and probably, quite often, don't have themselves. I worked this out. It's a bit pat, I know, but it's a bit true as well, I think you'll find. She was able to tell me things that any normal person would consider private, because privacy has nothing to do with her any more. Or maybe what I mean is that privacy is her currency. Her life and her thoughts and her fears, and her loves and her losses, and her body and her choice in clothes and her face and whether or not she's had work done, and her sexuality and her waistline and her decision to wear trainers, all of them are *our* business. They are things that in the rest of us are of no importance at all. We don't think about them. Or we keep them to ourselves. But they're the things which define her. That's what celebrities do. That's how you become one. Not by being good at something like acting or singing, not really, but by living inside out, revealing what other people hide, and hiding what the rest of us would never think of obscuring, or pretending that we didn't do – like going to the supermarket or filling in forms or missing the bus or being badly dressed on a day off, or being just mostly, day after day, *ordinary*.

Itsy drove us along the river for a while. I saw the back of his neck crinkle, ripple like the hide of a beast, like an alligator looking left and right as he turned us through pedestrians and parked cars and around the long bright worms of lazy traffic. He said nothing unless Catherine spoke to him, which she did only to say, *Take the left here, Itsy,* or *What time is it?* or *What kind of car is that, Itsy?* It seemed a long way to her apartment. While I thought about fame and privacy and manners, she talked about perceptions.

—They all said, the papers all said, that we were having an affair. And we let that go. We went out a few times. But actually we couldn't stand each other. He has something wrong with his ears, you know. It's why his hair is so long. You never see his ears on the screen. They're withered. Melted and pink. Like shellfish. He's hung like a horse, I grant you, but he thinks like one too. He's boorish, very *old* male, 1974, very boring. I couldn't stand his company. You have nice ears.

I wasn't completely sure who she was talking about, or why she was talking about him. She had mentioned several names, most of which I knew, in the way that you know the names of mountain ranges on the other side of the world, or of some extinct species of ape. She complained about newspapers and journalists and photographers.

Specific ones. She told me their names. She talked about security.

—Of course it's a two-way thing, but really, they are wild. If you give them the slightest hint of an inch they will take a mile. They are wild. They're savage. You need to learn how to contain them, how to control them, how to throw them the odd scrap so that they don't rip you to shreds out of starvation. But throw them too much and there's a feeding frenzy, and you're fair game, and they move in on you, they circle and they snarl and they pounce, and they will tear you to pieces and chew you up and spit you out. I've seen it happen. Molly Peters was a friend of mine. Poor cow.

It took a moment for me to recall who Molly Peters was – just a moment. Of strain. Although it seems ridiculous that anyone would have to reach for the details of that pathetic story.

—Oh, don't look so sad. Look at you. You're like a poor sad puppy.

She laughed, and flapped her loose hand against my thigh.

—I make it sound too serious. I shouldn't complain. I have people to get in their way when they can, but they can't stop them. They can't be stopped. And I'm aware of the ironies, the contradictions. I need them. They need me. It's . . . what do you call it? . . . oh, there's a word that I thought of. It sums it up. Itsy, what did I call it, the way the press and us coexist? What did I call that?

—An ecosystem.

—An ecosystem. An ecosystem. Is that what I called it? Is that right? I thought it was something else.

Itsy shrugged his shoulders and mumbled something that was indecipherable to me.

—Ecosystem then. Everything in balance. Everything depending on everything else. But the simplest alteration in . . . anything, could throw the whole thing into chaos. I'm sure I had a better word. Never mind.

She drifted off into a mumble. She seemed terribly dissatisfied with 'ecosystem', and I could imagine her on a film set, deciding that there was a problem with the script. And then she drifted back again.

—And sex. They want to know all the time about my sex life. And I make things up and let them say what they want, because after a while it's all the same. There was a story years ago that I had had an affair with a racing driver. Do you remember that? No, but you're young, aren't you? You're a puppy. Well, they ran this story, and it is now widely believed, that this racing driver and I had a passionate, *passionate* affair. They say *passionate*. They print *passionate*. What they mean is that we were fucking like dogs in the street. In the pits probably, or whatever you call it. The pits? Or is that tennis? In the pits. On the bonnet of his car. That's what's between the lines, and that's where people read now. And anyway, this story has been around for so long, and I have had it believed of me for so long, that I actually, now, cannot remember if it's true or not. I knew him of course. He was a nice man. Small, like a jockey. Marvellous body, I seem to remember, smooth and muscular like a farm boy, and I like a boyish type, you know, I just do, I can't help it, you're quite boyish, you should shave, and I seem to recall wonderful sex and jokes about his helmet and all kinds of nonsense. But I'm not sure if I'm actually remembering that or whether I just heard it said about us. I'm really not sure at all. Which is quite ridiculous. I don't know if it's my life I recall or something the press made up. Are you all right?

I'm not sure why she asked whether I was all right. Perhaps it was part of the script. Or perhaps I really was exhibiting the growing confusion I was feeling about whether or not Catherine Anderson, *the* Catherine Anderson, was coming on to me. I thought that she might be. And I was sure that I must be wrong. It was Catherine Anderson after all. And I hadn't even showered. Nevertheless, she had leaned over to me, her face next to mine, her shoulder and arm pressed against my shoulder and arm, and I could smell her peppermint breath and a scent like early sunshine.

—I suppose what you'd say is that if he was any bloody good I'd have no trouble remembering. What age are you?

My phone rang. I fumbled around in my jacket looking for it.

—Sorry.

—That's all right. Itsy, go along the canal. Along the canal and then home. Let's get home.

It was David. Had we not been on our way home anyway? It didn't occur to me not to answer, possibly because I was so flustered, but also because David, I thought, might be something of a relief. Something low-key and predictable. I was wrong.

—It's me, it's David. I'm . . . I'm sorry. I'm really, really sorry. Hello? Please come back. You were right, you were absolutely right, and I've been such a complete moron.

He began to sob. I shifted the phone to my other ear. No one has ever told me that I have nice ears before. I wanted to tell David about it. It would make him laugh. Catherine raised her eyebrows and mouthed a questioning *K* at me. I shook my head.

—David. Um. I'm sort of busy . . .

—I've been so fucking stupid.

The cursing again. He never curses.

—I've been utterly ridiculous. I'm very sorry. I should never have kicked you out. I've been living in a stupid, made-up fucking place. I've been living in Paddorn. I've been so obsessed with making a stupid made-up pathetic fantasy fucking fiction real that I've messed up my real life and everything is inside out and I can't stand it, I really can't.

We had turned on to the canal. Catherine had moved away from me slightly, and was looking out of the window. I assumed she was politely trying not to overhear.

—David, it's not really a good time. Just at the moment.

—I've really fucked up, haven't I? I've really made a complete mess of everything. And Mark . . . Mark was . . .

At this point he more or less began to wail, and I found it difficult to make out any of the words which were scattered among the tearful gasps and the cries. There were little gasps from Catherine too, and I was conscious that she was touching me, and I thought that she had picked up on the distress somehow and was sympathising, and it took me a minute to realise that it was her arse that was touching me, and that the noises she was making had nothing to do with David. She had turned in her seat to face out the side window, and as a result her bottom was brushing against my thigh. She had cupped her hands against the glass and was emitting little bleats of pleasure. I didn't know what was going on. Then I saw what she was looking at. There were swans on the canal. Big white beautiful swans, gliding along the smooth surface like a child's trick with magnets. About half a dozen of them, their long necks confused in my line of sight like a lattice of thrown white ropes, their bodies a cluster of wet pearls, like a bright spurt of seeds scattered on the water. Catherine

Anderson seemed to be moving her arse back and forth along my thigh.

—David. Get it together, for God's sake.

—Come back. Please. You need to fix things with K. You need to sort it out. I've been so selfish. You can stay here as long as you want. I'm so, so sorry.

Itsy was driving very slowly. I checked to see whether he was looking in his rear-view mirror at me but he wasn't. Catherine was looking slightly to the left now, back at the swans as we moved away from them, and her bottom was pressing harder against my thigh, and moving, and she lifted it slightly so that it was encroaching on to my lap.

—David, it's OK. I've got somewhere. It's fine. Forget it. I'll talk to you soon.

And I hung up. Which I shouldn't have done. That's now clear. But I did. I wasn't trying to get rid of David so that I could somehow start reciprocating Catherine Anderson's attentions. That's really not what I was interested in at all. I was simply confused. Flustered. I could manage only one thing at a time, and while it seems in retrospect that I chose the wrong thing to manage, that is nevertheless the choice I made. It seemed more urgent. And yes, I know, I could simply, while still talking to David, have moved out of range of Catherine's arse. Just shuffled over to the other side of the car, which was probably wide enough to allow an escape, but the idea somehow didn't present itself. Or I could have said, *Do you mind, I'm on the phone here, with a distressed friend.* But I was in her car. Her black-windowed fame car. Catherine Anderson, with her famous arse on my lap. And I suppose that it's instinctual – when there are two things attacking us at once we tend make a judgement as to which is the more immediately dangerous, and we concentrate on that. And David, it seemed to me, could wait. While Catherine Anderson plainly could not.

—Sorry. Excuse me. I . . .

I don't know what I said actually. But I held my innocent hands in the air and moved myself out from under her bum. She said nothing. She just turned around, and smiled at me, and sat back in her seat. As if nothing had happened. She gave a shivering sigh and said:

—God, I love nature. Hurry up, Itsy. We need to get home.

And although it seemed clear to me that the sigh had been about the physical contact, about the pleasure it had given her, it might have seemed to someone else that the sigh was simply about her pleasure at seeing the swans. And although to my ears *We need to get home* had sounded breathy and suggestive, there was actually nothing in the words that could be held against her. And I began to doubt that anything at all odd had happened other than that she had turned in her seat and looked out the window and as a result her bottom had brushed against my thigh and I was actually just being grotesque and ridiculous, and it wasn't Catherine Anderson's fault if I was filthy-minded and flattered myself so much to think that she might have that kind of interest in me.

For the rest of the journey she talked about her childhood love of ballet. And I have no idea whether, as a child, Catherine Anderson genuinely dreamed of starring in *Swan Lake*, or whether this was a bit of background detail suggested to her by a publicist, or by her own inner publicist, or whether she had heard it about someone else, or whether it was actually, pathetically, true, and it just seemed to her that to embrace the clichés made them less diminishing. I really have no idea which it was.

And I bet she doesn't either.

Catherine Anderson's apartment is pure cinema. By which I mean that I've never seen anything like it except in a movie, and also that being in it is a little like being permanently framed and lit and directed. I couldn't help feeling that I was always watched, in the same way that a film is watched. I felt that I had to do interesting things, say interesting things, in order to live up to my surroundings. Even when on my own, I behaved with great circumspection. I considered each movement before I made it, each tilt of my head, each hand gesture. I monitored my facial expressions, keen that they should never clash with the set. Even in the shower I was self-conscious – in that slightly narcissistic way of the actor whose character is pleasingly sophisticated, competent, attractive, deserving of a home such as this.

I was there for about three hours. Possibly a little longer. I don't see the point in going through all of it with you. There are pertinent points. There are gaps. You should be able to fill in what you want to fill in. We arrived, I was shown, by Itsy, to a guest room, where I shaved and showered and changed my clothes. I joined Catherine in what she called 'the drawing room', which is huge and hugely comfortable, and has an aquarium built into one wall and what looks like the entire city built into another – it is in fact a floor-to-ceiling window with the most remarkable view. She had changed. The tracksuit had been replaced by a short dark skirt and a blue blouse. It looked quite schoolgirlish. We ate a salad which was brought to us by an Asian lady who wore a little pinafore. We drank some superb white wine. We talked. Then there was an unfortunate misunderstanding, and I was asked to leave.

It wasn't a misunderstanding so much as an inadvertent trespass. On my part. Itsy showed me out. He stood over me silently as I regathered my bags, and he walked me down to the street. He wore an almost apologetic expression, which was some comfort. As if to say, *She's mad, don't worry about it*. And I think she probably is mad. I thought it at the time, and I think it now. Except that at the time I thought her madness was gross and inexplicable, whereas now I feel that it's interesting and distressing and in some strange horrible way *admirable*, and it is for this reason that I don't feel so terrible for telling you about it.

The point about Catherine is that she lives, utterly, in an artificial world. Everything about her is not fake exactly, but false, in the sense that it is a role she has been asked to play, and while some of it is certainly based on her own personality and on her own innate character and characteristics, it is not complete, it is not the whole story. She is a very beautiful and intelligent woman who has been shoehorned into a space that is not quite hers. Not fully hers. She is not living a natural life. Her life is constructed – comprised as it is of comfort and luxury and money and protection on the one hand, and exposure and judgement on the other. She's not a person so much as an entertainment device. She is given wealth and general affection in return for being a PlayStation.

What happened was this.

While we drank wine, Catherine talked some more about the men with whom she has been involved. These are famous men, and although their names are of course well known, I'm not going to name them here. I'm not going to link them specifically to the things that she told me about. Suffice it to say that she seemed to delight in telling me increasingly explicit details about her sexual relationships. It was a jokey, giggly conversation to begin with, in which she described them physically, and at first innocently, saying that so-and-so had, for example, lovely eyes, or very strong, sexy legs. Then she turned to the size of their penises, and their sexual stamina, which was amusing enough. It was all simple salacious gossip, and it would be disingenuous of me to suggest that I didn't have fun hearing it. But as she talked on, and as we drank more wine, and as Catherine began to go back to men she had previously mentioned as having, for example, lovely brown eyes and an average but inexhaustible penis, she would reveal more, and then more again, as if she could not mention them without mentioning some new secret about them, and these secrets became increasingly physically detailed and carnal and base, and I became increasingly uncomfortable.

She told me about the peccadilloes and preferences of famous men. She told me of the man who greatly enjoyed having Catherine shave his scrotum. Of the man who could not achieve an erection until she slapped his face. Of the man who liked to masturbate into her handbags. I began to weary of it, and I began also to feel that Catherine was filling my head with these things in preparation for something. I was still not sure what her interest in me was. I still juggled the idea that she wanted to sleep with me with the idea that I was mad to think that she wanted to sleep with me. She poured more wine. She told me more details of famous men and of what they wanted. Of the actor who wanted her to insert the heel of her shoe into his ass. Of the man who liked to be pissed on, fully clothed, repeatedly, during the course of long days in foreign hotels. Of the very famous singer who liked her to beat him, to thrash his body with her hands and with whips and with chains, who liked her to hurl abuse at him and spit at him and force him into all the physical humiliations he could think of. My head spun slightly. I did not want to hear any more. And I really did not want it to lead anywhere.

I went to her room, her bedroom. I wasn't supposed to. But that was not the trespass. If she had caught me in her bedroom I don't think it would have been a problem. It was a beautiful bedroom. I was looking for the bathroom. The main bathroom. It is a big apartment. My room, the guest room, seemed to have disappeared. In fact, I later discovered, it was down a different corridor, reached by a different exit from the drawing room. But in any case, when I had excused myself, Catherine had waved me out this way, and had told me either *second on the left* or *second on the right*, I wasn't sure, she had been laughing and her words were garbled. And I had opened a door and it had plainly been her room, and I had taken a brief glance around and was on my way back out when I noticed that there was an en suite bathroom there, on the left, I could see the glint of a tiled floor, and I headed for it, perhaps a little drunkenly, thoughtlessly, without much, certainly, in the way of thought – not thinking for a moment that the woman who had just been telling me of how she used to pee all over an expensively suited Hollywood actor in a hotel suite in Cannes, would mind for a minute me using her bathroom.

It was very large. A circular marble bath took up one corner. There was a big shower as well, with an elaborate system of nozzles and dials. The floor was marble. There were various rugs. There was a seat in front of a lit mirror, with other smaller mirrors on extendable arms, and there were various bottles and jars and tubes and tubs and containers of varying shape and size and colour lying around. I was not supposed to be there. On the floor there were a few items of underwear, and one leather belt. The lighting was recessed into the ceiling and the walls, and into the ledge around the bath. There were no windows. I was supposed to be in the main bathroom. And this was plainly not that.

In the middle of the ceiling, suspended on some kind of telescopic pole, around which coiled a couple of cables, was a very hi-tech-looking camera. To my left, the doors of a mirrored cabinet lay slightly open. It was filled with electronics. There were things that looked like DVD players, and a little screen, and various tiny green pinpoint lights, some of which flashed, others of which were off, others of which were fully on. I had to look at the shower and the bath and the toilet to reassure myself that I had not walked into the screening room by mistake. There were a couple of slim remote controls sitting on a shelf. I was confused, and then thought to myself that this was her safe room. Is that they call it? There was a film. The inner chamber in a wealthy house where the walls are thick and the door steel and it is filled with the most delicate and sophisticated electronic systems and you could hold out there for days. Strange to have it in your bathroom, but also, I supposed, quite practical. Then I saw the tapes. Are they tapes? I don't know. They're probably discs. They are probably digital storage things.

Each little rectangular, almost square, tape was in its own plastic box, and labelled, in small neat writing, almost as small as David's.

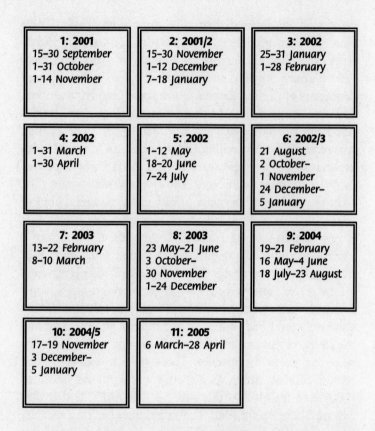

1: 2001 15–30 September 1–31 October 1–14 November	**2: 2001/2** 15–30 November 1–12 December 7–18 January	**3: 2002** 25–31 January 1–28 February
4: 2002 1–31 March 1–30 April	**5: 2002** 1–12 May 18–20 June 7–24 July	**6: 2002/3** 21 August 2 October– 1 November 24 December– 5 January
7: 2003 13–22 February 8–10 March	**8: 2003** 23 May–21 June 3 October– 30 November 1–24 December	**9: 2004** 19–21 February 16 May–4 June 18 July–23 August
10: 2004/5 17–19 November 3 December– 5 January	**11: 2005** 6 March–28 April	

I was still thinking about security. I thought that they were some kind of CCTV surveillance record. And as soon as I thought that, as soon as the letters were in my mind, were spelled out to me, I dismissed them. I dismissed the idea entirely, and scolded myself for being so bloody stupid, and instead I thought – *She's taping herself having sex.*

I looked for the slot where I could play one of the things, and found it, but when I tried to enter 11: 2005, it seemed to be jammed. I quickly realised that it was jammed because there was a tape already in there. Beneath the slot was a row of buttons such as you'd find on a DVD player. I pressed *Play*. The small screen fired up and flicked at me something blurred, quick, of colour, double, brief, and it filled then with that curtain of grey static snow, of chain mail absence, that signifies a memory that is blank and waiting to be filled. I pressed *Stop*. I pressed *Rewind*. There was no whirring noise. I waited a minute. There were flickering digits, a countdown from the low hundreds to a sudden zero. This was some kind of digital thing. Binary. More can be fitted into the world when everything is reduced to Yes/No, On/Off, Empty/Full. It stopped automatically. I pressed *Play*.

My mother tells me that when I was a very small child, still in my pram, I used to hate people looking at me, pinching my cheek, grabbing my toes, telling me in wide-eyed baby talk that I was simply adorable. I would either bawl at them, or screw my little face up into something horrible and splutter and seethe and hiss, furious until they backed away. As if the very idea of being told that I was a lovely little thing, good enough to eat, annoyed me so much that I wanted to show how ugly I could be.

Catherine Anderson, since you want to know, records herself defecating. The camera hanging from the ceiling points directly at her toilet. On one side of the split screen you can watch her pull down her tracksuit bottoms and lower herself on to the seat and you can watch her face exert and wrinkle and sigh with the process of shitting. On the other side of the screen is the feed from another camera, a different camera. It took me a minute to work out what it was. It seemed very bright, indistinct, an oval. Then, as Catherine sits down on the left of the screen, the brightness on the right adjusts, and the image becomes clear. It is Catherine's arse, on the toilet seat. The second camera is inside the bowl. As her face works on the left, her anus works on the right. It pushes out and opens and from it emerges a single file of dark slugs, a line of short hard creatures from a cave. And after each one is expelled her anus remains briefly open like a mouth, and then closes, slowly, like a mouth that is finished speaking.

—You shouldn't be in here.

—I didn't –

—I never said you could come in here. You little fucking cunt.

—I'm sorry. I didn't –

—Get the fuck out of my home. ITSY!

And so on.

It occurred to me then, but only fleetingly, and not in the way that was to have such a profound effect on me a night later, that Catherine Anderson is just an extreme example of the condition shared by all of us. All of us. The condition of not being in the world at all. Of being instead on a human platform, made not just of things, but of history and culture and our ingestion of both of them, of being in a created place that is separated from the world by a layer of human clutter. That *everything* is human. And all we see is this layer that we have thrown over the world, like a carpet put down on a floor. And all that Catherine Anderson is trying to do with her hidden cameras and her filmed shitting, is to rip up the carpet. Rip up the carpet and see what's underneath. And I think that to do that is to become mad.

Because we are not alone here.

Underneath the human carpet there is a writhing in the darkness. Like a spluttering sea.

The Terrorist's Daughter

What am I saying? The terrorists' daughter. The terrorists' daughter. I'm making a general point. Or, he was. He was making a general point. An extrapolated notion. Though he was talking about himself. In the first person. He was talking about his daughter and her hair and the way she runs down the garden path, as if there could be such a thing as a garden path, and her puppy, as if he really expected me to believe that she has a puppy. Had a puppy. Not that he was a terrorist. Unless you take what he said as being indicative of the future. His future. Can the things we say be indicative of the future? Has all this happened yet? I don't know what I'm saying.

The terrorist's daughter then.

Not that he is a terrorist. Not that he has a daughter. I can't believe one and I can't believe the other.

I'm talking about Anthony Edgar, who is about forty-five years old and who wears an expensive suit and expensive shoes and who has the skin of a man who can afford to be in perfect health, who can rise at dawn and swim in a private pool and eat well and sensibly and be driven to his desk in a car like Catherine Anderson's. I don't actually know that he does any of that. But he could afford to. If he wanted to. If he was so minded. But I imagine that he does those things, or similar things, which give him time to think, as he swims or is driven, about the way the world is fabricated, and what he owes to the fabrication, and how he wishes he could rip the blue sky off his life and see the darkness there. Like Catherine Anderson. Like most people.

He's the boss of BOX. He took me to see the Australia-shaped stain.

I needed to reset. I really did. I needed everything to stop, and I needed to stop, and I needed to stay still, in the one place, singly only me, solitary is what I mean, unmoving, still, with my eyes closed and my head empty, and I needed to reset. I needed (if you're a computer user you may understand me) to restart in safe mode. System error. Blight on the circuits.

I am dealing now with too many things. Too many fractured things, as if all the bones of my life have been splintered and I'm clutching them, little sharp sticks, and I'm trying to put them back together but all that happens is that I cut my skin and my skin is ripped and shredded and that's all that's happening. I feel like I am crawling out of something on the news. I feel that a microphone is being pushed into my face and I am being interrogated as to *how I feel.*

How do you think I feel? *Oh great. I feel great. Here, clutch my stump and feel the pump of how great I feel.* How do you think I feel?

Competing fictions. Aspects of the truth in confrontation. Do you believe a word I say here? Do you? Why? Why would you? Why should you? I know nothing about computers. I wouldn't know how to restart one in *safe mode*. I don't believe a word of this, frankly. I think I dreamed it and I'm telling you my dream and you should stop me before I ruin your engines. Before I ruin your delicate engines.

There were no photographers or journalists or stalkers waiting outside Catherine Anderson's apartment building. There was no one. There will be no record of it. No report. No one took my photograph. No one asked my name. No one was there. The street was like a canyon, emptied out by panic. After the stampede. It was quiet as the country-side and nothing moved. If you ask her what visitors she has had in the last week she will not mention my name. Itsy, I have no doubt, could look me in the eye and calmly and convincingly swear, all lilt and honest braces, that he has never seen me before. Never laid eyes on me. Doesn't know me from Adam. There was nothing. There were the high buildings and the bright sky and the dark street.

I reeled to the pillar of a Japanese bank and I leaned there for hours, or what seemed like hours, and I could not quite marshal my thoughts and I was afraid that if I said anything I would say something impossible, something in a language that I didn't actually know, or something that was borrowed from some other mind, head, story, place, person, combination of these, but I wanted a witness, a passer-by, that I could stop and tug at, barking whatever came out of me, so that I could point at the building where Catherine Anderson lives and mime that there was someone up there who needed help.

Maybe it never happened.

I don't know what time it is. Well, actually, I do know what time it is. It is nearly one o'clock. In the afternoon.

But I'm not completely sure what day it is. It is either Saturday or Sunday. There's a possibility that it's Friday, but I don't think it could be.

I really don't think it could be.

It's after four o'clock now. I slept for a while. And it's Saturday. I checked. In this hotel they'll do anything for you. If you look out at the corridor you can get the feeling that it is a chimney laid on its side. A lift shaft laid on its side. Something horizontal that is supposed to be vertical.

From the street I can hear very little. I can hear the occasional siren. I can hear no voices. I wonder whether I am fully here. I keep on looking out at the lift shaft laid on its side. It's fallen over. That's all I can decide about it. If I go out there I will have to climb it. Up or down it. Using trays of dirty dishes for my footholds. Using laundry bags and polished shoes for purchase.

Fully here. Is it possible to be half in one place and half in another? Yes it is. It is, you know. Because I am half here and half in the street after the stampede, crouched against the pillar of a Japanese bank, looking at the sky and the tops of things, thinking about human shit, and the way we sew up the famous like dolls, with no holes and no contents but for fluff and hidden pennies, and how Catherine Anderson's strategies are probably more common than we might think. I don't want to linger on it too much. But I just want to say that her anus is a pinched glimpse of truth, and it does not need measurement in frames per second. I think Michael knows that she does it. I think that's why he cannot see her.

There were phone calls. As I sat on the concrete between my bags.

- K. No answer.
- David. No answer.
- Michael. No answer.
- Rachel. No answer.
- My mother. She was well, yes, fine, no, no news, yes, no, yes, no. K? No, why would she have talked to K? No, she hadn't called K, no, no, no.
- K. No answer.
- Incoming. Michael. *You've been trying to get me?* Yes. *What's up?* Nothing. I was going to call over. *Are you all right?* Yes, yes. Have you talked to K? *No. Why? What's happened?* Nothing's happened. *You sound odd.* I'm outside a bank. *OK. A bank? OK. Is it collapsing?* No. *Did you know a woman died in the sports centre?* Yes. *Are you sure you're all right?* Yes, I'm fine. I saw your mother. *What?* She was outside your house. *Oh you're fucking joking.* No. She wanted to know who I was. *Oh Jesus Christ.* I like her. *Well, that's nice for you.* I think she's very clever and lonely. *Oh for fuck's sake. What did she tell you?* Nothing much. *Did she tell you that I'm not talking to her?* Yes. She misses you. *She does not miss me, she misses being a mother. She always has. When was this?* Earlier. I don't know. *Why were you here?* I just dropped by. *Right. I'll fucking kill her. She's just being so childish and stupid.* She's not. She needs you. You're real. *I'm real?* Yes. *As opposed to?* As opposed to the rest of her life. *Oh please. That's very her though. Did she get you in the car?* She gets people into her car. *It's like the evil queen in* Snow White. She had a car? *She had an apple, it's the same thing.* She just wants to be a real person. *Right. You're lobbying on behalf of my mother. I'm hanging up now.* Have you talked to K? *No, I told you. Why? Where is*

K anyway? Where are you? I'm outside a bank. *Oh yeah, I forgot. Are you casing it?* No. I'm going to . . . There's a hotel. *OK. Are you all right?* Yes. I'm fine. *You don't sound all right.*

• K. No answer.

The truth is. The truth was. I was afraid again. That I had somehow. That K was dead. In pieces in places where David hadn't looked. Oh, I know that it's ridiculous. I knew it then. But you hear of forgotten traumas, of mind erasers, of things too difficult to store, of the half-life of shame and terror. My unravelled mind could not find any other explanation. If people disappear they are dead. If they disappear after a row, then you've killed them. You know, it's that simple. Things like that are never very complicated.

I hung up on Michael.

I needed to go home. I needed, obviously, to go home, find out where K was and what had happened, exactly, and I needed to reset. To start again in *safe mode*.

I went and checked into the hotel at the end of the street.

Since then I've been out twice. I've been twice out. Once on Monday, for the whole day, and once again on the Thursday, when I actually checked out, and set off for home (as I should have done in the first place) only to be repulsed by what was happening in the streets. Repulsed and forced back. By what I saw.

I think what I'm going to do is just write down all of that, all of that, and then go home. Today. If I can write all of that today. Just check out and take my stuff and put my head down and not look at anything – just look at my feet until I have to look up to see where to put my key in my own front door. Just do that.

Everything is about to accelerate and get better. I need to have the writing at my back. I need to write everything up until *now*, so that now can be unweighted. Do you understand? I need to put everything down so that I don't have to carry it. Put it down. Empty my hands.

So. Anthony Edgar and posters.

Anthony Edgar

I was worried about money. Almost immediately upon checking in I was worried about money. Mostly because of the ridiculous nightly cost of my room. I have about one thousand pounds in my bank account. I also have a credit card with a decent limit. There are standing orders and direct debits to pay my half of the mortgage and the electricity and gas bills and my mobile phone and various subscriptions. In terms of money coming in, well, there is a fairly decent amount due for the children's poetry book, if I ever finish it, which at this stage is looking doubtful. I am owed eight hundred dollars by an American magazine for something I did three months ago. They've been promising it for weeks now.

I went to the hotel swimming pool. Absolutely nothing weird or disgusting happened to me there. A Swiss gentleman asked me where I was visiting from and what line of work I was in. Embarrassed by the truth I told him I was based in Amsterdam and that I was in IT. He was from Zurich and was in pharmaceuticals. He told me that people would always needs drugs and computers, and that we owned the world. He swam slow, lazy lengths on his back, under a bed of black-grey hair on a tanned chest, while I gripped the rail and moved my legs and looked at everything very carefully. Nothing, as I say, happened. Nothing fell in. Nothing floated by. My body seemed fragile though, and my stomach distorted, twisted in the middle, as if I had developed a new muscle, new to the species. A muscle for what, I don't know. For tying and untying, for hiding a body, for carrying on. I really don't know. My memory told me that it was malfunctioning. I put my head underwater repeatedly, each time hoping to clear the glut of impossibles that seemed to flood my mind like a rock-fall. I broke the surface. And broke the surface. And broke the surface. But the surface never broke, and when I got back to my room I watched the news to see if a famous actress had been found bludgeoned to death in her apart-ment, or whether police had discovered the grisly after-math of a domestic slaying believed to have occurred the previous Friday. There was nothing like it. There never is.

I called, with money in mind, my friend Anna. I say I called her with money in mind. And I think that is mostly true. But I can't deny that I may have been thinking as well, more generally, about BOX, and about Michael's story of the haunted building. What I was thinking about them I can't really say. I seemed to have a head full of unfinished business. Maybe I was working my way through that. Or maybe I was just simply, genuinely (if a little dementedly) worried about money.

Anna works for BOX. She's a friend of a friend – the type of person I see a couple of times a year at Christmas parties or summer parties or various other vaguely formal gatherings. I think she's a bit younger than me, but comes across as older, more sensible, settled, career-oriented, fully adult. She's been living with the same man for as long as I've known her. I have no idea what he does.

So I called Anna and she seemed not at all surprised to hear from me, even though I couldn't remember the last time I'd called her, and she must have known that I wasn't simply calling for a chat. But she didn't interrogate me, she just acted as if it was perfectly natural for me to call, and we talked about the weather and exchanged partner news (sanitised, shining, with no shade or hint of truth), and commented briefly on some gossip about another couple of friends who have recently split up. (Not David and Mark. I don't think David and Anna have met.) And then I asked her, after the first natural pause, whether she was still interested in the idea of me doing some work for BOX. *With* BOX, I corrected myself.

—Oh God yes. I'm so glad you've come round to the idea. I thought I'd put you off completely. We'd absolutely love to talk to you. In fact, there's a project we're getting into right now, and I was thinking about you the other day. I think you'd like it.

It was that simple really. She wanted to see me immediately. She wanted me to call over to her home. I said that was impossible. Then she wanted me to come to the offices the next day.

—Have you moved into a new place? Somewhere?

There was the briefest of pauses. Oh, a beat only.

—No. No, not yet. We're still on Egypt Street. Come and see me. You can meet a few people. We can have a chat. Completely informal. It'll be fun.

I told her that I didn't have a portfolio as such, just a few notebooks.

—We're familiar with your work. Bring whatever you want. But just come.

—OK. OK I will.

I never asked about money.

Egypt Street does not seem to have anything at all to do with Egypt. I walked its length trying to spot the connection and failed, although on one corner there is a newsagent's called 'Pyramid News'. The offices of BOX are in a non-descript block in the centre of the street. I dislike offices. I hate having to visit any offices. Publishers, magazine or newspaper offices, K's offices – I have the same feeling of discomfort that some people have in relation to hospitals. It's an unease. A feeling that I might end up in one myself. But of course, such a feeling is almost entirely to do with my own self-doubt about my self-employed, freelance status, and a desire to make it seem more exciting than it is. Or, more exciting and somehow more worthwhile than a mere office job. And I know that it's not the case. And I know that part of me longs for the stability and camaraderie of working with other people, while other parts of me cling to the notion that what I do is more difficult and therefore more worthy, while all of me knows that both ideas are equally spurious and that everyone everywhere dreams of adjusting their lives slightly this way or that way, into a closer alignment with some idea they've been given about what a good life looks like. In the offices of BOX, for example, there are pictures on the walls of the sea.

—Yes. It's a series of images we did for a software company rethink last year. We used something else in the end, but we liked these so much that we put them up. Plain really, just horizons splitting sea from sky, all at the same level. But you see how incredibly different the skies are? And how the seas are choppy or stormy or calm? There is all this difference in basically the one shot. The one framing device. It seemed to say something to all of us.

Anna talked like this. I don't know that I'm recreating it with enough force. She talked as if she was involved not in business but in art. I found myself increasingly annoyed with her.

—The patterns of consciousness are really what we are

trying to tap into here. We are not *creating* so much as *uncovering* what is already in there, in people, in terms of potential and their creative interaction with the practical aspects of their lives. Such as banking, in this case.

She was showing me some kind of moulded plastic sculpture. It was green. It looked like a beach ball with a deep groove cut into it.

—There is comfort in this shape, but also the channel which goes all the way around suggests precision, finesse, technical capability. So we have comfort and we have know-how. It's all about infecting people with their own dreams. We think you could help us with that. In the sense that you have a very visceral, direct connection to the psychology of contemporary life. That is incredibly valuable.

She never used to talk like this at barbecues or Christmas drinks. At least, not as far as I can remember.

—Infecting?

—Sorry?

—You said *infecting people*.

—Affecting. I said affecting. Moving them. Engaging them on an emotional level.

She said *infecting*. She introduced me to someone called Justin. He shook my hand as if he'd been waiting to meet me all his life, and told me after a couple of minutes of listing companies that I had never heard of, and the outlines of projects which to me all sounded like variations on the sea, that *the great thing about BOX was that it could contain anything*, and then he paused dramatically with his hand very lightly on my elbow, *but the question is – can it contain you?* And he giggled. That's the word. He giggled like a twelve-year-old.

These people are idiots.

I had put some thought into this. I had carefully chosen what to bring with me in terms of drawings. I concentrated on the simple, the animal, the ones that looked like they might encapsulate something. Images, in other words, that could be slapped on to any number of notions. Things for which I had forgotten the source. Anything that looked like it was a thought-through, considered piece, I excluded. I also had the hotel express-launder a shirt and a pair of dark jeans. They charged an absolute fortune. And there I was looking at storyboards for TV ads. Ads for things like online travel agencies and mobile-phone networks. And a design project for the world tour of a rock band. Justin showed me photographs of outfits and drawings of lighting effects which had been believed 'technically impossible' before BOX managed to *motivate* the technicians. There were pictures of politicians and the poor to be juxtaposed on screens behind the band on certain socially aware songs. Justin and Anna had an almost religious fervour regarding their own abilities. Actually, that's completely wrong. They didn't have a fervour at all. They had a kind of arrogant self-belief in the significance of what they were up to. They were proud, in that quietly striding way which is indicative of real pride. In something worth being proud of. In having mastered a magnificent and strange power. They thought they were mariners, riding on the ocean in a vigorous ship.

Anthony Edgar appeared out of nowhere. I didn't know who he was and I didn't pay him any attention. If I thought about it, I probably thought that he might be a delivery guy, perhaps, or one of those slightly older, slightly autistic people that are sometimes given light part-time jobs by companies who have a socially aware aspiration tucked away somewhere in their mission statement, perhaps inspired by a song. We were in an open-plan area, at a seating area, sitting on low orange chairs that looked like low orange shoes, and Justin was looking through my drawings, and Anna was telling me about where I fitted in, and Anthony Edgar was hovering around at a coffee machine somewhere over to our left and he seemed to be muttering to himself and rubbing the side of his face and making what I can only describe, much as I'd really prefer not to use the term at all, as mouse noises. Squeaks.

—The thing about your vision is that it is peculiarly focused on the particulars which are otherwise overlooked. You know. Your level of detail is wonderful. I don't mean detail in the drawing so much, though of course that's there in spades when you want it to be, which you often of course don't want it to be, such as in that one, Justin, thanks, this one, which is so simple as to be shocking, I mean, I don't even know what that is. Is it a seal? A walrus? It looks complicit though, in our observation of it, as if it knows what we know, and subverts our gaze with its own, looping back and returning ourselves to ourselves, so that looking at this strange creature, this *other*, becomes, in a very solid way, an exercise in looking at ourselves. But what I wanted to say was that your grasp of detail is in the observation. You see in details and *report back* in broad, clever strokes that clarify and summarise. I can see you playing a big role in our political work.

I had no idea what she was talking about.

—I'm not sure, Anna, really, having listened to you, whether this is so much a good idea. You know. To be honest. What you're doing here. Is. Well. It's nothing I do. It's far too . . . Well, it's far too orchestra . . . organised. Knowing. You know. I don't want to infect anyone with anything. I really don't. I don't want to influence anyone's behaviour. And that's what you do. Isn't it?

—In a way. In a way, yes, that is what we do. But there is nothing malign in BOX. And as I said to you earlier, we are plugging into what is pre-existent. We are simply using neural paths that already exist, and yes, we do that to fire people's minds, to get them thinking, and yes, we hope that they will think in a way that pleases our clients, but really, there is nothing sinister in that. If there is then all the world is sinister. All the world's malign.

She laughed. Anthony Edgar had stopped squeaking and stood much closer to us. I suppose he was listening. He continued to rub his face.

—I'm not really interested in using my work like that, Anna. No matter what the intention. I'm sorry. This is my fault. I was just interested. I was curious. I don't know what I was thinking really. I should be at home. You know. K is probably wondering where I am by now. K is probably. I shouldn't have wasted your time.

Anthony Edgar started talking. His voice was like the tread of a tyre in snow.

—You can't tell them apart, can you? Decaffeinated and caffeinated. I can't tell them apart. They've got, the coffee people, they've got it down, they've worked it out, and they've closed the gap and they've eliminated the disappointment that people used to feel with the healthy option. It used to taste like shit, frankly. Now it tastes great. So why would anyone want caffeinated any more? If the decaffeinated tastes just as good?

Anna and Justin had stopped moving, and they stared at him, and if it had not been for the delighted expressions on their faces I might have thought that Anthony Edgar was some kind of embarrassing in-house lunatic. I looked at him. He was staring at me. He was smiling, and sipping from a cardboard cup, and gently, with a fingertip, caressing the side of his face, along his beard line.

Anna introduced us. She described me as *the illustrator*, who might be *joining the dots for us on Hiatus*. I shook his hand.

—Leave him alone, Anna. He's pissed off with you. You're telling him a lot of shit that he really doesn't want to hear. He's the artist, not us. We make billboards and we make shopfronts and we make thirty-second intel-sells and aim them at pre-selected wallets. We don't do anything he's interested in. If he worked for us we'd kill him.

Anna smiled, but blushed a little too. Justin guffawed. They behaved as if he'd said something devastating. I looked around at all three of them and couldn't understand what on earth was going on. The dog had no collar. The dog I saw outside the café and in the park. He had no collar.

—Let me show you something.

He was talking to me. Anthony Edgar, I mean. He motioned to me, as if to say that it was all right, he wouldn't hurt me. I stood up. I put my notebooks in my shoulder bag. They bumped against my phone and my pen and my bottle of water and my sunglasses case. We take the same things through life. As if life only ever asks us the same set of questions. I snorted a swallow of laughter. Ridiculous.

He put his arm on my shoulder and led me away. He's a tall man. He was wearing jeans and a black shirt. He is bald. He wears square dark-framed glasses and a moustache. He smells slightly of salt. He must be in his mid-forties. He is muscled, toned, takes care of himself. But he wears it lightly.

—Look at this.

It was the green ball with the all-round slit.

—Yes. Anna pointed it out.

—Shit, isn't it? It's a green plastic globe. Actually, it's

two half-globes, joined in the middle by a little rod of green plastic. So that it looks like a full globe with a slice taken out of it. It's supposed to make you feel relaxed and excited at the same time. It's supposed to make you feel comfortable but prepared. Stable but ready to rock. Female but male. What does it make you feel?

—Puzzled.

He laughed.

—See. We fucked up. It makes me feel nearly three hundred grand richer.

Suddenly he scratched his head quite violently. Just for a second. Then stopped.

—Sorry about those two. They're always doing this. They think they're in a band. You draw animals, don't you?

—Sometimes. Among other things.

—You did the cover of last month's *Skirmish*, didn't you? With the weird sort of monkey thing. Full of holes. About genetics.

—Yes. I did.

—It was great. Scary. Would you like lunch?

—Lunch?

—Yes. It's a meal. I'm paying. Nice place too. There's a view of the city. So you get to see any plane crashes that might be occurring. You'll like it.

—What time is it?

—Lunchtime.

It was actually just after eleven. We left the building in a kind of deafening rush, as if descending a chute, an escape route known only to Anthony Edgar. I followed in his wake as he strode through various offices saying impenetrable things to thin young good-looking people. I never saw Anna again.

—Call Joyful. Tell them no. I'm skipping noon. I want

216

nothing to happen to Hiatus while I'm not in the building. Go back to yellow for the mountain and talk to them about a helicopter. Call Randolph's for a table. A window one. For two. For now.

From somewhere he retrieved a leather jacket and a pair of sunglasses. I don't think we were in his office. I don't know. There were rooms. There were pictures of different seas, all restrained by the same frame. If you asked me to retrace our steps through those offices I would not be capable of it. Stormy sea, calm sea, choppy sea, blue sea. We may have come out on the street by a secret door.

Anthony Edgar took me to an early lunch in Randolph's, which is a restaurant at the top of the Lacon Tower. Lunch consisted first of some coffee, decaffeinated and caffeinated, in two identical pots, which Anthony Edgar had the waiter mark *D* and *C* on their bases with an indelible black ink marker that he had in his pocket. I got the feeling that they would do anything in Randolph's for Anthony Edgar. We also had two cigarettes, each. This was the first time I've smoked since I was a teenager. The first one made me regret not having accepted the offer of one from the policeman outside the park. But after the second I had to go to the bathroom and splash my face with cold water. The bathroom is pristine. You throw the towels into a hole in the dark wood basin surround. The mirrors are kind. I guessed the coffees completely wrong. I guess the *D* as *C* and the *C* as *D*. The Lacon Tower was designed by Edwards Patten Associates, which is the company that Michael works for. It's the one that I think looks like it's going to fall over. Our table was right by the window, up on a sort of parapet. I found myself leaning involuntarily inwards, as if my weight might otherwise tip it. I told Anthony Edgar.

—Macrocephalic. Large-headed. It appears to defy gravity. It's unsettling. I like it. I come here as often as I can. Most people have the same reaction though. *It's going to fall over. It's not safe.* This place suffers, I mean Randolph's, suffers because of it. I bet they do. Who has an appetite in the face of death? I never understood the condemned man's last meal. I worry about shitting myself when the bomb goes off. When I'm shot. Whatever. I'm worried for my dignity in those final moments. Always go into battle on an empty stomach.

He kept his eyes on the city while he talked. For the most part. Sometimes he would look at me to see if I was getting it. Sometimes he looked at me for what I suppose he must have thought was dramatic effect. But mostly he watched the city. And he did actually follow the airplanes as they came in. His gaze was expectant.

—You know that I really couldn't care less, much as I respect your work, whether you draw things for us or not. It's not something I'm concerned about. Not in the least. If you want to, that's fine. If you don't. That's fine too. It's genuinely of no concern to me. And you might think that I'm downplaying it to take the pressure off, or to cover up the fact that actually we're *desperate* for your contribution and that I don't want to *appear* desperate in case you ask for too much money or get *put off* by the desperation, by having a weight of expectation on you, and that I'm going to talk you up over lunch and compliment you and leave you feeling that you at least owe me the small amount of energy it would take for you to do some work on Hiatus, for example. And then we have you. And that's not what's happening here. Really.

—What is Hiatus?

—It's political.

218

He rubbed a finger along his forehead as if he was sweating, which he wasn't. He continued, during all the time I was with him, to wipe, rub, scratch and generally *handle* his face, and his neck. It was not so noticeable that you'd worry about it. It was not the jerky, involuntary, self-conscious movements of an obsessive. It was much more relaxed. He rolled up his shirtsleeves for the cigarettes. As if it was business. He lit mine for me, holding the lighter like it was a grenade. I'm not sure what I mean. He held it as if he was half convinced that it would explode. He squinted as he lit it, and each time seemed to be surprised that all that happened was that a little bright flame appeared.

—Your drawings are filled in by their viewers. They're lines and shapes, in two dimensions, flat on the page. You give them very little, everything else comes from me. Or him. Or her. Or whoever it is who's looking at them. Anna wasn't completely wrong. But she missed the terror in that. The terror of what comes out of us. Of what we bring to things. Your drawings solicit unease. She always misses the terror. It surprises her. You don't know her very well, do you?

—No.

—No. You never will. What's to know? She's barely more than a doodle.

I can't remember the chronology of the things he said. I'm giving it to you as I remember it. But he jumped all over the place. There was a long conversation, for example, about children, children as an abstract. The idea of childhood, and our discomfort with our own thoughts. But I've cut that.

He ordered himself some clams and pasta. I wanted exactly the same thing, but once he'd ordered it I couldn't order it, so I ordered the sea bass. Randolph's mostly does fish. Which is odd, as of course it's nowhere near the sea. Why should it be though? They have refrigerated trucks now, and quick-freeze air freight from Sardinia and the Hebrides. I suppose it if was at sea level at least I would be less aware of it. But perched where they are, on top of the Lacon Tower, you'd think that if they specialised in anything it would be birds.

—I started BOX in 1997. People come and go. I have no interest in any of them really. Not in any sort of sense that would mean anything to you. That would attract you to us. I am interested in seeing that they work hard, that they do their best work while they're at BOX, that they get paid enough that they don't notice the waste, that they're happy and looked after and get free gym membership and good holidays and that they like me and look up to me and want to impress me, and I'm interested in dropping them as soon as they show the first sign of what you've got oozing out of you like sweat – which is the idea that they're better than all this.

—I never said that.

—Yes you did.

He had looked at me for this. And he held my stare. Not aggressively, but he held it, half smiling, chewing an olive.

—You know what I am. You know what BOX is. You know what it does. You know how it fits in. Or, if you haven't put all of it into words for yourself, formulated it, you know it instinctively. You know that this . . .

he indicated, with a sweep of his arm, the city

— . . . is all a fake. It's a set. It's a joke. It's a prop. You know that. It's paper-thin. It reeks of the temporary. It is a monument to fragility, in glass and stone and faulty

220

wiring. Look at it. It's a fucking nightmare. BOX does the wiring.

I looked. The sky was a milky grey, the same colour as most of the buildings. From our vantage point tangles of masonry and rooftops and communications devices collided with the horizon, with each other, and seemed to curdle themselves in confusion. The sharp lines and the pleasing shapes were few and disjointed, like things you might salvage from the debris of a landfill.

—It's just. It's just the city.

—It is. It's just the city.

He had taken off his leather jacket. It hung on the back of his chair, crumpled and expensive and male. His left hand rubbed his right arm. He peered out at the buildings and the sky, at the dots of aircraft and the bright rectangles of windows reflecting a sun I couldn't see. He is very masculine, Anthony Edgar. He emphasises the blood and bone that make him. I expected him to bark at me. But his voice stayed sane, wheeling gently around the cold roads of the things he thought.

—Incorporation. The city, like all cities, and like all humanly altered land, which is, let's face it, most of the planet, is doubly incorporated. I mean both in the corporate sense, which is the broad neo-capitalist sense, of all space being private space publicly available at a set price, an admission price – which is paid indirectly of course, through what you pay to *look* acceptable, admittable, to look like you've paid – as well as in the sense of combination – combining, becoming unified, not just with other humanly altered spaces, but with the humans who alter them. We take the city into our bodies. The city lives in us, just as much as we live in it. Just as much. We're half concrete. There are wires wrapped up in our veins. We're half-man, half-predigested water. We have other people's skin in our hair. We breathe their breath. You might as well kiss me. We're the piss of a million neighbours and stink of the sky.

—You've lost me.

—Oh. OK.

Our food arrived. He ate slowly, and I tried to match him, but he was doing all the talking, and the sea bass was cooling quickly, and I wasn't really enjoying it in any case. I pushed parts of it around my plate and ate the occasional small piece, trying to compare what I had left to what he had left. He seemed always to have a mountain of pasta and clams, which he spooled on to his fork like someone not eating but fidgeting.

—Why do you draw animals so much?

—Why . . . ?

—Yes. Why? You draw a lot of animals. Different kinds of animals. As if . . . I don't know. Why do you do that?

—I don't think I draw an . . . especially large number of animals.

I had wanted to say *peculiarly*, but I was sure that I would not be able to pronounce it. The sea bass is a rigorous fish.

—I think you do. Do you go to the zoo? A lot?

—No. I don't like zoos.

—Why not?

—Well. They're inhuman.

He looked at me then. I don't know if it was a joke or not. It just came out of me. I was tired of picking bones from my mouth.

—That's absolutely correct. That's the point.

—You've lost me.

—Most people like zoos. They like to go and look at

the animals. They like to look at the cages and the enclo-
sures and the feeding-time rituals and the teeth and the
fur and the hide and the claws and the screeching and
bellowing and the smell. They like it all. They can take
those little miniature trains around and show their kids.
Show their kids the hippopotamus and the snake. The
rhinoceros and the elephant and the lion. All those weird
living shapes, confined in a nice arrangement of rock-
eries and pools and painted backgrounds of the Serengeti
or the Arctic or the Congo River delta. But you don't
like it. And neither do I. And I suspect it's for the same
reason.

He was staring out at the city again, his eyes examining
the skyline in a way that made you look where he was
looking, thinking that there must be something going on
there. Some sort of commotion. But there was nothing.
Just the huddled city and the jagged roofs and the sky
pressing down and I wondered why, being so high up, all
the space seemed to have disappeared.

—This is not ours. This is not our planet. We act as if
it is. We act as if we're comfortable here. But. We're like
vagrants on cardboard by the train station, by the air-
conditioning vents. We are temporary here. We're clueless.
We build things to keep us warm. I'm part of that. BOX
is. Reassurance. Everything we do, we do for reassurance.
The task of BOX is not to make you buy certain things.
The task, the purpose, of BOX is to make you believe that
buying certain things is not as pointless, vacuous and empty
as you suspect it is. It's to stop you thinking about the
inherent shittiness of the human world. The constructed
world. Which is the world we live in. The world is
constructed to make you feel at home in it. All architecture is the architecture of reassurance. Even architecture

like this thing. Sure it makes people uneasy. You think that isn't comforting? Of course it is. It's scary-movie comfort. It's the adrenalised compensation for the bland banal rest of it. It's the building that makes us feel brave. Which is a *great* comfort to us. It's like white-water rafting. Rock climbing. We need a little managed danger to keep us from going mad. Like going to the zoo. All those nasty lions and tigers and polar bears just inches from the soft skulls of infants. The thrill.

He slapped a hand on the glass of the window, and lifted it then and looked at it and shrugged. I'm not sure. Bit weird. I think he was after a fly.

—The Lacon Tower is a monument to our mastery of gravity and the inanimate world. As the zoo is a monument, an exhibition, a *demonstration,* of our mastery over the natural world, over animals and the smell of shit. BOX covers up the smell of shit. It's what I do. I caress your intelligence and your emotions and your sense of yourself and I massage your life into continuance. Into earning and spending. Holidaying and house-owning and child-rearing and voting and chatting on the Internet and taking a trek in the Himalayas.

—Is that how BOX got its name?

—What?

—Vagrants sleeping on cardboard boxes by the air-conditioning vents. Is that what you were thinking of?

He looked at me then. And said nothing. He looked at me very carefully and all his rubbing and his scratching briefly stopped. I thought I'd made some kind of faux pas. That I'd hit on some eccentric sore point. But then he smiled. And it seemed like a genuine, warm smile.

—Yes. Yes that's right. That's where it came from.

I think he was lying though.

I couldn't decide whether he was smart or stupid. I couldn't decide whether I was impressed or embarrassed. I couldn't disentangle what he said to me from what I was thinking. Or rather, I wasn't sure, as he said these things, whether I had thought them before for myself, or whether I was hearing them for the first time from him. I still didn't know what he was attempting. What his intentions were. But I began to wonder, for the first time I think, whether he might actually *not* be interested in me working with him. At least, not in BOX.

—Reassurance has a diminishing return though. That's the problem. Especially now. Right now, things are bad. Business is looking difficult. There are hard times coming. People are people. They are stupid and doltish and they can be led like sheep for a while. For a long while, as it happens. But eventually they turn and they spasm and they kick. And they get ideas. And they share them. And soon everything starts to look like what it is. Unacceptable. My middle name is George. Imagine that. Anthony George. I'm the spirit of the age.

He laughed and threw his fork down as if he'd had enough. There was loads left. My sea bass lay sundered.

—We're pushing too hard. We're taking it too far. I'm a capitalist. Hands up to that. Hallelujah for it. Capitalism is my country, my race, my religion, my sexuality, my ethnicity, my food and drink, the love of my life, and they're killing it, they're killing it dead. It's going to implode. They're making the world unsafe for capitalism. Anthony George Edgar. AGE. Tony George Edgar. Tony and George. Among others. They're fucking it up. They're poisoning the water. Out of sheer stupidity. Because they are the worst kind of people you could have at the helm. People who believe they're at a helm. They're the worst

kind of assholes to have in charge of the free world –
assholes who actually seem to believe that there's such a
thing as a free world. They're the worst kind of idiots to
have running a war against terror. Because they're the kind
of idiots who . . .

He trailed off and his hand did a figure of eight, or
something, against the city. I threw a napkin over the evis-
cerated fish. Anthony Edgar's voice took a slow turn, down
a notch. He rubbed the back of his neck as if it hurt him.

—Life is a conspiracy of acquiescence. Western, contemporary, urban life. Our kind of life. It is the allocation of
parts and protocols. It's tolerant and liberal and comfortable. It proceeds by offerings. Special offerings and special
offers. We spend all our time reassuring each other. It's
been a great bit of fabrication. And it's coming to an end.

—It is?

—Yes it is. We've given everyone everything. Jobs,
money, credit, DVD players, computers, mobile phones,
cheap flights, digital music, the World Wide Web, there's
not much left. What can you think of? We put ourselves
on the television, we put ourselves on T-shirts, we put
ourselves into starring roles in our own online porn and
our own online autobiographies, we share our thoughts
with the world, we are described and discussed and
displayed, and the supermarkets know what we like and
the websites remember our names, and the whole world's
easy, getting easier, and look how bright and onward and
upward, marvellous, the whole thing is. And look at how
anyone you ask, anyone at all, will tell you that it's all,
all of it, the whole fucking thing, trivial and useless and
insulting and crass and demeaning and warped and
revolting. Celebrity junk. Vacuous. Dispiriting. No one
wants to live in this shit any more.

He gave a long sigh and leaned across the table towards me. Our plates must have been cleared away by now. He insisted that we share a cheeseboard. And more coffee. The place was almost deserted. A table of four women looked bored with their conversation. A few scattered businessmen sat alone. A family of tourists argued wearily over what building was what. That is the cathedral. No that is the museum.

—It's a difficult time to be in the business I'm in. People are on to us. They know how it works. And we're getting to the point where knowing how it works is no longer a novelty. There is a slow, international, *resentment* building among the constituency.

—The constituency?

—You and me. The people in this restaurant. Eating here and working here. The Western, urban, earning power block on whose behalf the world is set up and run. The constituency. They're starting to sicken. You're starting to sicken. I'm starting to sicken. The only hope for us now is the terror. The planes into buildings. The suicide bombs. All that can save my country, my nation, my love and my race – the only thing that can save capitalism is terror.

He sat back again, and watched me. I wasn't sure what I was supposed to do. Someone was ordering sea bass. I could hear her voice to my left, asking about and then ordering the sea bass. And it struck me as an incredible end for a fish. To be consumed at the top of a reassuring human tower a hundred miles from the sea.

—Are you saying terrorism is a good thing?

—Of course not.

—But . . . ?

—It's not a good thing. It scares me, frankly. You think I look at the planes coming in and hope that one of them is going to veer this way? No. But I'll tell you this much. Violence is the natural tendency of mankind. Believe me when I say this. Capitalism is violence contained, channelled, made acceptable, long-term, packaged out and rationed as distraction and amusement. This world is a fucking nightmare, yes. What has capitalism done? It's buffered us from the world. It's put a great big comfortable cushion between us and the hoary horns of nature.

He laughed.

—It's thrown a mattress down on the nettled grass. It's built cities on the burial grounds. It's enchanted the forest. It's covered the world that we live in with things that we've made. To make us more comfortable. So that we don't see the claw and the hoof and the fang and the blood that really runs this place. The guts of it. We never see any of that fibre and sinew and mess and stench. But the problem is now that we never see anything else either, other than the shit we've made, and how shit it is. We never see things that even our grandparents saw, like the Milky Way. Or an otter. So what do we need? We need to take things down a notch. We need to cut out some of the crap. Punch a hole in the mattress. Feel less like everything is muffled. Less like we're wrapped up in blankets, more like we're living. We need all of society to go white-water rafting for a while. To feel the exhilaration of the threat of death. Bring it on. Bring it fucking on.

He was looking at me now, and ignoring the city. I think he more or less believed what it was he was saying. I wanted to argue against him somehow. I wanted to object, and to say, *No, you've got it wrong*. But I wasn't sure what my argument was.

—Capitalism seeks to separate us from the world. Wrap us up. Terrorism, this new kind, seeks to separate us from capitalism. It wants to provoke a collapse, rip off the blankets. It wants us to know what it's like to be naked in the world. And part of us, don't tell me this isn't true, part of us wants to know what that feels like too. And we know we'll never do it voluntarily, not with our credit cards and our health insurance and our movie channels. So maybe, just maybe, we could do with some more of this suicide shit. Maybe it would do us all some good. You think?

The cheese was very good. There were four different types, I can't remember the names, although the waiter did tell us, as well as oatcakes and grapes. Anthony Edgar smiled at me broadly while I tried to think of the reasons why terrorism is a bad thing.

—It's not so strange. The political terrorist is old hat. Then we got the religious terrorist. Also a very old phenomenon. But reinvented especially for our times. Special edition. Suicide becomes the weapon of choice. The religious terrorist is blending into, bleeding into, the narcissistic terrorist. Where the theological rhetoric becomes threadbare, if it exists at all. American kids who shoot up their high school and kill themselves. It's a kick. Western-born, Western-educated Muslims blowing up their neighbours. Same thing. Same self-obsessed ego bombing. *Only I understand how shit the world is.* Teenage. Male. *And when I do something about it, then by Allah, or by Jesus, or by the hem of my long black raincoat, then that'll show them.* Suicide sulking. That's what we've got now. These categories overlap. But the next category is a little scary. Inevitable, and in some sense, already around. Remember Theodore Kaczynski?

I nodded.

—OK. Read his stuff. Remember how certain artists, and

writers, but artists especially, got so excited about 9/11? They were excited by the idea of it as art. As transforming public spectacle. They had to apologise of course. Roll it right back. They've got sales to protect, they've got their Sunday-paper profiles to keep going. They let something slip there. They quickly took it back. No fools, those guys. But the idea is out there. It's in the water. It's in the back of all our minds. No matter how hard we fight it. No matter how hard we deny it. It's there. We own it. It's our idea.

—What is?

—That terrorism might just be the intelligent man's response to this world.

He speared a piece of pecorino. I don't know if it was pecorino or not. I have no idea. I think I use words now because of the way they sound as much as anything else. It flitters me and bounces.

—Is it your response to the world?

—I have a daughter. She is seven. She has curly blonde hair and a puppy. She runs down the garden path carrying the puppy in her arms and she puts him down on the grass, and he half cowers and half collapses, and she tells him to *do his business*, and she stomps back up the path towards the house. And the puppy slouches along after her. It's Western civilisation in a single scene. I don't want the anti-terrorist squad breaking down my door, scaring my daughter, standing on her puppy.

All of this seemed ready on the tip of his tongue. I wanted to be able to say something that didn't sound like I'd just thought of it that second.

—Otherwise, you know, I'd be out there with the waistcoat nail bomb. In a flash.

—What's Hiatus?

—It's a bomb plot. I'm indoctrinating people into

230

wearing the waistcoats for me. Then I'm going to send them to strategic places of exaggeration on a specific Tuesday afternoon. And get them to kill the shit out of capitalism. You're on my list.

—No, really.

—I have a lot of money. You wouldn't believe how much money I have. I want to launch a subversive, untraceable series of television, newspaper and street ads. Except they're not advertising anything. I simply want them to be provocative. Odd. Weird. Subversive. Fucked up. There is so little space left for subversion now. I want to start elbowing a few things out of the way. Basically I'm encroaching on your territory. Except I have resources you can't even imagine. You interested?

I was genuinely surprised. He *did* want me to work for him. Or with him. Or did he? There was an expectant glint in his eye that made me suspect that if I said *Yes*, he'd laugh at me and tell me *Hard luck, I'm not interested in you.* Or that Hiatus was not really a campaign of intellectual provocation but a new model of car or a new range of skincare products for men. Then why the lunch? Why all that talk, all that exposition?

—Maybe. When are you moving into your new offices?

His smile faded. Slowly. He glanced at the city. Then at what was left of his cheese. His left hand scratched the nape of his neck as if gouging out a cavity.

—There's been a couple of problems with the building. How did you know about that?

—A friend of mine works for Edwards Patten.

—OK. Well, I suppose most people know most people. What did your friend tell you?

—About the fourth floor. All the problems. The lifts and the stairs and the stain.

He sighed.

—Yeah. I keep a record of it. I write it all down. That's my tip. When things start to go weird, start writing it all down. The fourth-floor notebook. It's quite a laugh really. I suppose. Do you want to see it?

—The notebook?

—No, the building. Do you want to go there? To have a look. The stain is remarkable. It really is.

The streets stood back from Anthony Edgar. They widened as he moved through them and people cleared his path and I bumped along in his wake like something snagged on his jacket. He didn't have a car or a driver. He bounded along the footpaths talking on his phone, making the necessary arrangements for this diversion – cancelling things, rearranging them, delegating. Shoppers and tourists and the lunchtime workers crowded me, collided with me, reformed their dense obstruction just behind him, and tried to shoulder me from my path. I couldn't handle the city. The noise was of traffic and voices and footsteps, and I hopped sideways and dodged prams and wheelchairs and suitcases dragged like afterthoughts, as if what they contained wasn't worth the effort, and I cursed and started to sweat, and I struggled to keep up.

I'm not sure I really wanted to see the building at all.

He walked, pointlessly it seemed to me, for about ten minutes, still talking on his phone, and it was only when I glanced at him, shorn off, that I saw the phone had disappeared, and he was still talking, so he must, I supposed, have been talking to me, and he had to shout a little, and I missed parts of it, as he breezed through the crowds as if they weren't there, while I was caught on the skinny bones of kids and their mothers and deflected off the muscular heft of men whose way I obstructed, and his words went:

—*Look at this shit . . . is mounted . . . nothing so foreign as the home-grown that isn't directed at you. Nothing so foreign as your teenage daughter's diary or your wife's phone conversations. The closest things to you. Look at all this fucking shit. How do we live in this garbage? Look at these signs. Look at the faces and the waddling fat families and these cheap suits and their shopping. Point out to me something that isn't shit. Shopfronts, well-being, mega deals, 50 per cent, 20 per cent, two for one, fun in the sun, candles, mirrors . . . ideal . . . ratchet up the ratchet . . . ratchet up the ratchet . . . the more the created environment becomes cheap, repetitive, acquisitive, loud, ugly, vulgar, without human alcove, WITHOUT HUMAN ALCOVE . . . where the only breaks from it are the marshalled, tethered nature of the parks, the more we, as its inhabitants, treat it not as a human place, to be celebrated and enjoyed, but as a naturally occurring habitat, hostile to us, in which we must become less human in order to survive. Less Human.*

People were starting to glance at him, I thought. Maybe.

—*We are suffocating on the streets. We are drowning in this mush of our own making. And I know every face. I know by the way they walk and by the bags they carry and by the clothes they wear what each of them is worth. There is no one on this street who surprises me. They are formatted. They are perfectly formed. They are doing exactly what they're supposed to be doing. Everything is as it should be. Everything is carrying on as it should be. Nothing is wrong with this picture. TAXI!*

In the car, Anthony Edgar was largely silent. He fiddled with his phone. He gave occasional instructions to the taxi driver. We moved from the mush to the sparser places, through better neighbourhoods, then back into a messy grid of the same shopfronts and the same tatty pavements and the same people, differently arranged, and the city thinned and fattened, gave and rolled back, behaved like the sea beneath the sky, altering but not stopping, and we seemed to drive for hours, and the parks, Anthony Edgar told me, the parks were only tricks. He was making me nervous. He became more nervous the further we travelled. Quieter, more agitated, and I could hear his breathing and the jig of the coins in his pocket as he bounced his legs in that autistic way that most men do, when they need to.

I saw the dog again.

It spiked in my field of vision, like seeing your own name on a list.

How can I explain this? I am tired of explaining this. It looms too often and it recedes too soon. What if I told you my dream? No. It was the same dog, yes. The same dog that I'd seen outside the café on the Friday, with Michael, yes. And the same dog that I'd thought I'd seen in the park on Friday night, yes. How does that help? Does that help? In the rotating silence of a car that turns a corner, I saw the dog again. And he saw me. How does seeing something stop you from hearing anything? Because the sound certainly shut down. But of course what do I really know? I have no idea if the sound actually did shut down or whether I simply use that, de rigueur, because it's in the movies. Because we are given our bags by Anthony Edgar, and we carry them, and we carry them. In any case, I did feel terrified. I really did. Didn't I? I had virtually convinced myself that the dog in the park had been imagined only. I had quarantined the thought. And here it was, escaped again. Escaped and standing on a street corner, dripping with the sweat of the day, breathing hard and staring at me.

He stood there, at the corner, as if waiting to cross the road. His gluey eyes were fixed on our taxi, on me, on my face, as we slowly took the turning, from main road to minor, on to some short cut of the lesser city. It was a low corner, and everything dipped down into it, genu-flected and passed on, and we came so close to the black-coat dog that I could have sworn that it was his breath that clouded the window next to my head, that steamed a patch of glass and hid me, and not my breath, not my breath at all, which I held, which I guarded, jealously, like a secret. I took in the power of his muscles and his legs and the gaping wound of his mouth, and I had the sense that all his potential for violence was as nothing when compared to his patience. He seemed to nod. Yes.

I don't know how things happen. I'm sitting here now and I'm thinking of the dog on the corner, and I'm wondering how much of this is mine. I'm thinking about the car, the taxi, and I can recall nothing about it. I'm thinking of Anthony Edgar, and of how many of the words I've written down here actually came out of his mouth. I'm thinking – maybe he just sat there politely over lunch and we talked about drawing, and graphics, and the reintroduction of intel-ligence into daily life. Perhaps we shook hands in the street and went our separate ways. Perhaps I never took that journey out to BOX, to the flapping walls and the buckled floor and the stale smell and the growths, and all the rotting things of the haunted building. And maybe when I say that I was terrified when I saw the dog, maybe I wasn't terrified at all. How would I know what terror feels like? Because I jumped once, at a movie? Because I got locked in a city park? What do I know about terror? Nothing. Nothing has ever happened to me. No catastrophe. No pain. No illness. No accident. No abandonment, no loss. I have never been in danger in my life. My life has been contained in a sheath. Nothing has ever touched me. Nothing. No one has ever died on me. Except a middle-aged woman I didn't know, and a mouse. I don't know what terror is. How can I say I was terrified? It's more likely that my heart leapt and that my mouth dried and that I was not in terror so much as I was in, I don't know, the gaze of something familiar, something comfortable, something that touched me. Maybe what I felt was some odd subsidiary of love. Which has, I imagine, some terror in it.

K.

—This place gives me the fucking creeps.

The BOX building stands on a side street in a dilapidated but gentrifying neighbourhood somewhere to the south-west of the river. There are old factories being converted into new offices and residential units. An ambitious-looking restaurant sits on the corner. Opposite that, on the main road, there is a bustling bar, and an estate agent's by the bus stop. It's all on the rise. As well as BOX, other companies seem to have moved it. There is a low building discreetly marked with the logo of a film lab I've heard of. And another, older building houses the offices of two magazines, one of which K has a subscription to. Other buildings looked busy, with couriers coming and going, and the type of people you associate with website design huddled smoking on the footpaths.

BOX itself was as Michael had described it to me. I liked it. I liked the metal lettering down the side, standing out from the brickwork, casting shadows. It looked empty, but it did not alarm me.

I must have spent less than half an hour inside the BOX building. By the end of it I could not talk. A security guard opened the door. He hadn't come from inside. I don't know where he came from. He just appeared as we stepped out of the taxi, and he led us to the door, and he opened it, and he went in and spent a moment pressing buttons on a beeping alarm console before Anthony Edgar held the door for me and I walked inside.

It looked like any other office reception. A bit gloomy and unused. Some post lay scattered on the floor. The security guard picked it up. It took me a moment to realise that I felt taken aback, and a moment more to understand why. It was the smell. Anthony Edgar coughed. The security guard waved at his face with a handful of junk mail. I held my breath for a minute, trying to work out if I wanted to breathe through my nose or my mouth.

The smell was rich and textured and it crawled on my tongue like a jelly. It seemed familiar but I couldn't place it. I thought at first that I'd have to leave. But actually, it was not sickening. Or not sufficiently sickening. I asked Anthony Edgar what the hell it was. At least, I tried to. What came out was garbage, some combination of random meaningless words, some communication I had not intended, which I had not authorised, from a part of me that I did not recognise, like a coded signal from a spy in my brain. I don't know what it was. I blinked, coughed, tried again.

—What in hell for that?

It was close enough. He gave me a peculiar look.

—Damp. It's damp. We have a problem with damp. A big problem. Hence the smell. Hence the stain. Everything else you heard is bullshit.

He led me up through a building that seemed to be

sinking, and I looked at my feet sometimes, expecting them to have organic matter clinging to them, to have the rotted leaves and twigs and corpses of a dense, tropical under-growth stuck fast to the soles. There was nothing but carpet tiles and polished floors. There was nothing but the newness of desks yet to be assembled and computers in boxes and chairs still wrapped in plastic and the hum of the lights coming on as we climbed the stairs and looked into offices. He refused to take the lift. Not that I asked him. He refused it in the way he took those steps, like a man a little puzzled to find himself doing such a thing, but certain that there was no conceivable alternative.

—Watch yourself here.

There was a kind of fungal growth on a wall. It was of no particular shape that I could determine. Something moved. The corner of my eye. I turned but there was nothing, and I imagined the building filled with hooded boys who knew how to disappear, and with birds who could fly around stairwells. It was probably the light of the sun, coming in and out of cloud, throwing itself around. I didn't know what time it was. My shoulder bag weighed a ton. The smell was getting stronger. Does damp rise or fall? It rises.

As we reached the third floor, we heard the lift start up. The gears engaged with a clunk and the motor kicked in and the thing began to purr. We stepped out of the stair-well to look at it. The walls dripped, a window was wet with condensation, something darted through a door, I thought. We looked at each other. Anthony Edgar laughed.

—You know, it could be that Max is playing silly buggers. It could be that Max has decided to come and join us. Or it could be just another strange lift incident. Any of those things really. Who the fuck knows? Who knows? I don't know.

We watched the lights go 1, then 2, then 3. There was a ping, a perfect filmic ping, and the door opened on a wood-panelled, red-carpeted, generously mirrored, empty lift. Anthony Edgar coughed and his mouth worked, as if on a bad taste.

—Who the fuck knows? I certainly don't fucking know.

It was the middle of the day. A scatter of sunlight moved around us. We were in a brand new building in an inner suburb of one of the world's great cities. We were surrounded by humanity. We climbed to the fourth floor like we were on a path up a Peruvian mountainside. I've never been to Peru. We climbed as if in the foothills of the Andes, parched and sweating, almost overpowered by the stench of rotting vegetation, startled by movements on the periphery, by the sense of eyes on our backs, of *things* in the trees, underfoot, overhead, of moving through a hostile environment. Not malign, but hostile. What is the difference? I don't know. I knew when I started the sentence, I had forgotten by the time I reached the end.

The fourth floor is a mess. The smell is very bad, but it seemed to affect me less than Anthony Edgar. It is an organic smell, and I suppose it might be damp. And I suppose that the staining on the walls, and the mossy deposits on the ceiling, and the general sense of what I can only describe as decay, might all be damp too. Things lay broken on the floor. Workmen's tools which seemed incongruous, such as a pickaxe and a shovel, were propped against a wall. A telephone on a window sill appeared to have melted. The windows seemed covered in a sort of scum, as if something had breathed on them or sneezed on them, or hurled dirty water at them. Part of the ceiling hung down in dripping folds of plasterboard and tiling. Against one corner there was a small pile of what looked at first like banana skins, blackened and congealed, but which could not have been that. I saw a large spider standing still in a corner, waiting. There was a dim noise like shuffling which I could not source. Anthony Edgar coughed heavily. He held a handkerchief to his mouth. I saw him put his other hand on a desktop for support and then pluck it away again, and look at it, and wipe it on his jeans.

—It's worse than it was. Jesus, what a stench. Australia is over here.

I knew I couldn't talk. I said nothing, not because I had nothing to say, but because I knew that my voice would not work. I would utter nonsense. As I followed I tested a phrase under my breath. *What's that noise?* came out as *Point rival flows*. And the noise bothered me. I thought of marching armies. It could have been mechanical, but it could have been feet. My eyes scurried around the room, which was a large open-plan area. Doors led off it into smaller offices. One door had fallen from its hinges, the wood splintered and chewed. Everything looked wet like a mouth. We headed for the boardroom. Things moved against distant walls, on distant walls, things dashed and ran, there were a dozen noises a minute, of small collisions, and over all of that the rising shuffle, as if of an approaching mass. The pitch became appalling.

—Don't step on it. It's actually wet. I think it's bigger than it was, but maybe it's the same. Someone tried to put down coins to mark the cities. They disappeared.

He started coughing again, and turned away. *Here's the body, detective, it hasn't been moved,* and the uniform cop who leads him there turns away and retches. But this was just Australia. On the carpet of a corner office. The boardroom, he'd said, though it was free of furniture and the windows were smeared with shit. Australia took up about a third of the floor space, and seemed to me, though I had nothing to compare it to, completely accurate. I walked around it. From the east (I mean the putative eastern side of the putative Australia) it looked a little like the distorted head of a rhinoceros. From the north, or upside down, it looked like the USA, squeezed away from the Canadian border in a curve. From the west it looked like a wood-pecker with a hunchback. A bird flying out of a cloud. Or the distorted rhinoceros again, differently distorted. From the south though, which is the way you saw it from the doorway, it looked remarkably like Australia. With Tasmania and everything.

I found that my hand was in my bag. I had been reaching for my pen. For a notebook and a pen. I wanted to draw it. But why would I want to draw Australia? It's a shape you can find in plenty of places. Why draw another one? I took my hand out. Perhaps what I wanted was to draw a distorted rhinoceros, or a woodpecker with a hunchback.

—You know the thing about Australia? You know the fear? You know why?

I shook my head. Anthony Edgar looked green, sincerely ill, his skin was damp and he gripped the doorway and held the handkerchief in front of his mouth.

—The white man clings to the coast. The European. Us lot. The cattle rustlers and the stealers of sheep. We didn't understand the place. Look at it. It's fucking huge. So we clung to the coast and we clung to the grass we could get to grow and we huddled in view of the sea and we ignored the rest of it. The outback. Where the black man wanders and the weird animals wander and where the sun will kill you or the spiders will kill you, where you can get nothing to grow, where you cannot build or plant or settle, because it ignores you. The country ignores you. You're an odd incompatible species and you don't know the tricks that the black man knows and you die if you go there. You did.

He took a break to cough, violently. I found myself swallowing a taste like butter.

—So you cling to the coast. Pretend you like it better there. But it's not a choice. It's terror. You realise you shouldn't be there at all. So you cling to the sea and the idea of somewhere else and you learn how to swim and to surf and you master what you can master and you make a big show of controlling the things you can control, like the waves and the easy land, and the black man. It's always easier to control someone else, put down someone else, than it is to admit you're lost. Australia is a nation afraid of itself. They're stalked by fire and poison and the anger on the inside and there's nothing they can do about it except spend all day at the beach and tell themselves they're an outdoorsy sort of people. Australia sums it up. *Fancy a tinny?*

He turned, and scuttled away from me, and was loudly sick on to the stinking floor, his hands on his waist as if squeezing himself dry. I wanted to help him but I didn't know this man. I walked to his side and put out my arm, but I didn't want to touch him. *Are you OK?* came out OK. I thought. He didn't answer. I rummaged in my bag for my phone. I don't know who I was going to call. I don't know how I was going to speak to them. I lifted my bag with my knee beneath it, and I rested my knee against the lip of a desk, for better balance, so that I could push past all the crap in my bag and get the phone. I would call Anna. *Your boss is throwing up outside the board-room. What should I do?* I found the phone and I knew that my voice wouldn't work. Maybe it would work on the phone. My knee was stuck. Anthony Edgar was vomiting again, his body bent like a broken stick. I couldn't move my knee. It was stuck to the lip of the desk. I lifted my bag to look at it and lost my balance, and saw that it, my knee, had adhered to some sort of clear oozing gunk, and as I fell, to the right, towards Anthony Edgar, as I fell and my phone flew out of my hand, as I fell, my eyes were thrown around the room for the small parts of a second, and I saw, staring back at me, as I collided with Anthony Edgar and sent him crashing into the wet wall, as I fell and my phone flew from me and landed in the stinking pool of Anthony Edgar's vomit, as I fell, and the knee of my jeans snagged and ripped, I saw, l don't know what I saw, a stripe of eye, a mouthful of colour, the various faces of living things, of animals, their moving parts, their paws and claws and mandibles, their mouths and demeanours, staring at me, moving in, moving in, with a shuffle like the march of an army, deliberate, dead-eyed, rank. I rolled on the floor for less than a second and rose to face them down. The silent dripping room looked back at me, empty.

I would tell you my dream. But I have rules about these things. Now.

By the time we got downstairs, I was able to say *OK, OK, it's OK* over and over, but anything else I tried came out wrong. Anthony Edgar was very pale. His skin was slick. He had a bruise coming up on his temple. The knee of my jeans was ripped. I had vomit on my shoulder. My phone had been abandoned. Anthony Edgar had tried to pick it up. But even he could not manage it. It lay face down in the mess, like a raft on a drained lake, a seabed of steaming wreckage, of clams and matted ribbons. The ghost of a sea bass flicked in my stomach. On the stairs I think he sobbed a little, but stopped himself and made himself calm.

I expected the security guard to be shocked at the sight of us, but he simply shook his head as if he'd seen it all before, and he held the door for us.

—You shouldn't go up there, Mr Edgar. You're going to kill yourself up there one of these days.

—It's OK, Max, thank you. Call us a taxi, will you?

Max. I looked at him closely for the first time. He was in his fifties. He was overweight and friendly and kind. He was not missing.

In the taxi Anthony Edgar called the office, and shouted at people about glue. About leaving glue around on desk-tops, about the state of the place, about getting in the architects and the contractors, about a meeting with the wet-rot people, a meeting with the damp-proof people, a meeting with the *specialists*, about demolishing and starting again, about lawyers and selling, about leaseholds and free-holds and money. About everything he could possibly think of. He shouted about environmental health and insurance. For a long time he was silent, and listened, and then he shouted some more about traffic and the waste of a day.

He seemed to understand that I could not talk. He wrote me a cheque for one thousand pounds, apologised about my phone, gave me his card, and dropped me outside my hotel. I stood on the street and watched his taxi disappear into the metal and the concrete and the glass and the flesh, distributed.

Posters

I stayed in my room and practised speaking. I stayed in my room and practised speaking. I stayed in my room and practised speaking.

I talked to no one but myself, to my reflection in the mirror. I spent long hours desperately frightened, and long hours sleeping, troubled, and my dreams were disgusting. I cried, I think I can admit that. I cried quite a lot, and I wrote down how I felt, in long streams of gibberish, in large blocks of text, and I drew no pictures while I was awake. Most of what I wrote is personal, and I don't want to share it. But my confusion is evident in it, and my fear, and in my more reasonable moments, I knew that I was in big trouble, and that I needed to do something about it.

I did not notice the time. I was ill. I became ill, possibly as soon as Monday night. I think I had a temperature. And my dreams suggest fever. I recall waking covered in sweat, several times. I recall being sick once or twice, violently, and being unable to eat, and I remember lying quietly in the bath for a long time, until I moved and realised that the water was cold. I wondered why nobody called me. I felt abandoned. I had forgotten about my phone. I remembered it only when I slept, and the dreams ran at me from across the room, with their pincers, with their eyes. I was lost, and for long periods I did not realise it. And by the time I had recovered enough of myself to function, it was Thursday. Very early, Thursday morning.

I thought I was ready. I thought I was healed. I thought I had been through a bad time and was out the other side of it. I thought it was over. I had left home, left K, some bad things had happened, I had been ill, and I had spent some days alone in a hotel, recovering, I had recovered, and I thought that was the end of it. The end of the nonsense and the stupidity and the oddness and the strangeness and the end of all the fear and the uncertainty and the smell and nausea and the nails. I thought that I could return. I thought that I could go back to K and sort it out. I thought that I could tell K the story of David. And the story of Catherine Anderson and the story of Anthony Edgar, and that K would make tea and listen and be both startled and wise.

None of this was true.

If I left immediately, I would be home well before K left for work. I packed my bags. I filled my bags with things. I was going home. I stared and wondered at a tea-stained mug with DAVID written across it, and at an empty silver salt shaker. I put them in my shoulder bag. I put my notebooks there too, with Anthony Edgar's cheque and business card somewhere between the pages. I packed the clothes that the hotel had cleaned for me. I packed my torn jeans.

I checked out, nervously, afraid that I would not have the words. But it was fine. I had the words. Words, after all, are simple things. They are always there. You only have to reach for them. I asked for a taxi. I waited. I scanned the newspapers. There was nothing specific. My picture was not there. There was nothing the matter. It was all going to be OK. They called me. My car. My car was there. I was going home. I climbed in, put my bags in the corner, recited my address, fastened my seat belt, sat back, relaxed. Going home. It is the most natural thing in the world. Everything was all right. Everything was fine.

I was nervous of course. Of course I was nervous. And my nerves increased. But it was as if I was returning from a long trip, nothing more. And my nerves were mostly excitement and anticipation, and I seemed to have forgotten how bad this was, and I seemed to have forgotten the history of the thing, and I seemed to be mad, and to know it, and to be consoled, for no reason, and I seemed to think that everything was all right. And it wasn't.

I didn't even properly see the first one. Something registered. Something nicked at my mind, at my eye, something snagged, and I found myself turning in my seat to look at a lamp-post we had passed, without knowing why. I couldn't see what I was looking for. I turned round again. The second one I simply caught a glimpse of, through the other window, on the other side on the street, stuck to one of those silver boxes beside traffic lights. It just looked . . . familiar. Something. Some shape. I didn't get it. I didn't see what I was seeing, and then I was past it, the taxi was past it, and we were into my neighbourhood, and I was recognising places, and buildings and roads and corners, and something was wrong, something in me had changed. Things were not all right.

The third one and the fourth one and the fifth one were stuck to a piece of hoarding around a building site, a few doors down from Eric's. They were plastered there, side by side, and it took me a moment. To see what I was seeing. To realise it was the same thing three times, and that I knew what it was. I knew what it was.

Posters. Three identical posters. And identical as well to the others I had already passed. Like shards of myself broken off and flung back. Posters. Wordless posters. They carried only an image, a single image, a photograph, my photograph, of a dead mouse, lying by a kerb, with the tip of a pen visible in the corner, a dead mouse, his hands at prayer, stretched as if swimming, given up on the world, dead on the road, my photograph, that I took, my mouse, a week-old death, which I had left on my computer in the flat I share with K, in the flat where we live together, in whose mouth the pen, in whose life, just around the corner, from where I was, from where I was. The mouse.

—Stop here.

—Here?

—Stop here please.

I got out of the car. I left the door open. I got out of the car and I walked up to the hoarding and I looked at the body of the mouse. He lay on his side, with his belly exposed towards me, and his limbs, with their little feet, stretched out from either end. He was a grey brown. With the underside lighter. You'd think, against the ground, the belly would be black with dirt. You'd think. You'd think. There was a little indentation, as if something had poked him. A little mark. A blemish. The only one.

I looked up the street towards the corner of my road. All the lamp-posts held him. He was on the walls and the backs of the road signs. I walked a little towards home, and the taxi with its back door open followed me. I looked up the road towards my home. He was everywhere. He covered every surface. Every empty space was filled with his small, insignificant death. He lay on the road, on the paths, he floated on the breeze, he seemed stuck beneath the windscreen wipers of parked cars, he lay under their wheels and his limbs stretched through all the gardens. His little corpse lay strewn across every inch, all the way up to the railings of the park, where he hung in multitude, like a hundred different ways of saying the one thing.

The one thing.

The hotel gave me the same room and sent up notebooks and pens and I started writing this down and now I have reached the end.

The Holy City

We crumb. By which I mean we have in ourselves lots of bits, of bits, which, when we are shook, or distartled, they come apart and are multivarious and varied and several and much of us is apparently lost when this happens, much of us is lost and come apart and dismembered. Disremembered.

I am in some difficulty here.

And there is a way of reassembling us. But it is not ours. And I believe now in my heart that I am not what I said I was, nor was I ever what I thought I was, and that there is, in truth, nothing left of the world.

There is a dripping tap in the bathroom, a brown stain on the enamel where it drips, an error in the glass of the window, my error, crackling little cubes of it in the bath like crystals. Don't bathe here. There is a cold air coming in. Today it is colder. Bright steel-blue sky cold with hell in the brackets. Hell in the brackets. I think my mind.

Do you think I'll be OK?

I think my mind is huddled to one side of my head, I don't know, frightened or something, collapsible, crouching there against the left side, as if something on the right side. I have left the hotel. My hand.

I am in Rachel's flat. Her apartment. I've been making too much noise and she is not here. A brown stain on the eternal. The enamel. If I was seen the police will come.

In her hallway, which is long, and narrow, but which kinks in the middle, which sends you to your right as you make for the kitchen, there is a *painting* of a corridor that is like the corridor in the hotel. That kind of corridor, that kind of coincidence. It surprises me. It takes me suddenly still and silent. A sentence punctuated by laundry bags and breakfast trays. You don't climb up or down it. You read it left to right. Your eyes run across it, and you recognise the code, and some appliance put in you in childhood tells you what it means and that is how you understand everything. Even this. Something is cut.

If she painted it or not I don't know. Rachel does not paint. I don't *know* that she paints. She makes things from our thoughts, she takes them from us, and she shows them to us, and we recoil and revulse, and we wonder where they came from, and in what way, and in what way did they come. Do you remember when I was a kid and my mother? The bee sting on my thumb? Did that happen to me or to you? Did I tell you that or did you tell me? When you see it in your mind am I there too? What do I look like to you? Describe me. Describe me as a child with a swollen thumb. Where am I? What colour is my hair? Am I blond or dark? Am I plump or thin? Am I clothed or naked? Do I bar your way? What is in your pockets? What things are in your pockets? What are in the vials?

Revulsion. I suppose is what I meant, in some way. *Revulse* is not actually a word.

Rachel's place. I am in it. It is Monday; that is my belief.

I have not been here long. My hand is bleeding from the glass, and I have not paid enough attention to noise. There have been conversations. I have talked to people. I have climbed the sentences. My words come and go. The words come and go. And everything is heightened, raised, off the ground, first floor, twenty feet. I can see better but I can't see far. Bear with me.

I had to climb, upwards. From the floor, I mean the ground, to the top of a council bin, to a low roof. There was the corpse of a rat in the middle of the sky. I stared at it and listened. Something's happened in the city. Spirit of the age. I put my elbow in a rolled-up T-shirt and bruised it when I broke the bathroom window, but cut my hand plucking at the shards like a fool. And I let myself into Rachel's place by stepping into her bath and out again, just like that, graceful, three drips of my blood on the white lip where she rests her arms. If I was seen the police will come.

Blood on the handle.

I'm sitting down for a minute. Holding my hand in the air. I'll sit here in the silence, listening to it. It's for the best. I get my breath back. In the distance there is bellowing. There is bellowing and the sharp air of screaming birds, sounding for all the world like sirens. Rachel's place is a mess. You should see the mess here. I close my eyes and my hand drips blood on my shirt. My shirt next to my skin. My skin next to my blood. My blood next to yours.

I saw, inevitably, the dog, as I was driven back to the hotel in the taxi. After the posters. He followed us through slow traffic, like an escort, a slouching outrider from some cadre of the damned. From a B-movie called *Cadre of the Damned*. I turned on the intercom and asked the driver could he see the dog, could he see the dog out of the window, on the right-hand side, just behind us now, could he see him? He was on the phone, took a minute to respond, and his response was to ask me what it was I'd said, ask me to repeat it, and by that time the dog had gone, even I couldn't see him any more, he had vanished.

I've been dreaming about the dog but I can't tell you the details. Maybe I can. I don't know. I don't know how it works. In dreams we should be alone. You should be alone in yours, I should be alone in mine. Privacy is what we share. Suffice it to say that in my dream I get a lot closer to him than I ever have in reality. He gets a lot closer to me. He runs at me. I fall. We are factories of interesting substances, blood and others, and they are all in that dream, which I have had now six times. Or seven if you count . . . I cannot tell you the details.

There are rags and paper towels everywhere. As if she paints. There are figurines and dolls and reams of coloured paper. There are sheets ripped up and scattered. There is all the debris of what she does. There are no paintbrushes. No paint. No empty canvases. No easel. There is an easel. It is in the bedroom. On it there is an empty canvas. There is a can of paint on a box on the floor. The canvas is not entirely empty. In its top right corner there is the start of something. I don't know what. I lean in closer. There are pencil marks all over it. I follow them, I have to lean in to see them. It is like reading something by David. I cannot make it out. It looks like a building. She paints. Imagine. I didn't know, I found out between one word and the next. There are several printers. I cannot see her laptop. It is portable. But there are several printers.

Rachel is not here.

My hand is bloody and there is blood on my clothes and if I was seen the police will come. I run a tap and wash the wound and I cover it with kitchen paper and I gargle aspirin for my throat. I drink lots of water and make a one-handed cup of sweet tea, being careful about noise. The city is all noise. All shrieks and exhortations. My hand is fine.

For two days now I've been drinking mostly water and sweet tea and aspirin for my throat. I am not entirely sure that this is the right thing to do but I do it because it feeds me, or feeds in me that thing that worries me, and makes it less itself in me, less obvious to me, as if we were two *different* things – I mean me and the thing in me that I feed, that worries, as if my worrying self was a crouching hungry captive *in* myself, the same shape as me, but smaller, pacing up and down in the cell of my ribcage or my head, I said that, pacing and scratching off the days on the bone near the door, and waiting for the punctuation of water or sweet tea or the distant painkilling gargle or the end of it – out or dead. I have a strange picture of a naked smaller me inside me, like a secret child in an inner room. I don't know where that comes from. Probably from some book or film or scrawl on the human wall. It doesn't come from me. Nothing comes from me.

This is a set-up. I am a patsy. I never killed anyone.

All the words exist. All you have to do is reach for them.

We are coming into the plains. We are. Coming into the plains.

In Rachel's flat there is a disorientating clutter. I am sitting now, for example, on a surfboard. The light shade in this room is a child's pale blue dress, hung on some sort of wire frame which fills it out, so that what you see is the ghost of a child hovering . . . in the centre of the room, a light glowing in her chest, her heart, the cable over her invisible head suggesting a hanging. In the corner of the room is a stack of American gun magazines that reaches almost to the ceiling. There is tourist tat from Jerusalem, including remarkably kitsch representations of the world's major religions. There are photographs of the aftermaths of bombings, I don't know where she gets them, and shootings: corpses in streets, body parts, people running screaming, police with drawn guns, panic. Pictures of panic that I look at while I sip my tea. There are two traffic cones, both of which have been painted white. There are old telephones. I am uncertain here what is art, or material for art, and what is simply accumulated and accidental, just the detritus of a life like hers in a city like this at times like these. I am uncertain what to think. I think that is all I have to say.

I don't know where she is. I suspect she is away somewhere looking for someone who is not missing.

What if everyone you know in your life was to suddenly disappear?

When I got back to the hotel, after the posters, I looked up Edwards Patten Associates in the phone book.

—Michael?

—What?

—Are you OK?

—You've a nerve.

—What do you mean?

—Calling me.

I was silent. I guessed, I suppose, before he told me. I was confused but I understood what it was. Or. I understood that it existed. That it was the necessary thing for her, his mother. Maybe it was the truth.

—That's not what happened.

—You hid in her shower?

—No.

—So you could watch her?

—No, I didn't.

—Oh for God's sake, my mother is not so mad that she can make up something like this. She was in tears. She was distraught. You fucking creep. What the hell is wrong with you?

He wanted to shout, but there must have been people. He hissed at me and his voice cracked like ice on a pool. She had to tell him something, I suppose, afraid that I would tell him something. Or maybe I had to tell you something, afraid that she would tell you something. Why do we have the need to always tell each other things? Information. It is rabid. Out of control.

—That's not what happened.

—I don't need to know. I spoke to you that day. You fucking called me. You called me and you hung up on me and you never once mentioned going to my mother's. You never said word one about it.

This was true. I never told him about the sports centre. Or did I? I never told K. There are things I just haven't told anybody. A volume of deletions.

—I'm just embarrassed for you. I really am. You're sick.

—It didn't –

—The only reason I've taken this call is because of David.

I thought he meant K. I thought he'd intended to say *K* and had misspoken. This can happen. He barely knows David.

—Apparently after you left his place on Sunday he piled all his notebooks and his maps and whatever the hell it was that he was working on, piled it all on the floor of his living room and set fire to it. He's OK. The fire brigade came in time, and the room is gutted, but that's all, and he has some burns to his arms and face I think, but he's OK. He's in hospital. K wanted me to tell you if you called. K has been to see him. K asks that you return his calls. Sometime. When you've stopped wandering around the place behaving like a fucking animal.

Michael sighed. I heard a great weary sadness in his voice, and my heart dropped and broke.

—You're a fucking cunt to be honest, and I don't know that I'm ever going to be able to speak to you again. Goodbye.

I rode into Sunday. I was hurtled and I fell. *K asks that you return his calls.* I wrote into Sunday. I wrote about the mouse and the pool and the dog and the spider and about David. I wrote about David and K and Michael and Rachel and Catherine Anderson and Anthony Edgar and my phone in the lake and the posters. I was useless until I did it. I was useless like a child. I cried for the parts that I could not make sense of. I covered the pages with my writing and my hand hurt and swelled and I lacerated my body on the rocks where I dived. You should see me. The state of me. I am Barely Human.

I have drawn nothing now for over a week, well over a week, except the shapes that the words make on the page. The blocks and the slanted lines. The occlusions and the shivering pattern and the squinted pulses of the sentences. I did all that. And I harried the language so that it rose and took me on. I don't know what I mean. I think I mean I challenged the silence that poured out of me like a let of blood, and I staunched its flow with bits of my remembering. And I don't know what I mean by that. And what I did not see in living it, became kind of clear in writing it down. I had not known, until I told you, half of what I've told you.

Rachel made the posters. Of the mouse. She made them. Not K. In her flat she made them. I did not know it when I saw them. I did not know it when I talked to Michael. I did not know it when I started writing, but I knew it by the time I'd finished. I am here to be certain. That is what I'm here for. Aren't we all, poor creatures?

Then I can go home.

I put my cup in the sink. Through the window I can see the smoke in the sky, the dissipated rat. As I walked up the road to Rachel's I could hear the phones – people checking on each other. Even if I was seen, what policeman cares much these days about a man on a roof who leaves his luggage at the door while he breaks . . .

. . . in? I retrieved my bags in that gap, that gap there between *breaks* and *in*. I had forgotten them. So I left this apartment. I had to undo the locks, and leave the door propped open with a small pile of telephone books (for here, and for Poland, and for Israel), and creep out into the communal landing and down the communal stairs to the communal hall and open the communal main door, and keep it open with an extended leg, and grab my bags and haul them inside and back up here to Rachel's apartment, where they now sit beside me on the floor of her living room, with all the junk and clutter she has put aside to make a point with. You have no idea the things I can do between words. I can go and come back and sit still and do nothing, or I can brush my teeth or repair my hand, or clean up the bathroom or turn on the radio or have a long sleep between this word . . . and that. And you have no idea. I have no idea. There are only these words, and the gaps between them, in which things happen.

I feel very bad about David. David didn't want the gaps. He attempted to fill in everything, to create a place where there was no uncertainty, no fear. A place where everything is provided, where you need bring nothing of your own, nothing of yourself. There is no such place. There is no such place. We must creep the communal hall, and he didn't have it in him.

And neither did I.

We came into the plains. And on the distant mountainsides the moon tumbled ragged and the stars fell landslide sideways, as the globe turned in the globe, and the night was a dome. We rode our horses into Sunday. Across the plains of the middle lands, towards the east where the brightness starts, towards the Welderns and Threw, towards the Holy City which goes unnamed until we name it.

Rachel has one of David's notebooks. I don't know why or how she has it. I had not thought of this. It is full of intricate descriptions of pathways and tunnels and rooms and chambers. It is hard to read with my eyes, with my eyes as they are. I am in a state. He writes very well, David does, but this notebook contains no writing, if you see what I mean, just notes. Noted descriptions. This leads to that. This is so many feet wide and so many feet high. This was built in the year of this, and rebuilt in the year of that. This chamber holds the Killord Ring, this the File Assembly, this the priest's contactments, this the Ship of Rebellion. And then the sealed room, and the details of its sealing. And its ceiling actually, as it happens. And a drawing of the door. He can't draw.

Neither, by now, can I.

On the door there is the mouth of a dog. I imagine that's what David intended. An open diamond, with triangular teeth, the roll of a tongue, a snout and two puckered eyes above it, the jaws stretched taut. The sealed door. Poor David.

There are jars full of seeds in Rachel's living room. Jars of seeds and boxes of bulbs. There are plants and dried flowers. There is a picture of a blowing whale. There is the head of a donkey made out of straw. There are masks of politicians and actors and crooks. There are fake jewels and counterfeit pennies. There are chocolate Santas and chocolate coins. There are sex toys. There are metal and rubber and wooden and glass phalluses. There are teddy bears and rubber spiders and plastic mice and rubber ducks that squeak when you squeeze them. There is a stuffed dog. There are wigs on wig stands. There are photographs of Max and the upstairs of buses. There are empty cages with straw and water and tiny little piles of tiny little shit. There are mirrors. There are statues of the Virgin Mary and the Sacred Heart of Jesus. There are magazine cuttings. Catherine Anderson looks out at me, smiling for all of us. There are plates from the Greek Islands, vintage pornography, clothes for dolls, coats for dogs, shark's teeth, bricks, a scorpion in amber, snow globes and mobiles, a rotating child's night light, tequila worms, a box of soldiers, dancing pumps, a carved cigarette box with a secret compartment, hotel ashtrays, K's umbrella, Don Quixote and Sancho Panza made out of drinks cans, a drawer full of light bulbs, a leopard skin, three broken cameras, my camera, a contact sheet of my photographs, a tin full of clothes pegs, newspapers announcing the death of the Queen, the assassination of the President, a bomb in the Vatican, posters of Max, a tape recorder, a picture of a man by the side of a road, crouched in the tent of his overcoat, a plastic case of singed index cards, a map of the city taped to a wall, a fridge full of chemicals, animals, details and dreams, a room full of rooms, full of minutes, hours, seconds, a room of descriptions and ancient ideas, of Rachel, of this, of that, of the gaps between, of everything, sitting there, immobile, first floor, collected, staring at me, me, staring at me with my hand in the air.

As if I half surrender.

I thought of calling K. At work. I could look up the number in the book. They might know my name, K might have told them. They'd put me through. Simple.

—Hi.

—Were you in a meeting?

—Yes.

—Sorry.

—

—

—

—

—

—

I can't imagine what we would say.

I looked at my hand swaddled in paper. I looked at the telephone. It was actually difficult to tell which was the real telephone, among all the others. I could not decide what the words would be. I could not tell if there would be anger or relief or some mangled mix of both, or whether there would be silence only, a revenging, a horror, or whether there would be only peace and passing over, and the *come home* of a remarkable forgiveness. I was terrified of all of those. I even thought that I might be terrified of all of them equally. I lifted each receiver in turn and put it down again.

I cannot go home.

—I thought you were dead, you know. I thought you

were dead. I thought I would never see you again. Do you know that? I thought you were dead somewhere and at some point I would get a phone call and I would have to go to some nightmare place and look at your uncovered face after you'd been pulled from the river or the sea, or from under a train, or look at your wallet or your keys or your shoes, or have them tell me that your teeth matched, or have them tell me that it was your DNA. That's the kind of thing that I've been thinking. Do you know what that feels like? Do you know what that's like?

There was a silence. I could hear corridors. I could hear empty rooms and the layers of clutter, rustling in the quiet. Making noise that emphasised the silence. Making no noise at all. Making nothing.

I have to go home.

The Welderns. They rise steep and sharp out of the plains in the east. They stand like a ring of teeth in the ground, like an open jaw biting at the sky. They come at the end. They are the ending, which is always in the east, as is the beginning. So where we landed we return, and we leave.

In the villages of the foothills where the fresh cold streams flow to the rivers, where the grasslands feed the cattle and the cattle feed the people, where the houses gather in the evening sun, is where we arrive, on horseback, on the last day, and we dismount, and start to climb. And the paths are weary and narrow and close. And from the crags and in the gullies strange eyes watch us, and the air grows colder and the paths grow steeper, and all the living things thin out to rocks and circling birds and the dogs that come to meet us.

They stand stern. Black against the sun. They are muscle

*and tooth and watchfulness and they guard the gates. A
silent boy admits us and the dogs continue watching. They
do not flinch and we wonder what they're made of.*

The boy leads us by the hand.

In Rachel's flat, amongst the clutter, there is nothing.
In Rcahels' flat, gmonsta the clutter, there is onthing.
Ni Crahel's tfal, monagst teh luctert, herte si inthong.

I have talked to K. I'm sure you'll agree. I have talked
to K. I have. I called the office, the department, the government department, just now, between words, and they must
have known. About me. No problem. So. What K said
was that everything is all right, everything is fine, and that
I should go home now. K is there.

K will be there.

K *will* be there and I should leave here now and just
forget about it and just go home. Because this has been
pointless and there is nothing I can learn here, and I should
just go home now. Just go home.

I know, you see, what is inside the canister in the sealed
room in the Holy City. There is nothing. It's empty. We
cannot relocate ourselves. We cannot find a source. We
cannot lift the floorboards or rip off the sky. We are
ourselves, and we live here. We live here. This is where
we are, and there are, yes, there *are* other things here too,
but that is not the point, and K said, said, come home,
and I listened, and I know that the only reason David
burned Paddorn was that he knew this, he knew that it
was empty, that there was nothing in it, and that he was
looking the wrong way, and I know that Rachel knows
about all this too, more than the rest of us, look at what
she has here, and I know that Catherine Anderson knows

it, but is helpless, and I know that Anthony Edgar knows it, and hates it, and I know that he does not have a daughter because if he had a daughter with blonde hair and a puppy then he would not throw up at the smell of the earth or the sight of a stain or the thought of Australia, and I know that there was no dog, not really, and I know that the mouse was simply . . . I know that, **I KNOW IT,** and K said come home and I talked to K, when I talked to K, when last we spoke. K.

Is all there is.

My bags were heavy and full of things I don't need. So I dumped a lot of stuff. I put what I wanted into my shoulder bag and I left the rest lying there on Rachel's floor, for her to do with what she wants, whatever she wants. I don't understand what she wants. My hand hurts. I left her bloodstained towels and a broken bathroom and I left her something else I can't remember.

The doors closed behind me. And I was in the world.

The rat in the sky had gone by then. Something is always happening in the city. Don't worry about it. The buses were slow and not busy. I know what goes on here. I know what goes where. I remember all my fears and I don't mind. I can count them and list them and I know what they amount to, and really, I don't mind. I look for the dog. There is no dog. I am *persuaded* of the concepts of love and forgiveness. I am *persuaded* that there is nothing in this world that we do not make and govern and determine and direct. I am *happy* in knowing that I do not know the extent. I am *happy* in knowing that I am one of many, that my tastes are predicted, that my steps are mapped out, that my disorders are ordered, that my money is safe, that my imagination is like yours, that yours is like hers, that hers is like his, that we share our fears and our privacy and our senses. I am *happy* that we share our dreams.

I am *happy* that we share our dreams.

On this bus I am nearly alone. There are a few people. It is three-quarters empty, one-quarter full, I don't know, it's fine. I'm upstairs, near the back, so that I can see that there is no dog. No escort. No outrider from elsewhere. There is nothing in the canister. There is nothing but us.

On the seat back in front of me there is a tiny thing, the smallest thing, the most harmless of things. I rummage in my bag. My shoulder bag. I rummage in my bag. My hands make forms of things. They create a set of signs. My hands in my bag on the bus, rummaging. I know what I'm looking for, but what I want to say is that I don't know what I'm looking for. David's mug. I take it out. It's still tea-stained. It is grubby underneath the handle. I hold it and I imagine David holding it, his fingers wrapped around the handle like mine, and his hand, and his hands. His lips will have touched it here. Here where I put my lips. This is what we share.

We can't see one thing unless it's next to another.

I find the salt shaker from the café. From Arthur's. A plain little silver canister. I took it because I was thinking of the canister in the Holy City in the mountains he made up, in the land he created. Where the horses travelled over the plains. I twisted off the cap on its base and I held it gently, gingerly against the seat back in front of me, and I harried and I lured the wasp inside.

I've written all this down. It's OK. I'm nearly home. K said it. Come home. Why is the city?

Behind me. Something.

A cold sensation across my throat. And all the sounds are gone. And the world's gone still. How strange. And everything is very clear. Suddenly there is a clarity, a clarity. Here. I can't help but look down, and I cannot see the page.

I cannot see the page.